DEADLY RELICS
Grave Diggers Seri
- Book 4 -

by
Chris Fritschi

DISCLAIMER

This is a work of fiction. Names, characters, businesses, places, events and incidents are either the products of the author's imagination or used in a fictitious manner. Any resemblance to actual persons, living or dead, or actual events is purely coincidental.

Deadly Relics
by
Chris Fritschi

V3

ISBN:
ISBN-13:

Click or visit
chrisfritschi.com

To Karen. Your encouragement, honesty and belief in me fuel my spirit.

ACKNOWLEDGMENTS

The pages of his book are the result of all the people who gave their input, guidance, and knowledge. Thank you all.

A special thanks to all of you, you know who you are, for the encouragement and finger wagging that kept me on my toes through the development of this book. The critical, but honest, input from my beta-readers Cinnamon, Becka, Samantha, Lauren. You guys make me look good.

Enough can't be said for my wife who spent endless hours listening to me brain-dump over this book. Her patience and support never flagged.

1

SEEDS OF REVENGE

February 7th, 2018
US Army mission support base - Al Khabour River in Syria

Every day was an unwelcome competition between the boredom of isolation and soul sapping heat. Today's competition was entirely forgotten by the appearance of advancing Russian tanks.

Soldiers tried to ignore the adrenaline surging through their bodies as they stuffed extra ammunition into their chest rigs. They distracted themselves from thoughts of being shot at by turning their focus on inspecting their weapons. It was critically important everything worked. Where they were going, there wouldn't be anyone to back them up if their weapon jammed.

Nearby, four MRAPs rumbled indifferently. Their big 380 horsepower engines idled as crews ran back and forth, hastily stocking the big machines with supplies of food and water. Others stacked anti-tank missiles wherever they could find room. The big Mine Resistant - Ambush Protected vehicles looked like oversized, armored SUVs.

Twenty-five miles away, a Reaper drone circled high above the source of the high alert. Everyone without an immediate job crowded around a large, flat panel screen showing the live feed from the drone's high resolution digital eye.

Corporal Decter tried to elbow his way through the soldiers gathered around the display to see what the excitement was all about. On the screen was a large column of vehicles snaking their way through the city of Khasham.

"That's a tank," said Decter.

"A T-55," pointed out one of the Green Berets. "And there's lots of them."

"They crossed the Euphrates?" said the corporal. "They can't do that. That's our side of the river."

"Why don't you go tell them that," said a sergeant.

Close proximity between Russia and the United States was like rubbing two sticks of dynamite together and hoping for the best. It was always a bad idea.

When both superpowers moved their armies into Syria, a country half the size of Nevada, their strained nerves would be tested to a new level.

Even with the terrorist group ISIS as the common enemy, the US and Russia still ended up backing conflicting interests in the Syrian civil war.

The Russian-backed Assad regime had been grabbing oil fields and enforcing its authority under the guise of stamping out the dwindling band of ISIS terrorists. The US threw its support behind a multi-ethnic force known as the YPG.

Ironically, ISIS served as a buffer between the two superpowers. As the terrorists lost ground, it brought Russian and US forces uncomfortably close in the oil-rich province of Deir ez Zur. To reduce any 'misunderstandings', they had agreed to use the Euphrates river as a natural divide. Each country was supposed to stay on their own side. Nobody was shooting at anyone, but that looked like it was about to change, fast.

Earlier in the day, a column of eight hundred troops and twenty-seven vehicles, including T-55's, T-72's, armored personal carriers, artillery trucks and rocket platforms had crossed the

Euphrates using a pontoon bridge. They had attempted to mask their movement by sinking though the city of Khasham. The Syrian general leading the force refused to believe the American UAV posed a threat. He was disastrously ill-prepared for how wrong he was.

Klaxons came alive, sending US forces into action at the Al Udeid Air Base in Qatar. It was a mad scramble as ordnance and fuel crews rushed supplies to their respective aircrafts. Weapon packages of anti-armor and high explosive bombs and missiles were released from the munitions lockers. F-15 Strike Eagles, capable of going 2.7 times the speed of sound, F-22 stealth fighters and AH-64 Apache helicopters were quickly equipped for battle.

A transport designed specifically to carry multiple ordnance left the storage locker and headed to a row of AC-130 gunships. The aircraft was a four-engine machine of staggering destruction. Protruding from the port side of the fuselage was a trio of bad news for anyone on the ground. The first was a 25mm Gatling gun, capable of firing 1,800 rounds a minute. Next to that was a 40mm Bofors auto-cannon. Both of these weapons were highly effective against ground troops and lightly armored vehicles. But, in case those two weren't up to the task, the gunship mounted a 105mm howitzer. Originally engineered as an artillery piece, this weapon fired a multitude of twenty pound airburst and impact shells. The AC-130 gunship wasn't as new, sleek or pretty as the other attack aircraft, but no other aircraft inspired as much fear in her enemies.

The ordinance carrier headed for the rear of the gunship, lovingly named Nurse Betty. Under the cockpit window was a painting of a pretty nurse aiming a huge gun. Under the painting were the words, "This is going to really hurt".

The carrier stopped at the lowered ramp and several men with pallet-jacks came out of the cargo hold and began transferring the boxes of ammo.

"This is nuts," said Airmen Daulton, as he grabbed a clip of

40mm Bofors shells. "The whole base is hopping. Are we going to war?"

"My buddy in comms told me the Russians are attacking," said Airmen Sandies.

"Shut up," said Daulton in disbelief. "The Russians wouldn't do that."

"Tell that to Secretary of Defense," said Sandies. "He's the one who told the base commander to get our birds ready."

"No way," said Daulton, impressed. "But Russians? That's like World War Three stuff."

"Russian, or not," said Daulton, holding a 105mm shell, "someone's about to have a really bad day."

Tension in the Pentagon had just jumped another notch. The Secretary of Defense slammed the conference room door hard enough to make the floor to ceiling windows rattle. The conference room looked out over the Operational Situations Room and the intelligence analysts, looking up, could see him shouting into the phone.

"Keep your noses to your screens, if you know what's good for you," said Jill Williams.

She was the site intel supervisor and had just left a group briefing with the SecDef. There was no mistaking the intention of the enemy forces that had crossed the Euphrates. They were preparing to take the Conoco oil fields. This sort of thing typically played out with them occupying an oil field. There'd be the usual outrage, sword rattling and posturing. Eventually, things would settle down and the US would throw a handful of sanctions at them.

This wasn't typical because there were thirty United States soldiers hunkered down in the direct path of the enemy column. The small contingent of US soldiers were occupying a post on the edge of that oil field and desperately calling for support.

The intel supervisor's warning was enough for the two analysts to whip their heads around.

"They're turning again," said Todd Shelly. A new analyst, he was just as troubled by how quickly things were escalating.

On his screen was the same drone feed everyone else was intently watching. The column of enemy military vehicles was taking a path through the city of Khasham, trying to hide its movements from view.

"Don't these bozos know about drones?" chuckled Todd.

"Is that your professional analysis, Mr. Shelly?" asked Williams.

"Uh, no, ma'am," said Todd, stiffening up.

"What happened?" asked Mike Robertson, taking some of the heat off his new partner. Mike had been an intelligence analyst for several years and had never seen the SecDef so keyed up.

"The big guy called Moscow," said Williams. "They deny knowing anything about this."

"But we've intercepted radio chatter from that column," said Mike. "Last time I checked, Afghan Shia's don't speak Russian."

"Moscow categorically deny they have any forces in that column," said Williams.

"The radio intercepts..." began Todd.

"The Secretary isn't going to tell Moscow we can de-encrypt their comms," said Williams. She looked up to the conference room then back at her analysts. "He'll want another update soon. What have you got?"

"Between the infantry fighting vehicles and troop trucks, I make it about two battalions strong," said Mike. "They've got a company of tanks. It's a mixed bag of older T-55's and T-72's. There's two platoons of mobile arty and a platoon of wheeled rocket launchers."

Williams dictated on her notepad. "Over a thousand infantry, sixteen tanks, eight artillery and four rocket platforms. Anything else?"

"Anything else?" grinned Mike. "Yeah, there's a guy in the back of the column carrying a kitchen sink."

"You're a funny guy," said Williams, before walking back to the stairs leading to the conference room and an angry Secretary of Defense.

Mike turned back to his screen and Shelly leaned over to him. "What about our guys stuck in the outpost?"

Outpost Samson was intended as an observation post and provide limited security against small bands of raiders. Its total complement was a mixed force of thirty Delta Force and Rangers working alongside a small contingent of Kurdish and Arab forces. The few not watching the drone footage were looking at the enemy armored column through their binoculars. Everyone could feel the pit of their stomach knotting up.

Behind them was the now abandoned oil field and beyond that, miles and miles of open desert. Their only fortification was the low berm of sandbags ringing their position and a handful of foxholes scattered around.

The two teams who would be manning the heavy .50 cal machine guns had already inspected them and were playing cards to keep their minds off the approaching battle. It wasn't working.

The few shoulder-fired anti-tank missiles they had had been distributed, but even if every one of them scored a hit, it wasn't near enough.

Sergeant Franks had been on the radio, requesting support and giving updates. He'd been told command was aware of the situation and were 'taking steps'. The hollow reply left him feeling even more isolated and exposed to the enemy than before. He would have been surprised to know his lack of confidence was shared by some of the approaching enemy soldiers three miles away.

"This is stupidity," swore Luka, on the edge of motion sickness as the troop transport truck bounced and squeaked.

Being the fourth truck behind a platoon of tanks meant they were downwind and constantly assaulted by the exhaust fumes of everyone ahead of them. All the men in the truck were in full battle gear and wilting under the sweltering heat, regardless of the truck's canvas cover.

Several of the men in the truck frowned in agreement, but one of them laughed.

"How do you see the humor in this, comrade Kilmonikov?" asked Luka.

Misha Kilmonikov leaned against his battered AK-47 and grinned. "Luka, my friend, you complain about being idle on the base. You complain about the cold when we are home. And now we are neither idle nor cold and you still find something to complain about."

The other men chuckled.

"It is Luka Noskov's special skill," joked Mitya. "When we all joined the Spetsnaz, Luka was a terrible marksmen, couldn't use a compass and folded in hand to hand combat. The military directorate couldn't allow him to graduate without any ribbons on his chest. He would be a national embarrassment."

"So they invented an award for complaining," said Misha, knowing the rest of the joke.

"Spetsnaz," spat Luka. "I didn't put myself through all that difficult training so I could be whored out as a mercenary."

Months earlier, all of these men had been transferred from their official status as special forces under the direction of the GRU, Russian military intelligence, and passed into the ranks of the Wagner Group. They asserted to be a private military company, separate and unconnected to Russia, or its agendas. But it was well known in the intelligence communities that the Wagner Group was a proxy army of mercenaries under command and control of the Russian Ministry of Defense. This gave the MOD the advantage of complete deniability.

"Are you suggesting our leaders are making foolish mistakes?" asked Colonel Genrich. Attached to the unit as the Political Officer, the colonel watched and reported anyone whose actions, or words, reflected negatively on Russia's leadership.

"No," said Luka begrudgingly.

"Watch what you say, comrade Noskov," sneered the colonel. "Talk like that is bad for the morale of your fellow Spetsnaz. The Deputy Director is a busy man, but not so busy as to ignore malcontents."

"Comrade Colonel," said Misha, his grey-blue eyes looking sincere. "Luka Noskov has proven his loyalty and bravery many times over. You, yourself, have seen this with your own eyes. But he is a man with little education for words."

"What words would you have me put in my report about him?" asked the colonel.

"It is not his confidence in Moscow he disagrees with," smiled Misha. "This attack scheme of the Iranian general is a fool's errand. After crossing the river, we should have immediately attacked the Yankees. Instead, he's got us skulking around the city, wasting time. We have seen the American's drone above us. They know we're here and the longer we crawl through the city, the more time the Yankees have to prepare."

The colonel couldn't help but reflect his own troubled thoughts about the general's tactics. "There may be some truth in what you say, comrade Kilmonikov." The colonel caught his slip and quickly eyed the men hunched in the truck with him. "But we are Spetsnaz," he blustered. "The Americans are soft and lazy. They fight from behind their machines, but they are about to get a real lesson in combat from six hundred Russian warriors."

Bolstered by his words, the men in the truck cheered, all except Misha and Luka. Each traded looks of worry from under their helmets.

An hour later, the column had left the confines of the city and turned towards the oil fields and Outpost Samson. Less than two miles between them, the column deployed in a long line. On either end, the mobile artillery crews jumped out of the trucks and quickly set up the cannons.

The men of Outpost Samson watched as their mouths went dry and fear clenched their guts. Any instant now they were going to be eating enemy fire. Losing grip on his control, the radio operator began shouting for calls of support.

The first enemy tank round ripped over their heads, exploding a hundred meters behind them.

Seeing the distant explosion, the Iranians began cheering and pumping their fists in the air.

The Russians looked at each other with open contempt for their allies.

"You'd think we'd just won the war," scoffed Misha.

"The first enemy bullet will wipe the smiles off their idiot faces," said Luka.

One of the Iranian officers began shouting, twirling his finger in the air. Taking his meaning, the troops prepared for their assault.

Misha looked around and spotted the colonel farther down the line, issuing orders to the second of the two battalions of Spetsnaz. The next senior officer, Misha took command of the first battalion.

As he ordered the men to prepare, he nodded to Luka who quickly split off to join a small group of men.

"Stay behind the tanks," shouted Misha, his voice projecting from his barrel chest. "Use them for cover. If our artillery starts hitting close to you, report to your commander for them to adjust fire."

Several of the men nodded, acknowledging they'd heard him. Misha saw several of the Spetsnaz looking at their battered AK-47s with disgust. As contract mercenaries they weren't allowed to have their Russian-issued weapons, nor anything else that could connect them, officially, to the Russian government.

"Keep your Iranian comrades nearby," said Misha.

"What are they good for?" said someone in the crowd. "They'll run off as soon as the real shooting begins."

"If your guns stop working," grinned Misha, "stuff your magazines in their mouth and shoot your bullets out of their arses."

Laughter rolled through the ranks of men, some of them clapping the Iranians on the back. The Iranians looked around in confusion, not understanding Russian, but smiled along with the burley foreigners.

Luka appeared with a handful of men and Misha lead them a short way from the crowd.

"Where are the rest?" asked Misha, concerned.

The ground shook as the artillery batteries fired their first salvo at the American outpost.

"They got stuck in the colonel's battalion," said Luka.

Misha threw a quick look over his shoulder at the colonel's distant battalion.

"We can't get them," warned Luka. "The colonel will get suspicious."

Misha nodded gravely before looking at the other men.

"We've all seen enough battles to know the Iranian general's walking us into an early grave," said Misha quietly. "My brothers, we have sworn our lives for Mother Russia and would willingly die for her without hesitation."

"Our loyalty is without question," said one of the men proudly.

"And nobody does, Vitaly Ustinov," said Misha respectfully. "I don't believe Moscow knows what this fool general is about to do. I tried telling him that we can take this oilfield with a handful of men. But this puffed-up clown wants his moment of glory at the cost of all our lives."

The small group of men agreed.

"We won't pay that price," said Luka. "When they call for us to attack, make your way to the left flank. There's a dry riverbed that runs parallel to the Yankee outpost. If there's any hope for our survival, that will be it."

"We must move quickly ahead of our main force," said Misha. "As soon as we're behind the outpost, we'll spring on the Americans like hungry wolves on lambs. Wound them. Only kill if you must. We'll take them prisoner. The American commander will stop any counter-attack on our main force to protect their captured men."

"Will it work?" asked one of the men.

"If it doesn't," said Misha sternly, "hundreds of our brothers will needlessly die today."

Artillery began falling down around the outpost, drowning out the calls for help, but their message was understood.

The Secretary of Defense sat at a large conference table, rubbing his temples. He'd called Moscow, hoping they would call off the attack, but they staunchly denied any knowledge of it and refused to acknowledge any involvement of Russian forces.

The SecDef had done everything possible to avoid a fight, but the Russians had backed him into a corner. Seated at the same table were members of CENTCOM, the United States Central Command, responsible for direct combat action by the Army, Air Force and Navy.

The tension was like brittle glass. They could almost hear the air cracking.

The SecDef looked at the men and women who were intently staring back at him. He let out a long sigh, lowering his head. When he looked back at them, his expression was grim and unflinching.

"You are authorized to engage the enemy," said the SecDef. "Attack until they are destroyed or made combat ineffective."

A moment later, each member of CENTCOM was on a phone. The advancing enemy forces were about to learn the full might of American forces had just been unleashed.

In a cloud of dust and fire, a salvo of Iranian missiles swarmed from their tubes, screaming into the sky. Before the trails of smoke had been swept away, the missile crews quickly worked to reload the launchers.

The massed blow of artillery had slowed to staggered fire with long lapses in between. Their lack of training evident as the men shouted confusing directions at each other.

The Iranian general decided the American outpost was effectively suppressed and gave the order for the armored platoons to roll forward. The Russians scowled in distain as the Iranian troops whooped and cheered.

Four hundred meters to the west, Misha hurried down the dry riverbed, followed by his twelve men. The riverbed was shallow, forcing them to crouch, frustrating their urge to run. Their desert camo would not be enough to conceal them from detection.

Misha chanced a quick look over the edge of the riverbed. They were pulling well ahead of the advancing tanks. Thankfully, the Americans had not responded.

He began to wonder if the outpost had been abandoned after all, but that question was answered an instant later by the chugging of a Browning .50 caliber machine gun.

He could hear the sound of the shells hammering against the tanks protecting his fellow Spetsnaz and allies. The Iranian's celebration had stopped now that the Americans were fighting back. Looks of fear began to spread through the Iranians.

A couple of them broke ranks and began running back to the troop trucks.

One of the heavy .50 rounds hit a luckless soldier, blowing his leg off. The limb cartwheeled, throwing blood and panic. The Russians watched in disbelief as the Iranians threw down their guns and ran.

Misha and his men sneered as they watched the spectacle.

"We can't waddle like this anymore," he grunted. "It's all or nothing."

He and his men broke into a run. Suddenly the air was shuttered as it was torn apart. Instinct gripped the men and they dived for cover.

The ground bucked with the sound of distant explosions. Misha jumped to his feet and looked at the line of friendly forces. His ragged breath caught in his throat.

Clusters of American artillery fire rained down, exploding in the air above the men. Clouds of razor-sharp shrapnel sliced into the tightly-packed soldiers.

They were sitting ducks on the flat, open terrain. He heard another long rip, quickly getting louder. The air above the distant men exploded, cutting through swaths of men. The shockwaves slapped Misha, blowing grit into his face and eyes.

Swearing, he fought to clear his vision. "Attack the Yankees," he shouted.

Every one of them broke into a full out sprint, hoping to save their friends, the sound of American artillery driving them on.

Soon they saw the tops of the American soldiers glancing over the edge of their fortifications. The first Russian close enough threw a grenade, but his aim was off and it fell far short.

They began shooting, their rounds kicking up puffs of dust on the wall of sandbags. Aware of the new threat, the Americans turned their fire on Misha and his group.

Kneeling in cover, Misha racked his brain for their next move. They were being pinned down. His assault was failing. The radio buzzed in his ear with orders, counter orders and cries for medics. Above the sounds of bullets zipping over them, he heard the muted drone of aircraft. His heart sank as he looked up and saw a pair of B-52 bombers.

Under the wing of the B-52, the Sniper Advanced Targeting Pod fed a crystal-clear view of the massed enemy forces 15 miles away from its high definition imaging camera.

The Electronics Warfare Officer sat in his station behind the pilot. The EWO toggled the targeting pod to laser track and target marking mode. Using his joystick, the EWO shifted the aim of the laser to a large group of enemy infantry and pressed the Track button. He repeated the same action on the cluster of tanks and artillery. The onboard computer fed the location and movements of the multiple targets into the individual guidance processors of every smart bomb in the weapons bay.

The computer calculated the aircraft's speed, direction, distance to target and weather conditions in less than a second. The computer told its human counterpart it was finished with a green indicator light on the EWO's panel.

The weapons bay doors opened with a smooth whine and locked into place.

"Pilot, EWO," said the warfare officer with sterile professionalism. "Targets are locked and weapons ready."

"Roger, EWO," answered the pilot. "You are clear to release."

"Clear to release," confirmed the EWO, and pressed the release switch.

Even from his distance, Misha could see a black swarm form beneath the bombers. He watched in horror as the two bombers released a combined one hundred and forty thousand pounds of laser-guided bombs.

"Bombs," yelled Misha, throwing himself to the ground.

A moment later, the earth was rocked in a ripple of shattering explosions.

The ground violently bucked, like the fists of gods were hamming the earth in rage. Misha and his men were jolted into the air. Shockwaves slammed them back down, over and over. The massive pressure waves blew out eardrums, bursting capillaries in their eyes and noses.

The sun was blotted out as tons of earth and dust were thrown into the air.

Then suddenly the earth was still.

The men in the riverbed could only groan, their senses ripped in tatters. They choked and gagged on dust-clogged air, covered in grime.

Misha fought against the protests of his battered body and forced himself to get up. Smoke and dust hung thickly in the air, blocking his view. He tried calling out, but his shout was nothing more than a ragged gasp.

He thought it would suffocate and his vision began to tunnel. A sweet breeze kissed his cheek and the gloom began to thin. At last he could breath and he painfully gulped in fresh air.

In the distance he saw the blacked hulk of tanks, belching smoke and fire. The entire area was cratered and scorched. Two minutes before, there had been over a thousand men. Now there was nothing but a few ragged figures shambling, directionless.

The Americans focused their wrath on the broken survivors.

They obliterated the artillery and missile positions. Secondary explosions popped mutely in Misha's wrecked ears. He slumped into the dirt as bitter tears streaked his face.

How could Moscow callously throw away so many lives? Is this how we're repaid for our loyalty?

Betrayal and hatred welled up in Misha as he thought of the years of sacrifice he'd given to his country. And in return they turned their back on him, casting him into the hands of an imbecilic general, careless of his fate.

Lost in the depths of his own thoughts, he hardly took notice that Luka had half carried him back to safety and into the troop truck.

A week later, Misha was approved to leave the hospital and sent back to Russia.

As they sat in the cargo bay of the aging Antonov An-22 military transport, Luka looked at his friend, concern etching his face. Misha had hardly spoken since the tragically failed attack.

"Be seated and secure your seatbelts," ordered the pilot over the loudspeaker. "We are making our final approach for landing."

Luka patted Misha on the shoulder. "We are home, Misha. No more sand to chafe your bits. Tonight I will take you out and we'll get drunk on the best vodka Moscow has to offer."

Misha didn't respond, but kept his gaze fixed on the floor at his feet.

The Antonov touched down with a squeal as its tires met tarmac. Soon it had taxied off the runway and stopped next to a secluded hanger. The beleaguered solders unbuckled from their seats and stood, waiting while the rear cargo ramp opened.

Cold, fresh air swept into the cargo bay as the men walked down the ramp into the bright, crisp day and came to a sudden stop.

Ringed around them were heavily armed soldiers of the GRU.

Two men in suits waited for all of the retuning Spetsnaz to exit the plane.

A man in a suit stepped forward, looking down on the soldiers over his hawk nose.

"I am Savva Savinovich Yegorov," he snapped. "Assistant Deputy of military intelligence. All of you are under arrest for violations of article 359 of the criminal code of the Russian Federation. Engaging in mercenary service."

"We are not mercenaries," protested Luka.

"You were operating in Syria, under the employ of the Wagner Group," said Yegorov.

"At the direct order of GRU," countered Luka.

"Do you have any evidence of your claim?" asked Yegorov.

"You know we don't," said Luka. "We are loyal soldiers of the..."

"All of you will be transported to the Kovkiv penal colony," said Yegorov, raising his index finger. The surrounding guards lifted their weapons but didn't point them at the stunned soldiers. "The sentence for your crimes will be determined at a later date. *If* you prove yourself as a useful and loyal citizen, you will, eventually, be released."

Yegorov and his companion turned and left without another word. The guards herded their prisoners towards the waiting trucks.

Luka looked at Misha, who had displayed no reaction to what had just happened. If anything, Luka could only detect a darkness in Misha's eyes. Something black and cruel had gripped his heart.

2

CODES AND TRUST ISSUES

P **resent Day**
      United States Army Base Fort Hickok - Panama
    Tate carried his bottle of water to his desk and sat down in front of the monitor. He looked at the small lens staring at him from the top of the monitor and self-consciously ran his hand over his close-cut ash, blond hair.

Turning his attention to the keyboard, he typed in a series of numbers and letters, then looked up expectantly at the screen.

Nothing happened.

He frowned, mentally going over the pass code. He jabbed at the keys again. This time the screen flickered and his face appeared, looking back at him. His image shrank to a small window in the bottom corner of the screen and Nathan appeared in the central window.

The corner of his brown eyes creased with a hint of a smile as he looked at Tate.

"Good to see you," said Tate.

"You, too," said Nathan. "I wish we could avoid communicating this way."

"I thought you said it was secure," said Tate. "I mean, you set the encryption feed."

"It's secured," smiled Nathan. "But it's harder to hack into a one on one meeting."

"You're giving me mixed signals," joked Tate. "It's secure. It's not secure. We meet. We shouldn't meet."

"I can tell you're having a good time with this," said Nathan. "Do you want to get on to more serious business, or should I let you run with this?"

"Wow. Are all bio-neural, lattice crypto hackers as touchy as you?"

"No," chuckled Nathan. "I'm one of a kind."

It struck Tate how they were talking with the ease of old friends, but he could still remember their first meeting. The setting was starkly different with Nathan tied to a chair and Tate interrogating him.

Nathan had been attached to a squad of soldiers sent to ambush them and was dumb luck Tate and his team survived.

Tate's team was completely inexperienced in combat and were no match against the highly-skilled attackers. With the enemy hunting them, Tate and his team ran into the jungle. They finally escaped by leading the pursuing enemy, including Nathan, into the hands of the cartel king, Nesto San Roman.

Tate wanted to know who was behind the ambush, and when he learned Nathan had survived, Tate made a deal with the drug lord. San Roman agreed to let Tate question Nathan, but there were unforeseen strings attached. Strings that would put Tate under San Roman's thumb.

Nesto San Roman was a power-hungry sociopath, but he wasn't dumb. Having a contact inside the local military base was too good to pass up.

He sent Nathan, under guard, to be interrogated. That's when Tate learned Nathan was too valuable to return to the drug lord.

He freed Nathan and in exchange for his life, agreed to collaborate with Tate against The Ring.

The mysterious organization was working covertly and quietly to recruit powerful members to its ranks. Their offer was a noble one, laced with patriotism and the love of the country; or that's what they told the unsuspecting members. By using their combined influence, wealth, and resources, they could circumnavigate the current political stalemates and bureaucracy to speed up the recovery of the country, enact selected laws that would work in their favor, and entice politicians to vote against laws and policies that were counterproductive.

The real truth, what Nathan had revealed to Tate in that dank basement, was that The Ring was, in fact, making use of its member's power but using it for their own purpose. The core founders of The Ring were planning the systematic overthrow of the government and once they wielded enough power, they would take over the country.

Who they were and where they came from was a mystery. What they planned to do after seizing power was open to speculation. But Tate knew the only way to strike a fatal blow was to discover the core members. With Nathan's help and the recent capture of the Vulcan 4 database key, they might be taking a big step in that direction.

"Okay," said Tate, turning serious. "What have you got?"

"Nothing," said Nathan.

Tate could only look at him with confusion and impatience. He'd learned that Nathan wasn't a 'to the point' kind of person. Tate was and didn't shy away from making it known.

"Nothing," repeated Tate. "As in the opposite of something."

"Almost," said Nathan.

"Do I have to hunt you down and yank teeth anytime I want a complete answer?" grumbled Tate.

Nathan smiled again and gestured with his hand for Tate to calm down. "The reason we have the database key is because The Ring hired me to piggyback onto the NSA's communication satellite."

"Right," said Tate, taking a drink from his water. "They wanted to use it to send and receive communications to their contacts without being detected."

And that's the 'nothing' I found," said Nathan. "There's no record of The Ring sending communications to anyone."

"None?" said Tate, straightening up in his chair. "What about receiving."

"No," said Nathan. "They didn't send or receive anything."

Tate glanced up at the ceiling, trying to come up with a plausible explanation. The Ring had paid Nathan a lot of money to be linked up to Vulcan 4. It didn't make any sense that they'd never use it.

"Maybe the satellite was only part of the network," offered Tate. "They might need something else in place before the connection's complete."

"I thought about that, too," said Nathan, "but I was hired to design the system, end to end. I know they had everything in place to use it."

"Maybe they wiped the records when they knew the satellite's orbit was decaying," said Tate. "In case they couldn't retrieve it after it crashed."

"They never got the chance," countered Nathan.

"What about communications system tests before it went live?" asked Tate. "Were those gone too?"

"That's where things get interesting," said Nathan.

Tate stared at him, wishing he could reach through the screen and smack him. Instead of getting to the point, Nathan had led Tate through the process of deduction until he had caught up.

"San Roman thinks you're dead because I lied to him to save your life," said Tate. "If you string this out much longer, I might develop a guilty conscience and tell him the truth."

Nathan accepted the empty threat, understanding his lack of social skills was beginning to wear on Tate.

"Sorry," said Nathan. "I have a hard time finding the right level to talk to people who... "

"Aren't genius criminal hackers?" said Tate.

"Aren't technologically current," said Nathan.

Satisfied he'd made his point, Tate gestured his acceptance of Nathan's apology.

"Getting back to the system tests," said Nathan, referencing something in his hand. "There's several records of tests. A lot more than I would have expected. I had recommended a bank of five tests." He looked back up to Tate, pushing his lanky, brown hair out of his eyes. "All of those tests ran successfully, but they went completely off script. Each test was designed to trigger a return of the satellite's onboard computer. It would send a set response acknowledging the communication was received. But they sent what looked like random commands, each one slightly different than the previous one."

"If the satellite sent back the same reply every time," said Tate, "why would they keep sending it?" His expression suddenly changed as the answer dawned on him. "They wanted the satellite to send them something different."

"Exactly," said Nathan. "I skipped to the record of the last systems test. That one activated a different subroutine. In response, it sent a string of codes."

Nathan's image was replaced by a series of alphanumeric codes. Tate studied them for a moment, but they didn't look like anything he'd encountered in his time with military intelligence.

"Do you know what they mean?" asked Tate.

"Not what they mean," said Nathan, "but who used them. What I worked out is that the request The Ring sent was for a catalog listing. This is what they got back."

"Hang on," said Tate. "The Ring has these codes?"

"Yes," said Nathan, "but I doubt they know what to do with them. I can't read them, but these look like military cyphers, not NSA. Someone high up in the Department of Defense might know what they are."

Tate's expression changed as he began to make connections in his mind. He might very well know how to find out what these codes meant, but it would require exposing Nathan. Maybe not Nathan by name, but that Tate had access to someone capable of penetrating government security protocols. In a relationship where trust was tenuous, this was going to test that trust more than any time in the past.

"Send me a copy of those codes," said Tate.

"There's an encrypted copy already on your computer," said Nathan.

Tate pursed his lips, but resisted protesting about Nathan blithely accessing his computer without permission. They'd cover that topic another time.

"Thanks," said Tate.

"One other thing," said Nathan.

"Let me guess," sighed Tate.

"Kaiden," prompted Nathan. "She broke into my safe-house."

"I know," said Tate, lacking anything else to say.

"With an assault team," pressed Nathan. "With weapons."

"I understand what assault means. It could have been worse," fumbled Tate. "You weren't hurt."

"I wasn't hurt because I wasn't there," said Nathan. "I'm not the lucky one. Kaiden is. If my security had been armed, she and her crew would've been blown to bits."

"While I'm glad that didn't happen," said Tate, "how did someone like you forget to arm your security system?"

"Because I didn't," said Nathan. "She's a different animal than most people."

Tate laughed. "I haven't heard it put that way before, but it's true."

"She's a problem," said Nathan. "Let me clarify that. She's *your* problem."

"Hang on," said Tate.

"I can't work with you if she's involved. It's too much of a risk," said Nathan. "She can't be trusted. If you want my help, do something about her."

"I've run dozens of ops with her," said Tate. "I trusted her with my life."

"I won't make the same mistake with my life," said Nathan. "It's only a matter of time before you get between her and what she wants. That's a terminal place to be."

Tate stared at his ghostly reflection in the monitor. Nathan had hung up.

Before the double doors had closed behind Tate, Teddy Moon was greeting him with a friendly handshake.

"Jack," grinned Teddy. "It's been ages. Welcome back to the Blue Orchid. The place just isn't the same without you, pal."

Walking into the Orchid was like taking a step back into a Humphry Bogart movie. There was nothing modern about the decor. Leather, brass and wood in rich hues made for the perfect ambiance of a 1940's speak-easy.

Light jazz flowed through the club from the live band on stage, the pleasant music easily mingling with the low hum of conversations.

The owner of the club, Teddy Moon, loved the golden era of the 40s and it showed from the retro, double-breasted jacket and immaculate white shirt to the black bow tie he wore. His cologne was a warm mix of tobacco, citrus and leather. Tate had never known Teddy to wear anything else.

"Good to see you, Teddy," smiled Tate, uncomfortable with the sudden attention. He'd been here several times but getting used to Teddy was like wading into a cold pool. It took a while to adjust.

"We're friends, Jack," corrected Teddy. "Call me Commodore." He walked Tate into the club and snapped his fingers. "Louie."

Instantly, a man with slicked back hair and black suit hurried over.

"You're looking very trim these days," said Teddy. "Is there a new dame in your life?"

"I just felt like I was out of shape," said Tate.

Teddy nodded and turned to Louie. "I want you to take special care of Mr. Tate."

"Yes, sir," said Louie.

"A table in the back," said Tate, looking for the least crowded area.

"I'll see to it immediately," said Louie before leaving.

"Louie's the best man I have," said Teddy. "If you need anything, say the word."

"Thanks, Commodore," said Tate.

Teddy shook his hand warmly, then was gone, quickly mingling with other customers.

Tate made his way across the club to a table Louie was waving him to.

"What would you like?" asked Louie.

"Whisky," said Tate.

"Make it two," said a voice behind Louie.

Louie headed off to take care of the order with a quick nod of acknowledgment.

"Good to see you, Colonel," said Tate. "Thanks for coming all the way out here."

"I needed to get away from DC," said the colonel. "I like this place."

Tate had to grin. In another time, Colonel Earl Hewett would have fit right into the 40s. Stocky, gruff, but fair. He looked like someone who believed that a man's word and a firm handshake was all the bonafides you needed. But, as a career officer in the US Army and years of service in the Department of Defense, he understood people were rarely who they seemed to be. It helped that Hewett had a keen ability to judge a person's character.

That same ability had worked against him, leading Hewett to join The Ring and recruiting Tate as a private team of covert operators.

Hewett had been increasingly frustrated with the state of government mismanagement, political in-fighting and the kind of incompetence that can only come from lack of experience. A trusted friend approached him about The Ring and their desire to guide the country's leadership focus back to the improvement of the country and its citizens.

Hewett had known his friend for decades and after considerable thought agreed to join the secret society of patriots. Shortly afterwards, the real truth came to light when his friend was murdered attempting to tell Hewett that he'd discovered the true aim of The Ring.

Understanding now the threat The Ring poised to the country, Hewett and Tate agreed to remain with The Ring and sabotage it from the inside. Both understood the grave danger they were putting themselves in should The Ring ever suspect what was going on under its very nose.

"What's going on," said Hewett, getting to the point.

"We've had limited success getting anything off the database key," said Tate.

"But you have had success," said Hewett.

"That depends on you, sir," said Tate.

A waiter appeared next to their table with a tray holding two drinks and set them down.

"Can I smoke here?" asked Hewett to the waiter.

"Yes, sir," said the waiter and produced an ashtray and lighter.

"Got my own," said Hewett, waving off the lighter.

"Can I get you gentlemen anything else?" asked the waiter, tucking the tray under his arm.

"We're good, thanks," said Hewett.

The waiter left as Hewett reached into his jacket pocket and took out a leather case containing two cigars. He offered one to Tate.

Tate considered it for a moment. He decided he'd reward himself with one after he dropped another fifteen pounds.

"You do this in Washington," said Hewett, clipping the end of the cigar, "and people act like you throat punched the Dali Lama. I've served to protect our country for most of my life and look what they've done with it."

This was a well-picked bone of contention with Hewett. Tate's own feelings weren't much different, but they weren't as close to the skin as Hewett's.

Tate took a sip of whiskey and let the rich fluid breathe on his tongue before swallowing. The vapors filled his mouth with complex flavors as he felt the warmth of the alcohol begin to radiate inside him.

"This is very good," said Tate, hoping to derail Hewett's rant.

The colonel flicked on his lighter and puffed on the cigar until the tip of it glowed a bright orange. He leaned back, savoring the experience with a deep sigh. It was only then that Tate noticed the creases of strain lining Hewett's face. For reasons of security, they communicated as little as possible, and saw each other even less. The casual exchange of everyday life was a luxury their relationship could rarely afford.

Tate could only speculate that the double life he was living as a loyal member of The Ring and the demands of the Pentagon were taking a toll. Tate wanted to make this meeting as brief as possible but saw what a respite it was to Hewett. As one soldier to another, Tate knew the value of those rare moments of peace. He didn't want to be the one to take it away from Hewett.

The colonel blew out a long stream of cigar smoke then leaned forward.

"All right," said Hewett. "Show me what you have."

Tate took a printed list of the codes out of his pocket and pushed it across the table. Hewett held the cigar in the corner of his mouth and unfolded the paper. The change in him was nearly imperceptible, but Tate could see Hewett was rattled.

"How did you get this?" said Hewett.

"From Vulcan 4," said Tate.

"I didn't ask where you got it. I asked *how* you got it."

"My contact. Accessing systems is what he does."

Hewett took a drink of his whisky and tapped his thick finger on the paper. Tate hoped whatever questions Hewett was thinking about asking, it didn't force him into a position where he'd have to lie to keep Nathan's identity safe.

"You better start at the beginning," said Hewett, puffing out a cloud of smoke.

Tate told him everything he'd learned, keeping Nathan's personal details out of it.

Hewett looked at him with his stony gaze, not giving away what was going on his in head.

Tate finished and waited.

"Now The Ring has these," said Hewett.

"What are they?"

"Evidence codes," said Hewett. "Any time a bureau executes a raid, runs surveillance, takes a witness statement, it becomes evidence. Each branch of the intel community logs and stores their own evidence. NSA, CIA, whoever. These codes were used by the FBI."

Tate utterly failed to keep the surprise and worry from showing on his face. Hewett quietly nodded in agreement.

It had been five years since the country was rocked by an explosive investigation that had blown the deep roots of FBI corruption wide open. Evidence of blackmail, abuse of power, false flag operations, witness intimidation and falsifying evidence were only some of the grievous practices being directed from the 7th floor of the FBI. Nearly all of the upper echelon of the organization had been fired. Several were tried and convicted. Of them, a few fled the country. What remained was a law enforcement agency riddled with crooked agents. Weeding all them out was impossible, and the worry was even a single bad apple could be enough to begin the rot of the organization all over again.

After vicious infighting, suits and counter suits, Congress abolished the FBI. Of the more than thirty-five thousand employees, only those in specific departments were banned from being employed by the government or law enforcement. The remaining were slowly merged into other agencies.

The event was a national disgrace and, in the eyes of the public, threw suspicion on everyone in law enforcement.

Any association with the FBI was considered taboo and a quick way of being ostracized.

"What's The Ring want with FBI evidence?" whispered Tate, glancing at the nearby tables to see if anyone was listening.

"See this?" said Hewett, pointing to a reoccurring string of numbers appearing in each set of codes. "That's a classification number used for highly sensitive items. Things involving national security. I spent a year running with bureau field agents on a joint investigation. Tough sons of..."

"Do these codes reference a location?" blurted Tate, worried The Ring could already have what they were after.

"Affirmative, but I couldn't tell you where," said Hewett. "And I seriously doubt The Ring knows either. But before you breathe a sigh of relief, keep in mind that they could have a loyal member who was in the bureau. Maybe someone who knows what they mean."

"If they don't," said Tate, "they're turning over every rock to find one."

He dropped his gaze to the lights reflected in the surface of his whisky. He was at a complete loss where to go from here. Maybe Nathan knew how to find the location of this evidence. Maybe Kaiden, but his thoughts came to an abrupt end. For a moment, he'd forgotten she'd tried to steal the database.

What was he going to do about her? Whatever it was, he had to do it soon.

3

DEADLY CARGO

The water lapped quietly at the algae-caked sides of the dock. The morning air was cool with a fresh puff of wind that brought the smell of the sea.

Misha's broad chest expanded as he inhaled deeply, enjoying the rare quiet as he walked along the dock. The thick wooden timbers felt solid and unmovable under his feet. They were weather-worn; their edges crusted with sea salt. The dock looked like it had been built a long time ago, and he guessed the stout beams would be there for years to come.

Perhaps they'll outlast the human race has, he pondered.

Misha walked up the plank of the only ship moored to the dock. The forty-foot fishing trawler hardly moved, the water in the bay being almost still.

It wasn't until he set foot on the ship's deck that he spotted the armed guard. He gave the man a nod of greeting, who returned it then went back to watching the dock for unwanted visitors.

Misha's boots rang on the metal stairway as he made his way up to the bridge.

"Good morning, Luka," he said.

"Morning?" said Luka from under a console. "When did that happen?"

Misha looked around at the disheveled condition of the bridge with an appraising smile. "You've been working too hard."

The navigation console had been stripped of all its covers. The old ship had been liberated of some of its instruments over the years and new instruments were being installed.

"There aren't enough hands to go around," grumbled Luka. "Did I not tell you we'd need another electrician?"

"We need loyalty more," said Misha, pouring a cup of thick coffee. He placed the steaming cup near Luka, looking at the tangle of wires snaking across the floor.

"From these prison rats?" scoffed Luka.

Too many of their Spetsnatz brothers had died in prison and Misha needed men. It was no secret that Luka didn't like having part of their crew made up from recruits from the penal colony.

"I'd rather be surrounded by Russians," said Misha.

"Maybe so, but with hired labor, we can shoot them when the work's done," chuckled Luka. He squirmed free of the console and sampled the coffee.

Misha laughed loudly and patted Luka on the shoulder. "That kind of thinking would have made you a deputy director of the GRU. You missed your calling."

Luka motioned for Misha's help in lifting a large control panel off the floor. The two men grunted, Luka more than Misha, as they positioned the console into place.

Misha studied the panel with interest, not sure what it all meant.

"This will give me control over the cameras," said Luka, pointing to a number of small joysticks. "The rest of these will be the digital instrumentation of the normal ship's controls. Speed, steering and so on."

"You don't cease to impress, comrade," said Misha.

Luka wiped his face and leaned his lanky body against the control console. "We all have our talents," he said, taking the coffee cup. He eyed it, trying to decide if the horrible taste was worth the energy boost.

Overhead they heard the sound of a saw cutting steel, making them look up at the ceiling. Luka shook his head, visibly annoyed.

"Still no word?" asked Misha.

"It should have been here a week ago," bristled Luka. "This place. It's primitive. Show me one machine that isn't held together with sticky tape and wire."

Misha frowned at the bad news but kept his anxiety from making further progress. "What's the last you heard?"

"Tomorrow," said Luka. "Maybe."

"We'll have to move forward without it," said Misha. "Our timetable can't be adjusted."

"It's too dangerous," said Luka. "The antenna's the only way we can operate outside of their radar. If they detect us..."

"We don't have a choice," said Misha. "If it's not delivered in time, we'll have to adapt our plan."

"We're not there yet," said Luka. "I'm doing as much as I can without it. Once it shows up, installation should go quickly."

"But with little or no testing," said Misha.

Luka raised his coffee cup but thought better of it and put it down. "Have you tasted this?" he said.

"That?" said Misha. "No. It's horrible."

"What's the status of the other ship?" asked Luka.

Misha looked out the window of the bridge, into the distance. Through the morning haze he could see a hulking shadow moored to a dock.

"It's still there," he said with a grin. "Not everything is working against us."

"If it was gone, we'd know it," smirked Luka.

"Everyone would know it," chuckled Misha. He pushed himself off the console and swatted away a fly. "I'm going over there now," he said, bringing a frown to Luka. "Don't worry so much. The Black Rat couldn't kill us, neither will this."

Luka's mind flashed back to their arrest by the GRU. When the bus pulled up to the gates of the Kovkiv penal colony, he couldn't remember a more desolate and foreboding place.

He took a mouthful of coffee, purposely burning the inside of his mouth. The distraction of the pain was a small price to take his mind off that prison.

"I'll be back in time for lunch," said Misha. "We'll go out and get something good to eat."

"Since when do they have anything here that's good to eat?" asked Luka.

"It'll be an adventure."

"I'm busy," said Luka.

Misha stopped at the hatch and crossed his thick arms over his chest. "It would hurt the men's moral to see you dragged off the ship by your boots," hinted Misha.

"In that case, go away so I can get some work done," said Luka. "You chatter like a fishmonger."

Both men smiled. Luka returned to his work and Misha left the bridge.

Misha's destination was over a mile away, but the drive was far from direct. The old truck was a battered shell, but the engine had strength to spare and easily carried everything Misha could demand of it.

As he made the last turn in the road, the large ship came into view. He was struck with the same apprehension and distrust as reaching out to pet a strange dog; never sure when, or if, it will suddenly attack. Misha had been onboard the ship many times, but in this case, familiarity was not a source of comfort. The thing was a necessary evil.

Unlike the wooden timbers of the other dock, this one was concrete; its foundations driven deep into the seabed in order to withstand the pull of larger vessels.

Beneath the surface he could see the sunken dead hulks of other ships. Left to rot, they'd been moored here until their hulls rusted out. Their weathered superstructure climbed above the water like the bones of some leviathan, long since dead; their true size visible just beneath the murky water.

Misha stopped the truck near the gangplank leading to the main deck of his cargo ship. The ship's name, Vixen, stood out from her black hull in rust-streaked block letters along her bow.

In a former life she was a bunker barge cargo ship. Only two hundred feet from bow to stern, she was tiny in comparison to the over-thousand-foot cargo ships that once crisscrossed the seas, but that was before the outbreak.

For Misha's needs, she was perfect and came at the right price.

Parked on the other side of the gangplank was a flatbed truck stacked with barrels and sacks of material. Men were going up and down the gangplank, some with a sack over their shoulders, others pushing trollies, muscling fifty-five-gallon drums.

The growl of the gas-powered crane caught his attention and Misha looked up as a pallet lifted off the flatbed.

Everyone had stopped what they were doing, intently watching the pallet gently swing as the crane hoisted it into the air. Misha couldn't help but glance at the crane's greasy, grey cable. Strands of frayed wire stuck out along the length of it, but it was strong enough for the work he required.

On the deck, a crew of men waved to the crane operator, guiding the pallet. The operator put it down with practiced skill. With the pallet safely down, everyone went back to work.

The sun had cleared the horizon and it was already warm. The ocean breeze did little to keep Misha from sweating as he went up the gangplank. He walked towards the tall, squat bridge at the stern of the ship. The bridge sat fifty feet above the deck with a sweeping 360-degree view. Lightly panting after the zig zagging flights of stairs, Misha walked into the bridge and instantly shielded his eyes.

"Pavel," called Misha.

Intense white light, like a bolt of lightning, blazed from a cutting torch. The torch turned off with a pop and Pavel flipped up his welding mask.

"Welcome aboard," he said warmly.

"Good to see you, Pavel," said Misha.

"It's good to be seen," smirked Pavel. "Another day, another breath."

Misha looked around the bridge, or the skeleton of what the bridge once was; holes had been cut in the decking. Cords of electrical wiring ran through them and into the naked navigation console.

Around the windows of the bridge, metal shelves had been welded into the bulkheads. Each shelf held a mounted camera, having their own area of the world to observe.

"You are making great progress," said Misha.

"I have great incentive," said Pavel. "The sooner I'm done, the sooner I can get away from this death-trap."

"Skittish talk from a decorated Spetsnaz?" teased Misha.

"And I'd like to be an old Spetsnaz when I draw my last breath," grinned Pavel.

Misha looked out the bridge window to the open cargo hold doors in the main deck. "Is Gerasim here?" he asked.

"Da," said Pavel. "In the belly of the beast."

Misha left the bridge and returned to the main deck. The sun hadn't reached high enough to throw light directly into the cargo hold, but weak, yellow lamps lit the catwalk that hugged the interior of the hull down into the depths of the hold.

Misha's boots rang dully on the steel stairs as he finally reached the bottom level. The cargo hold was smothered in darkness except for a pool of light around a battery-powered lantern.

A tall man glanced between his clipboard and the front of the hold, checking his list. A handful of local workers stood nearby, watching him expectantly.

"What's the status, Gerasim?" asked Misha.

"You," said Gerasim to one of the bystanders, "go forward and tell them we need another ton in between the second and forth bulkhead."

The worker nodded, ready to race off, but Gerasim stopped him.

"Just solids. No more drums, you understand? No more sloshing containers."

The worker nodded quickly and took off.

"I was having trouble reaching you," said Misha. Beads of sweat quickly formed on his face in the stifling heat. He looked up to the open cargo hatch, thinking about the fresh air so far away.

"We can't use radios down here," said Gerasim. "No signals of any kind."

"You're making progress then?" asked Misha.

"Da," said Gerasim. "By the end of tomorrow, we'll have the first layer evenly placed throughout the hold."

Misha picked up a flashlight and tested it. "This should be interesting," he said. "I know you're uncomfortable with running the lights…"

"This old wiring?" said Gerasim, nodding to the string of wire connecting the overhead lights. "One short and…"

"I understand," said Misha, waving off Gerasim's sudden concern. "But I want to get a proper look. Give me a few minutes and then turn on the overhead lights."

"All of them?" balked Gerasim.

"Yes," said Misha firmly. His expression overruled all of Gerasim's objections.

Gerasim nodded his head in acceptance but said nothing.

Misha turned on the flashlight and walked into the gloom. He kept the beam of light on the deck ahead of his feet. Several times he had to step around and over cables of wires, stacks of rope and other debris.

He'd gone far enough and turned off the flashlight. The stuffy dark of the ship's hold collapsed around him.

The moment transported him back to the Black Rat, the name given to the penal colony; a small pocket of Hell, lovingly crafted for the single purpose of inflicting punishment on those who offended Mother Russia.

On arrival, Misha and his men had been split up to the individual colonies in the area, each one the absolute domain of the warden. Misha had watched as his squadmates were shoved into lines apart from his.

His first lesson in life at the Black Rat had come when a guard punched him in the ribs for not keeping his eyes forward. That was the first of many unspoken rules Misha would learn through harsh punishment.

By day the guards ruled with an unforgiving and iron fist. Orders weren't always delivered by verbal commands; a nod, snap of a finger, or tap of the hard, wooden baton was sometimes all that was given. It didn't matter if you were a 'lifer' in the prison or fresh meat; you were expected to understand what you were told to do. The consequences of failing to obey were harsh.

When the guards retired for the night, the prison was handed over to the inmates. Inmates had separated into tribes, like rivaling packs of wolves. The new inmates were fresh meat for the taking.

Beatings, rape and sometimes murder were never questioned by the guards, unless the inmate served their interests.

If an inmate had been wealthy, before they were arrested, they could bribe the guards for protection from the other inmates, and better living conditions. But may the gods help them if their money ran out.

Nothing was known about the inmates other than what they told each other.

Misha had walked through the building of cells to the shouts, threats and insults of the prisoners. On the floor above had stood an inmate who's face was covered in tattoos, surrounded by several men, all of them eyeing Misha with cold malevolence. Misha and the tattooed inmate had locked gazes. This had been one of the gang leaders. Judging by the size of his enforcers, Misha doubted there was anyone else in the prison that was higher on the food chain.

The new inmate in front of him had trembled with fear, hardly able to lift his feet. The guards didn't care that the man feared for his life; he was slowing down the line and got punched in the gut for his insubordination.

To the prison population, Misha was just another target. To the guards, he was garbage.

At five foot nine, he wasn't an imposing figure. His baggy prison clothing did nothing to betray his powerful frame or iron will forged in the fire of some of the hardest, most unforgiving training any military had ever devised. As part of the Spetsnaz training, Misha had overcome levels of mental and physical endurance considered excessive by the military of other nations.

Let other counties put their faith in technological machines of war. Russia's true might flowed through the blood of its soldiers; warriors who could endure longer, push harder and charge into the teeth of the enemy.

Misha remembered flicking a bedbug off his hand as he'd sat on his prison cot, immune to the howling and shouts of the other inmates. It would be night soon. The guards would be gone. The wolves would come.

The evening horn had sounded and the guards filed into the cell block as the loudspeaker croaked out a scratchy recording, tediously reciting the prison rules.

The prisoners all fell silent. The recording wasn't a warning to them; it was a dinner bell. The guards marched out, the thick steel door echoing through the building as it slammed shut.

They came slowly. The tattooed gang leader had claimed Misha as his property. The main lights had shut off, leaving a few dim bulbs to allow the video cameras enough light to see that the prisoners weren't trying to escape. As long as that didn't happen, nobody cared.

Faces had appeared outside of Misha's cell. Calloused hands gripped the steel bars and someone pulled open the cell door.

Misha had sat unmoving on his cot as if he wasn't aware of the danger moving into his cell.

Four of the leader's enforcers came in, glowering down on him. For a moment they'd paused, confused that he hadn't reacted at all. It was something they weren't used to, but it was only a curiosity.

One of the men had slapped Misha on the side of his head with a powerful hand. The blow knocked Misha over. The four brutes laughed, watching as Misha sat back up without a word.

The spectators outside the cell whistled and cat-called, cheering on their friends.

Misha had looked at the gang leader standing at the open cell door. "Your man hits like an anorexic whore."

The surprise in his attacker's face had been quickly replaced with a murderous scowl as the others laughed at Misha's insult.

With a snarl, one of the brutes had swung his fist.

Misha lowered his head and pushed off with his powerful legs. He'd driven his skull into the man's fist. The bones in his hand crunched and snapped and the brute wheeled away with a howl of pain.

Misha drove his hand into the next man's throat, snapping his fingers closed like a bear trap. The spectators gasped as Misha pulled, ripping out the man's throat.

The other brute had panicked and tried to run from the cell, but Misha caught him by his hair and pulled. The man's head snapped back, mouth open in a cry for help.

Still holding the mangled flesh, Misha had rammed his fist down the brute's throat. The inmate's eyes rolled back as he gagged for breath, quickly turning purple.

The last enforcer had ran, plowing into the other inmates to escape the cell. The gang leader was sent sprawling to the floor.

Taking his time, Misha had wiped his bloody hands on the suffocating inmate at his feet. Everyone backed out of the way as Misha walked through them and grabbed the leader.

The next morning, the guards had funneled into the prison, bored and malicious. A second later, one of them was hammering the alarm button. The other guards gawked at the dead body of the tattooed gang leader. Someone had shoved his head through the bars of his cell, crushing his skull in the process.

The guards had vented their wrath on Misha for six months. He'd killed their pipeline to the Black Market. Hard labor, forced starvation and beatings were only the start of his punishments. Chained by the neck, they'd left him out in the snow until he almost died.

While regaining his health in the medical ward, he'd recognized the patient in the next bed.

Illia was heavily connected to the Black Market and was treated like a king in the prison.

That night, Misha had paid a visit to Illia. By the time the sun rose the next morning, Illia was missing several toes and his Black Market business had been transferred to Misha.

With preferential treatment from the guards and no other gang leaders willing to stand up to him, Misha had taken his place as the new boss of the Black Rat.

When the ship's lights snapped on, Misha's face was a mask of hatred as the memories of those long, dark years played themselves out. He blinked away the fog, returning to the present.

His rugged face creased with a smile of satisfaction as he looked at the magnitude of Gerasim's work.

Packed against the hull of the ship was an eclectic mix of the most volatile explosives he could lay his hands on. Bags of RDX, pentaery-thritol nitrate, glyceryl trinitrate and other chemical agents were being loaded and placed with special care. Mixed in were barrels of gasoline and kerosene.

Something metallic winked at Misha from between the bags and he crouched down for a closer look. Gleaming in the light was a 102mm artillery shell. Securely strapped to the shell were several wires with a small detonation device. If Gerasim had done his job right, and Misha knew he had, those wires connected fifteen more shells. Each shell was packed into the stacked-up explosives and ran the entire length of the ship's hold.

The Vixen was the largest floating bomb history had ever known.

4

FRIEND OR FOE

By midnight, the army base was just how the MPs liked it; quiet. For new recruits it was lights out, shut up and in your rack. Those rules didn't apply to the noncoms, enlisted and officers who were quartered in another area. They could travel around the base as they liked. The MPs tried to discourage people from being out after dark; nobody like the idea of patrolling a dark base built on the edge of Vix-infested territory.

New walkways and roads were being added as the base began to see growth in personnel and strategic usefulness.

This delightful armpit of the world was the primary operating base for Mortuary Affairs and its detachment, All-Volunteer Expeditionary Force.

The role of the AVEF was to systematically clear the Vix from strategic areas of South America.

Called Victus Mortuus, Latin for 'living and dead', the nightmarish monsters came to be known as Vix. They were fast, strong and unrelenting.

While the United States was not suffering from overcrowding, the acquisition of South America through the United Nations treaty opened a wealth of other resources.

In the beginning of the Vix outbreak, South America was the

worst of worst-case scenario. Confused and contradicting leadership, panic, erratic communications and a failure to comprehend what was happening resulted in the obliteration of entire populations. The governments that tried to stand firm and guide their people were gutted of resources within hours. Police, military, even civilians who tried to band together couldn't accept the nature of what they were facing.

Millions were slaughtered, swelling the ranks of undead. Swarms of Vix grew to unimaginable sizes. It was suggested that a nuclear war wouldn't have taken the toll in human life equal to the outbreak of the Vix.

The population of South America had all but been exterminated.

In an effort to preempt the swarms from reaching North America, the United States convinced NATO to annex South America to the US. Shortly after, the AVEF was formed.

Primarily manned by volunteers, the men and women were put through a program called Fast Emersion in Weapons and Survival. In short, they were taught how to use a weapon without being a danger to themselves and their fellow soldiers.

No other competency was required. The AVEF would take anyone; anyone at all. The rest of the armed forces considered the AVEF the dregs of society. The Pentagon considered them disposable.

It was within these ranks that Jack Tate had hoped to disappear, forget his past and hope the world would forget about him. Those plans were short lived.

Now he was running a covert team gathered from the best of what the AVEF had to offer. It was worse than it sounded; they were unexperienced, untrained, and far below the skill level of even the most rookie special forces team he'd ever seen, but they had heart and grit.

He'd devoted his time and knowledge to training them, and they were steadily improving. They'd been tested in some risky operations and were lucky to be alive. But experience brought wisdom and skill.

To their credit, they never shied away or let him down. At Tate's request they had been unofficially sanctioned as The Grave Diggers. The reason for their existence was a secret so dangerous that only a handful of people knew.

They were to sabotage and undermine The Ring's expansion of power.

This is where Tate's past as a member of Delta Force would serve him well. He and his team continued to operate out of the AVEF, staying under the radar.

Except for the constant heat, the humidity and endless jungle of dangers, Tate couldn't complain. His base quarters were spartan but clean. The air-conditioning almost never failed. His team had recently broken into a broadcasting nexus and tapped into a television feed, so now they had all the junk TV and sports anyone could wish for.

If he wasn't so exhausted after the day's exercise, he might have gone to the Rec Room and seen what was showing. Instead he decided to stay in and get some rack time.

Outside, two MPs patrolled their sector of the base's living quarters. Even though it was nearing two in the morning, the MPs didn't mind the late shift; the weather was at its coolest then. The MPs felt bad for the poor suckers who had to walk a beat in the middle of the day.

The patrol paths of the two MP's intersected a few yards from Tate's quarters. They spoke in quiet undertones to avoid the complaints, in case any of the noncoms were awake. One of them gave his friend a stick of chewing gum. With a nod of thanks, they parted ways to continue their patrols.

Once the MPs were out of sight, a shadow parted from the well-manicured hedges. It stopped at Tate's living room window and went to work on the lock.

The window slid quietly open and the dark figure climbed in without effort.

Inside Tate's quarters, the figure paused, their hand resting on the butt of their gun. Tensed and ready, the still figure melded with the dark.

Remaining motionless for a long time, the figure decided they were satisfied the quiet rhythm of the night hadn't been disturbed. They crossed the room to a small space near the far wall.

Their gloved hand reached down and felt along the floor, gently sweeping back and forth until they detected a defect in the surface of the wooden tiles. There was a seam that didn't lay perfectly flat.

The muted light from outside glinted off a knife that appeared in the figure's hand. With the careful movements of a surgeon, the figure probed the seam until they found what they were looking for and leveraged up the flooring, revealing a dark void under the floor.

The knife disappeared into its sheath and the figure reached in and removed a thick, metal box. The top of the box was hinged with a numbered keypad and display in its center.

Under their black balaclava, the figure smiled to themselves, amused at the unintimidating security measure.

Taking a roll of silicon from the pocket of their cargo pants, the intruder laid it out beneath the keypad. With practiced movement, they attached four fiber optic connectors from the sheet of silicone to the box. On the face of the silicone was a compact keyboard and a polycell display. After typing in a series of commands, the sheet's onboard AI began sending intricate pulses to the keypad. Normally, a press of any of the keypad's buttons would have activated it, back-lighting the keypad's screen and emitting a series of tones to signal it was ready to receive the biometric input of its owner.

The hacking AI instructed the box's security system that none of that was necessary and fed an error code to the security's internal maintenance chip. The AI then flooded the chip with a rapid series of pulses, overwhelming the chip's syntax matrix. The chip's algorithms switched into maintenance mode. Used by the manufacturer's repairmen, the diagnostic mode shut down all processes before further damage was incurred. The box unlocked in three seconds.

The figure opened the lid and reached inside. It was empty. The box wasn't large and the object the figure was expecting would have taken up most of the space. But something was there.

The figure stifled a sigh as they recognized it was a piece of paper. They took it out to read it and the room filled with light.

The figure moved, lightning fast. A gun appeared instantly in their hand. The business end was aimed at Tate, who was lounging in an easy chair across the room. His one hand was on the light switch;

in his other was his Colt .45, the big mouth of the barrel pointed directly at the intruder.

"Evening," said Tate.

The black-clad figure sat down on the floor, keeping their gun steadily pointed at Tate. "Evening."

"Lost?" asked Tate.

With their free hand, the figure slowly pulled off the hood. Long black hair spilled out, framing a female face with high cheekbones, gentle yet defined features and almond-shaped eyes of Kaiden Benedict.

Tate's long-time and trusted friend swept her hair back out of her face. She looked at him with an expression of nonplused amusement.

"Would it help if I told you I got lost?" she asked.

Tate considered the question a moment, not taking his eyes off her. "Not really, no."

They looked at each other, both content to let the silence fill the room. Neither moved. Neither entertained a distracting thought; both on the razor's edge, ready to act.

"Is that loaded?" asked Tate, breaking the quiet.

"Yes," said Kaiden. "Tranq darts. Fast acting, but without the annoying after-effects of a headache."

"That's thoughtful," he said.

"Is yours?" she asked.

"Yes," said Tate flatly. "Hundred and ninety-eight grain, hollow point. Also fast acting. But without the annoying after-effects of a headache."

"Ouch," said Kaiden.

"The safety's off, too," said Tate.

"That hurts," she said, looking wounded.

"So does breaking into my home," he said, leaning forward. "And stealing from me."

Kaiden looked down at the paper she found in the safe. *You owe me a new safe.*

In a gesture of surrender, she put down the gun and moved her hand away from it.

Tate did not mirror her actions. His .45 was still aimed at her.

"You broke into Natan's," he stated. "After the database from Vulcan 4, I'm guessing."

"I didn't think he should have it," said Kaiden.

"And you should? He thinks you're a threat. Not just to him. All of us. This situation strongly reinforces that argument."

She only looked at him, saying nothing.

"What really troubles me is that you had an assault team with you," he said. "Full gear, modern looking stuff. Don't tell me you hired a bunch of derelict mercs who brought their own equipment."

"I wasn't going to tell you anything," said Kaiden, holding up the note. "But that plan didn't work out and here we are."

"Why are you after the database?" growled Tate. "Who are you working for? And before you try dodging the question, consider I've spent a lot of nights in this chair, waiting for you. I'm tired, uncomfortable, and pissed off. Most importantly, and I can't impress this on you enough, the only way tonight ends is with me getting the answers I want, or you getting a bullet."

Kaiden studied Tate for a moment, calculating; gauging. "Seems like there's no middle ground," she said.

Tate came out of his chair, his face tight with anger. "I gave you middle ground," he yelled. "I turned a blind eye to the secrets you wanted to keep because I trusted you. Now you're trying to steal a database that opens the door to our country's most classified communications, exposing covert agents, and who knows what else. I swore to protect this country and I promise you, you do *not* want to put that oath to the test."

The room vibrated with the brittle energy of Tate's anger.

Kaiden looked up at him, the strain clear in her features. Her brown eyes reflected a cold seriousness. "I swore an oath, too," she said.

"To what country?" said Tate, his voice sounding like the grinding of granite. The knuckles of his gun hand were white, his grip squeezing hard enough to make the gun shake.

"The same as yours," she said, her eyes not wavering from his. "And no one else's."

Tate glared at her, processing her words through the torrent of half-contained anger. He resented her for his outrage. Feelings of loyalty and trust teetered over the bottomless pit of suspicion.

He realized his finger had tightened on the trigger and eased the pressure.

His was on the tipping point leading to disaster and death, or a return to sanity and calm. With all his will he clamped down on the storm in his mind, demanding calm.

Tate's thumb moved. Sliding up the checkered grip of the Colt, it pressed against the safety until the lever clicked into place. He held the gun rigidly aimed at Kaiden for a second more, then let his hand drop to his side.

Kaiden visibly drew a breath and relaxed.

Tate sat down and rubbed his eyes.

Putting the gun on the side table next to him, he rubbed his tired eyes against the throbbing headache that was thudding through his brain.

Kaiden stayed on the floor and watched him. She waited, giving Tate room to decompress before she spoke.

"I can answer your questions," she said tentatively. "All of them."

Tate's laugh was a mix of weary cynicism and irony. "You're joking, right? After all this, you're asking me if I'm sure?"

"What you want to know comes with a responsibility," said Kaiden. "There's a bigger picture of what's happening."

"And what?" said Tate. "I'm too fragile to know the truth or some BS like that?"

"Okay," she said, standing up. "Be ready to leave in a few hours."

"I'm exhausted," he sighed. "Enough cloak and dagger. Just tell me."

"Pack for a couple of days," said Kaiden. She picked up her hood and gun and headed to the door. "I'm sorry it went this way," she said over her shoulder, and closed the door behind her.

Tate looked at his gun laying on the table and shook his head. "Yeah. Me too."

5

RATS IN THE BASEMENT

Tate and Kaiden left the base just before dawn. Three hours later they were touching down on runway 4/22 at Ronald Reagan International airport. Hardly a word was said between the two. The awkwardness was dialed up even more when they had boarded a private jet. Except for the pilots, it was just Tate and Kaiden.

He stuck a piece of chewing gum in his mouth to help his ear pop as the air pressure increased. Looking around, he didn't see anywhere to throw away the wrapper and stuck the wadded foil back in his pocket.

Access to a private jet only fed the number of questions swirling around Tate's head. The more Kaiden revealed of the resources at her disposal, the more he was both impressed, and suspicious.

It wasn't just that she had been hiding another side of her life; it was the magnitude of what she was hiding.

The jet's wheels touched the tarmac with a squeal and the engines reversed the thrust, bringing a shuddering end to their smooth flight.

They rolled onto a taxiway that took them away from the main terminal. Out the window, Tate saw a black SUV parked next to the taxiway and guessed it was meant for them.

The jet came to a stop and the door opened up, extending its stairway to the pavement.

Kaiden got up and retrieved her duffle bag. With a nod to Tate, she exited the plane. He followed and smiled to himself as she put her bag in the car. Nobody else was in sight.

He climbed in the passenger seat as Kaiden pressed the starter. The SUV silently came to life. Outside temperature, engine status and location appeared on the windshield's heads-up display.

"Hello," said the SUV's Artificial Intelligence. "I'm Sam. I see you've already set your destination. Would you like me to drive?"

"No," said Kaiden.

"Your drive time will be..."

"I don't care," she said.

"Your passenger seems tense," said Sam.

"Hey," protested Tate.

"There's sensors built into the seat," said Kaiden.

"I have a great selection of relaxation music."

"What are you tense about?" she asked.

"I'm not," said Tate, frowning.

"You look like someone who enjoys jazz," said Sam.

He didn't know how the AI could know that, but Tate didn't like being analyzed.

Kaiden tapped a small dot on the dashboard in front of Tate. "Camera."

Taking the gum out of his mouth, Tate stuck it over the lens.

"Bug off, Sam," said Tate.

"We don't need any company," said Kaiden.

"Shutting down," said Sam.

Tate left his gum in place and buckled his seat belt. "This is what they're doing with technology?"

"Some people like it," said Kaiden, pulling away from the jet.

As they past a row of hangers, Tate watched an airliner come in for a landing; once a common, nearly unnoticed symbol of everyday life.

He didn't know what to make of it now. It made sense that people still traveled, but how common was it? All he ever saw were deserted and ravaged towns and villages; places only the dead inhabited. But here were real people, doing normal things. It made him wonder if they even thought about the horror still prowling outside the defensive walls that surrounded the city.

For over two years he had been living on the outskirts of humanity. He had no concept of what was happening in the rest of the country. He didn't read the news or attempt to keep up with current events. Tate had been there before; keeping tabs on world events, politics, all of it. Staying informed was his way of being ahead of the game if a new mission came through related to what he already knew.

A side gate opened as they approached the airport's security fence and soon they pulled onto George Washington Memorial highway. It was a culture shock to see all the cars

So many cars. Images from post-apocalyptic movies flashed through Tate's mind. Rusted, abandoned hulks littering a weed choked, cracked highway didn't mesh with what he was looking at. It was as if the Vix had never happened.

"It's real," said Kaiden, reading his expression.

Tate mentally swore to himself. He hated her talent for guessing his thoughts. It was like there was nothing private, even in his head.

"Inside the city life goes on," she continued. "Don't let it fool you. It isn't like nothing's happened. People like to pretend it didn't. When they test the emergency broadcast system you can see the fear in their eyes. Even with all the countermeasures in place, something could happen. An accident, a sudden death and they don't catch it in time. Next thing you know, Vix are ripping people to shreds."

"Has that happened?" asked Tate.

"Not for a while, but yes," said Kaiden. "In the beginning there were some pretty bad outbreaks. The government wised up fast but putting the countermeasures in place took time. Getting people onboard with the changes..."

"Intrusions into their privacy, you mean," injected Tate.

"No man is an island," she answered. "Everyone has to wear bio monitors. It's not like they track you."

"Sure," he scoffed. "Don't tell me you believe them."

"I *know* they don't," said Kaiden. "They don't have the capacity to track everyone. The manpower alone..."

"Come on," said Tate. "They don't need people. AI that can run rings around humans. Remember when everyone had a smart home? The tech companies didn't just spy on people. They studied them like lab rats."

"I remember when they got exposed," she said. "The backlash was ugly."

"People didn't like learning they were being manipulated through psychological targeting," he said. "They used it to influence policy in Washington."

"They got shut down hard," chuckled Kaiden. "Some of those CEOs are still doing time."

"Just the ones that weren't murdered in the streets," said Tate. "They should have stuck with bribing politicians."

Kaiden glanced at the wade of chewing gum on the dashboard. "That's why you don't trust AI?"

"They say AI is strictly machine made," he said, "but somewhere in all that code is a speck of human contamination. Something that will create an agenda in the AI."

She shrugged off the debate. "Believe what you want. The biometric monitors couldn't care less about you, except when your heart stops beating."

"Then they care a lot," finished Tate. "So if they aren't tracking you, how do they know where to go if your heart stops?"

"The monitor sends out a location," she said. "That only happens after you die. Then emergency services begin broadcasting. Everyone knows what to do, depending on the condition level."

"I was wondering what those things were," said Tate.

Along the way he'd noticed tall posts lining the highway. They looked a little like tall traffic lights, but they weren't on.

"When someone dies, those'll come on, depending on how far away the threat is. The color will change with the level of threat."

"I'd hate to see what would happen if someone hacked into that as a prank," chuckled Tate.

"Someone did," said Kaiden flatly.

Tate's expression turned serious. He looked at her to fill in the blanks. He could see her brow furrow as the tragic memories came back to her.

"This stupid kid thought it would be funny," she said finally. "Nearly the entire city went condition black. It means the city can't be saved. Evacuate or die."

"Oh my gosh," he gasped.

"Yeah. The city tore itself apart," said Kaiden. "Traffic jams, riots, looting. But the worst..." She paused, struggling with the tragedy of it all. "The worst was the suicides. So many people killed themselves it nearly created a real condition black. It sounds cold, but thank goodness for the people who hung themselves, or blew their brains out. If security hadn't acted fast enough, they would have scorch-earthed the city."

"What happened to the kid?" asked Tate.

Kaiden shook her head as if trying to dislodge the memory from her mind. "It was so pointless," she said. "That stupid kid."

"Kids do stupid things," he said. "Making mistakes, learning from them."

"They had to send a message," she said. "Make sure that nobody ever did that again."

"They executed the kid?" he asked in shock.

"I wish they had," said Kaiden.

Tate waited. He wanted to know, but something in her voice made him dread what she'd say next. He changed his mind and was about to change the subject, but she spoke first.

"They dropped the kid outside the city walls. They slaved a couple of drones with cameras to follow him. They televised it 24/7."

"Outside the walls?" said Tate. The kid would have been scared out of his mind; dropped in a land of monsters. His own heart began beating faster at the image of being isolated from any help. Surrounded by prowling nightmares.

"It was hideous," said Kaiden. "But the message was received. Nobody's messed with the system since."

"Who approved that execution?"

"Ha," she laughed. "Like anyone would tie their name to that. We don't even know who was in the room when that decision took place."

Tate was groping for something to say when Kaiden interrupted.

"We're here," she said, catching him by surprise.

He instantly recognized where he was as they came down N. Rotary Road. Looking to the south was the entrance to the Pentagon.

"You're kidding me," he said in disbelief.

"You wanted to know," said Kaiden. "Your answer's inside there."

They found a parking place and quickly crossed the lot and up the steps to the entrance. Kaiden handed him a lanyard with a card hanging from it.

"This one's yours," she said.

Tate was familiar with the common access card. Worn by civilian contractors, government and military personnel, it would grant access to all but the higher security floors.

They stopped while the Pentagon Force Protection Agency inspected their credentials. The PFPA took their job seriously and made sure everyone knew it. All of them were dressed in tactical gear. They carried a sidearm with an assault rifle slung across their chests.

The Pentagon was the heart of the Department of Defense. Everything that happened, every mission, covert operation, troop movement, new piece of equipment... everything originated from this building.

The PFPA officer held up Tate's card and look at his face. Satisfied, he let it drop and nodded his permission to enter.

Stepping into the wide, bustling hall reminded Tate of his time as a Delta Force operator. He had come here to present after-action reports after completing a couple of highly classified missions.

At first glance it didn't look like anything had changed. The wide halls, drab-colored walls and matching floors, still the same as he remembered. But then a couple of details caught his attention. Strong metal frames were bolted into the walls and ceiling. Attached to them were reinforced doors. Each door was controlled by two large pistons.

"They added those after the outbreak," commented Kaiden.

Tate's jaw clenched in annoyance. Was she that good or was he that easy to read?

"If there's a report of Vix inside the building, the doors automatically close."

"Keeping the Vix from spreading," observed Tate.

"Sucks if you're on the wrong side of the door," said Kaiden.

They stopped at the double doors of an elevator and she pressed the 'down' button.

The five above ground floors were used by the twenty-six thousand employees and contractors. The two sub levels were used as a catch-all for storage, archives and maintenance facilities to keep everything running. It was new territory for Tate.

The two moved out of the way as the elevator doors opened, emptying its passengers. They stepped inside and Kaiden held her card in front of a sensor. The doors closed and with a slight shudder they felt themselves going down.

When the doors opened, they were looking at another hall, this one empty of the bustling crowds.

Kaiden led the way past several unmarked, nondescript doors until they came to one that was open. She went inside with Tate behind her.

The inside was set up like a small classroom. Three rows of rectangular tables with the same yellow, fake wood grain laminate tops he remembered as a kid.

"Have a seat," said Kaiden, pointing to the first row of chairs.

Tate picked a chair and was mildly surprised as she walked to the back of the room and leaned against the wall.

The only sound was the decades-old clock on the wall. If the drab walls and yellow-tinged lighting was designed to make every second feel like an hour, they had achieved their goal.

Tate was beginning to feel restless. He checked his watch and decided he'd wait another five minutes before pressing Kaiden for answers.

The door opened up and two men dressed in similar black suits walked in. One of them put a stack of file folders on the table next to Tate, then joined his near twin in the front of the room.

Tate had been out of special operations for a few years, but he knew a spook when he saw one. These guys were so cookie cutter it was enough to make him chuckle, but he ignored the urge.

The two men looked at Tate with the same disinterest of watching paint dry. They never looked in Kaiden's direction.

Tate knew their type. With these bozos everything was a game. It irritated him to have to play along if he wanted answers.

They were waiting to see what Tate said, or asked them.

Spook psychology 101; making him come to them.

A load of bull, Tate knew, but these guys were going to do things their way.

Tate decided to cut to the heart of the matter.

"What do you want with Vulcan 4's database?" he asked.

One of them began to speak and Tate raised his hand, cutting him off.

"Before you start, I'll set the bar for you. If you say, 'need to know', 'above your pay grade', or 'that's classified' I'm out, and you two will die of old age never knowing where that database is."

The two men looked at each other then nodded to Tate as they re-appraised the man in front of them.

"Look, uh..." said Tate, dropping a hint.

"I'm Smith," said the man, "and this is Jones. What do you know about Vulcan 4?"

"I asked first," said Tate, already feeling his patience growing short.

"This isn't a one-way street," said Jones. "We'll tell you about Vulcan 4, but that means you give us something in return. We're not asking for a lot..."

Tate got up and walked out of the room. He was waiting for the elevator when Kaiden caught up to him.

"Just to clarify the situation," she said. "You put a gun to my head and demanded to know what's going on. It wasn't easy getting them to meet with you. After all that you're leaving?"

"These guys stink of FBI," hissed Tate.

"Truthfully," said Kaiden, "I can't tell who they are."

"What's your gut tell you?" he challenged.

Kaiden shrugged. "I've worked with slimier people than these two."

"I don't like it," spat Tate. "I've known drug addicts more trustworthy." He jabbed the elevator button several times, swearing under his breath.

"Right," she said. "This isn't your first time you've had to get into the muck to get the job done. You handled it then. Handle it now."

"And what?" he said. "Agree to their terms without even knowing what I'm getting into?"

"These guys are scummy," she said, "but they've never thrown me under a bus. I think they're afraid of me."

Tate looked unconvinced as the elevator doors rumbled open. Before he could step inside, Kaiden grabbed his arm.

"You're not making this easy for me," she said, as he looked at her quizzically. "I'm asking you. Please."

"Why should I?" he asked. "Why is this important to you?"

"How else will you ever know you can trust me?"

Tate studied Kaiden's eyes. Her deep, walnut-hued gaze possessed a hardness and intensity he seldom saw. She kept his stare, daring him to reject her.

He exhaled loudly and headed back to the room.

Neither of the men seemed surprised to see him walk in.

Too keyed up to sit, Tate paced by his chair.

Kaiden walked in and nodded to the two men as she returned to the back of the room.

"This situation is highly classified," began Smith. "Your previous clearance level lapsed..."

"Oh, screw that," snapped Tate. "You know who I am. My file's right there." He pointed to the stack of folders. "I was cleared for above top secret and I never violated it. I'm not going to start now." He stared at them, waiting for them to continue.

The spooks shared a look then nodded in agreement.

"We knew Vulcan 4's security protocols were compromised," said Jones. "We're the ones who did it. We baited the hook and we got exactly what we were looking for."

"Which was?" prodded Tate.

"There's lots of elements out there who are a threat to our country," said Smith, sitting against the desk. "We leave the other agencies to handle the amateurs. We're only interested in the smart ones. The top tier dangers with the TTPs to exploit our bulletproof systems and use it against us."

Tate frowned for a moment as he recalled the 'Pentagonese' that people used to make a point of showing they worked at the Pentagon and you didn't. Tactics, Techniques and Procedures was part of how enemy threat levels were assigned. The better trained and capable of applying those skills, the more dangerous a person was.

"And someone took the bait," said Tate. He began to wonder if they were talking about The Ring. That possibility came with a rat's nest of complications. There was no way he was going to tell these spooks he was effectively a double agent for The Ring. If they knew half the things he was into he might end up in a black site interrogation room for the remainder of his life.

He kept his expression neutral but interested, waiting to see where all of this was leading.

"Ever hear of the Wagner Group?" asked Smith.

"Yeah," said Tate. "Officially they were a private military contractor, but they took their orders from the Kremlin. When they wanted something ugly done but didn't want to be blamed for it, the Kremlin would transfer teams of Spetsnaz into the Wagner Group."

"That's exactly what happened in Syria," said Jones. "The Kremlin had inserted two battalions of Spetsnaz for an op we still don't know much about. They used an Iranian general to attack a US outpost. The attack was supposed to mask the Russian's real mission."

"Smart," said Tate. "But risky. We pulled a couple of those. Both of them almost went sideways on us."

"No almost here," said Smith. "The attack blew up in their faces. That wasn't the worst of it. If any surviving Russian soldier admitted they were following orders from the Kremlin, it would prove Putin ordered an attack on US forces. The optics would destroy Putin and his power base."

"Of course, Putin disavowed the whole thing," added Jones. "He threw the surviving soldiers in some hell-hole to rot."

"We thought they all died there," said Smith. "Then Misha Kilmonikov appears on our radar."

"Should I know him?" asked Tate.

"Unlikely," said Smith. "But the Kremlin does and they're scared of him."

"An angry Spetsnaz, betrayed by his country?" said Tate. "If he's after revenge, they should be scared."

"We had an asset in Moscow who reported the head of Russian military intelligence was blown up in his car," said Jones.

Tate marveled that even though the world was nearly destroyed by the Vix, the spy game kept on living. They were like a cockroach; nothing seemed to kill them.

"After that, four more high-level types were killed. We thought someone was making a power play until Kilmonikov publicly posts a hit list with the names of the dead guys crossed off. Moscow mobilized the army and went into lockdown. Nobody in or out and a 'shoot on sight' curfew."

"He's Spetsnaz," said Tate. "That won't stop him."

"This is where Vulcan 4 comes into the story," said Jones. "Two months ago, someone finds the exploit we planted and a new communications feed appears on the satellite. It's a group of Russians and they're talking to people in the Black Market. Crime bosses, bad guys. Someone slips up and we catch a name. Kilmonikov. There's a whole lot of chatter that he's planning something big."

Tate looked over his shoulder at Kaiden as the last piece of the puzzle fell into place.

"You were monitoring him using Vulcan 4 before it dropped out of orbit," said Tate. "And you're thinking there might be more intel about him stored in the database."

"We *did*," said Jones. "But we don't care about that now. The situation has become fluid. Vulcan 4 is old news. We got a location that Kilmonikov's in Nigeria."

"What did you hear that's making you nervous?" asked Tate.

"For the time being that information is out of your lane," said Jones.

Tate clenched his jaw against the unfiltered thoughts colliding with the back of his teeth. The intel community enjoyed the snobbery of a class system. They used expressions like 'need to know' or 'above your pay grade' to make sure you knew where you fit in the food chain.

He took a deep breath and filed away the slight.

"We need someone downrange who can give us real-time intel on what he's doing," said Smith

Suddenly, Tate could see this meeting was going in another direction. He was there to learn why Kaiden had been after Vulcan 4. The situation was shifting from a briefing to a sales pitch. One that involved travel.

"Kilmonikov has advanced training in urban combat, sabotage, counterterrorism, diversion and reconnaissance," said Smith, counting off on his fingers. "He's adaptable, intelligent, and highly motivated."

"The best person to recon him has to be someone with similar training and experience," said Jones.

The agents finished what they had to say and looked meaningfully at Tate.

"You want me to go to Nigeria?" he scoffed.

"And Kaiden," added Jones.

6

PLANES AND TAXIS

"Collision. Collision, warned the airplane's robotic voice as Tate and Kaiden were thrown around in their seats.

"Break right," yelled the co-pilot.

The Gulfstream banked hard right as the pilot pushed the throttles. The twin Rolls-Royce engines roared as they pumped out enough force to push the plane's passengers back in their seats.

"This place is a death trap," yelled the pilot over his shoulder. "We should land somewhere else."

Tate looked out his window, down at the Murtala Muhammed International Airport and shook his head. He unbuckled his seatbelt and made his way to the flight deck.

"Anywhere else will be too far away," he said.

"You're seeing the same thing I'm seeing, right?" asked the pilot.

Outside, the sky was a jumbled crowd of small planes, climbing, swerving and cutting each other off. Most were beat up, nearly vintage bush planes; DeHavillands, Cessnas, Murphys, Lockheeds and others. Many of them were patched and rebuilt from other aircraft pieces so it was impossible to tell which part was the original plane.

International flights had become rare to nonexistent after the outbreak. The airport had been abandoned for a short time. The bush pilots saw a perfect opportunity to make money busing people and supplies.

Located on the West African coast, Lagos had been a vital shipping port before the Vix came. Few cities possessed the extremes of poverty and wealth as Lagos. The poorer areas lacked running water, electricity and even paved roads. That didn't stop people from flocking to the city once the Vix appeared. Lagos was better than being ripped apart.

"Tower," said the pilot, switching the radio to the cabin speakers. "This is GS-774. We had clearance to..."

"Yeah, man, I know," said a frustrated voice. "The rest of you idiots listen up. This is the tower. I'm telling you, that white jet is the next one to land."

The speakers filled with several people arguing about why they needed to land next.

Out of the window, Tate could see planes dodging each other, trying to drive off another pilot and take their place in line to land.

"Shut up," yelled the tower. "If anyone lands before the jet, I'll have your plane impounded. Jooko, that means you, too. Okay? Okay."

The airwaves quieted down and the planes veered off to a safer distance.

"Okay 774," said the tower. "Land now and hurry up."

Tate looked down and saw a string of people jogging across the runway, chased by someone in an orange vest.

"Hang on," said the pilot.

Tate gripped the bulkhead as the Gulfstream banked hard and dropped its nose. The windscreen filled with the ground below as Tate's stomach dropped.

"Pull up. Pull up," said the onboard computer as several warning lights began to blink.

The ground zoomed up at them and whatever confidence Tate had in the pilot was disappearing at the same speed they were racing to the tarmac.

At the last minute the pilot pulled back hard on the stick.

"Throttle back," snapped the pilot.

The co-pilot pulled back on the thrust controls, keeping one hand on the stick.

"One hundred, sixty, forty, ten," said the computer, counting their altitude.

"Flaps," said the pilot.

The co-pilot toggled the lever setting the flaps in landing position.

The Gulfstream banged down hard on its landing gear and bounced. The pilot pushed the plane back down, the wheels hitting with a thump.

"Reverse thrust," said the co-pilot, pressing another switch.

Outside, two doors opened on the rear of the engine, redirecting the engines thrust forward. The pilot increased power to the engines and abruptly slowed the Gulfstream.

"Okay 774," said the tower. "You park by that green Cessna on your right."

Looking to their right, they could see a beat-up, bright green Cessna with flat tires in a dirt field.

Tate and the pilot traded looks of exasperation.

"When in Rome," said Tate. "That was impressive flying."

"Navy," said the pilot. "You land on enough carriers during storms, you pick up a few techniques."

"Go Navy," said Tate.

The pilot taxied the Gulfstream quickly off the runway, making an opening for the next small plane to land.

Tate made his way back to Kaiden, who was looking very pale. Her eyes were closed and she was taking deep, controlled breaths. Her fingers were white, clutching the armrests of her seat.

"We're down now," he said. He'd never seen Kaiden so shaken up. He admitted to himself that his legs were a little wobbly but forced himself to ignore it.

Kaiden opened her eyes and looked at him, expelling her breath. She looked at her hands before letting go, as if they were fighting against her.

"That was a rough one," said Tate kindly. "Want some water?"

She nodded and he handed her a bottle after taking off the cap.

After several sips, her natural color returned.

"I can't wait to see what the rest of this place is like," she said with a lopsided grin.

"You haven't lived until you've been to Lagos," chuckled Tate. "You have a little bit of everything here. Like diametrically opposed ecospheres, and yet it all works together."

"Sounds enchanting," said Kaiden.

The Gulfstream bumped to a stop.

"It's magical," said Tate. "Don't forget your gun."

The hatch opened, lowering the stairs down to the ground. Warm air mingled with a complex swirl of smells that filled the cabin as Tate picked up his bag.

"We'll be done here in five days to a week," he said to the pilot. "I'll call you on the sat phone when it looks like we're wrapping up."

"Take your time," said the pilot. "We'll be here."

"You're staying?" asked Tate.

"After what it took to land, you think we're going through that again?" scoffed the pilot. "That's a negative."

With their feet on the ground, Tate and Kaiden took in their surroundings. In the distance was the airport terminal. Scattered around them were small aircraft either dropping off passengers or picking them up. Men and women in brightly-colored hazard vests herded people at the edges of the runways.

In charge of controlling foot traffic, the crossing guards watched the planes taking off or landing. When there was enough time for everyone to get across the tarmac, the crossing guards would blow a whistle and it was off to the races.

Tate and Kaiden joined a crowd of travelers who chatted excitedly with each other. The crossing guard blew her whistle twice, putting her hand in the air. Everyone went quiet and waited. The crossing guard blew a long trill, dropping her hand and the crowd took off. Some laughed with excitement, while others swiveled their heads like field mice looking for a hawk swooping down on them.

Tate and Kaiden made the dash two more times before reaching the doors to the terminal.

Small in comparison to other international airports, the building was constructed twice as large as needed in anticipation of future growth that would never come.

Tall windows reached to the high ceiling twenty feet above. A second-floor shopping arcade looked down on the open terminal and its arriving passengers. Banners hung from the arcade advertising foods, clothing, and various goods.

The air conditioners rumbled above the buzz of the crowds, but hardly made a dent in the heat.

Once inside, Tate motioned Kaiden off to the side and they took a moment to study their new surroundings. This was a foreign place where government infrastructure was fractured, if not entirely broken. There weren't just cultural customs to be aware of; it paid to watch and learn from those who lived and survived here.

People had lined up at three of the Customs Agent counters, though it was anyone's guess if the uniformed agents were authentic. The fourth terminal was closed, but the fifth was open. In an attempt to look official, the man at that terminal had pinned a fake badge to a stained Fed Ex shirt. Smiling, he was waving at the new arrivals, trying to draw people to his terminal. Nobody was in line there and Tate and Kaiden instantly knew something there was wrong.

Not everyone was paying attention. A woman struggled through the door, trying to keep track of two impatient children and their bags. Tired and exasperated, it wasn't difficult to choose between the long lines and the friendly man at terminal five.

Tate and Kaiden could see the concerned expressions of people in the longer lines. Something bad was happening.

They were too far away to hear but saw that the man let the children pass. When the woman tried to follow, he stopped her. As soon as she started to protest, the man's smile vanished. He started shouting at her, demanding payment. She pulled a couple of wrinkled bills from her bag and slapped them down on the counter. Confused and scared, the crying children called for their mother.

The man at the counter wasn't a match for her as she pushed past him.

He shouted something and two armed men appeared and took each child by the hand.

Tate and Kaiden casually rested their hands on their concealed pistols.

"We're here five minutes and already doing something stupid," said Tate.

"I bet they don't have backup," said Kaiden.

"That's your first thought?" said Tate. "Nothing about shooting with kids downrange?"

"Aim high," said Kaiden. "Problem solved."Barricaded from her children, the mother reached into her shirt and pulled out more bills. The money must have been enough because the skinny man lost interest in her. The armed men went back to wait for the next unsuspecting traveler.

The mother grabbed her kids and quickly disappeared into the crowd.

Taking their hands off their guns, Tate and Kaiden relaxed and got into the long line.

As they waited, vendors walked up and down the lines hawking hammers, pipe wrenches, clubs and machetes.

"Good for evil dead," said an old woman with a sack of hammers. "You need for the city."

"No thanks," said Kaiden, waving her off.

Others prowled the lines selling whistles. A small boy came up to them with a thick bundle of whistles piled around his neck.

"You see them," he said, contorting his face to mimic a Vix, "blow for help."

With a crowded line of potential customers, it didn't take much convincing to turn him away.

In spite of the crowds, the line moved quickly. Two men and a woman worked the *official* terminals. They hardly looked at Tate's passport. Their only interest was collecting the governmental fee required to enter.

The walk to the exit was a quick one, without incident. The curbside was jammed with taxis, scooters, bicycles towing seats bolted to axels; if it could carry people, it was there. All of them were shouting their fees, competing with the others. It was like a non-stop bidding war.

Tate spotted a handmade sign with a surprisingly good drawing of a yellow taxi on it. Several men, bored from hours of loitering, sat around the booth looking at Tate with new interest.

A dispatcher stood behind the scuffed, thick plastic window and nodded a greeting.

"Iganmu," said Tate, pointing to a faded map on the wall.

"No," said the dispatcher. "Nobody will take you there. Drivers aren't safe there. They will go as far as Ikate."

Tate frowned at the map. Ikate would knock a long way off their destination, but it was still too far to walk from there.

"These are good drivers," said the dispatcher. "All good drivers. Friendly. Work hard."

"Okay," agreed Tate, passing a couple of bills through the opening in the window. "Ikate."

"Louie," called the dispatcher.

Tate turned around and Louie was in front of him with his hand held out.

"I'm Louie," grinned the driver. "Hello, sir. Hello, Ma'am."

He grabbed their bags in one hand while sticking his free hand out to Kaiden.

"Welcome to Lagos," he said warmly. "My taxi is over here."

Tate and Kaiden had to pick up their pace to catch up to Louie before he disappeared into the crowd. They soon reached the other side and Louie opened the door for them.

"See?" he said as they climbed in. "Very clean inside. Very professional."

The taxi squeaked as Louie slammed the trunk closed on their luggage.

"Okay, where are you going?" he asked as he started the engine.

"As close to Iganmu as you can," said Tate.

Louie's smile faded and he pulled out into traffic. "I don't go into Iganmu," he said. "They have bad unions there. You have to pay a lot to drive through there."

Kaiden looked at Tate curiously.

"The gangs call themselves unions," said Tate. "The gangs flash their driver's license saying they're authorized to 'police' their territory. They extort money for protection, general hoodlum stuff. It's been this way for as long as I've been coming here."

"You know about area boys?" said Louie. "That's good. That will help you."

The taxi swerved around several cars waiting to turn in a crowded intersection while Tate and Kaiden held on. Traffic moved with its own rules of chaos. Bicycles and scooters darted between the cars with daredevil speeds, seemingly unconcerned by the honking and swearing.

"I didn't expect so many cars on the road," said Tate.

"Lagos doesn't ship oil like before," said Louie. "The ships hardly come. Now we have lots and lots of gas. Everyone drives. Everyone."

"What happened at the outbreak?" asked Tate.

"The what?"

"When all the Vix came," said Tate.

Louie shook his head, not understanding. "Who?"

"The, uh, the mmuo ojoo," said Tate, using the Igbo word for demon.

Everyone in Lagos was Nigerian, but the country was made up of several tribes. People held their tribe of the highest importance. It was their heritage. Each had its own customs, culture and history.

Unfortunately, it was also a point of division between people.

"The evil spirits," said Louie. "They stay mostly outside the city. Many watch towers were built. I tried to get a job doing that but ended up driving a taxi. The watch towers make sure the mmuo ojoo stay out. Everyone carries a whistle." He showed them a small, wooden whistle he wore around his neck

"Everyone carries a weapon," he said. "It's the law. When someone sees those creatures, they blow their whistle. Everyone comes running and attacks with their weapons. Everyone. The monster dies very fast."

The taxi bounced and squeaked through the dense city. They had traveled out of the fresh, clean architecture of the modern city into an older, poorer quarter. They hit a pothole that sent a jolt through their bones. In some places the roads were relatively smooth, but in others they were badly deteriorated. The pavement had been replaced with crushed rock, but every time it rained, which was often, the constant wear of trucks and cars would turn the dirt underneath to mud.

Planks and boards spanned deep channels between the street and sidewalk to keep runoff from the rain from building up on the streets.

The sides of the road were packed with parked cars. Beyond them were three- and four-story apartment buildings shouldering each other for space. The buildings were painted blue, tan, green, brown and everything in-between in an effort to brighten the rundown, shabby living conditions. Every window and balcony had bars over them.

Power lines ran between tall poles, crisscrossing haphazardly with no rhyme or reason. Broken cables hung from the poles with no telling if they still carried electricity.

Louie caught Kaiden looking at the tangled mess.

"Nobody counts on city power anymore," he said. "It comes. Stays a couple of days and goes. Poof. Sometimes there's power for twenty minutes then gone for days. Everyone had generators. Everyone. Gas is cheap to keep them running."

To Tate's eyes, little had changed from his memory. The thing about Lagos that always impressed him was the indomitable spirit of the people.

No matter what was thrown at them, they found a way to adapt and overcome. That sort of thing could make people bitter, but here, the people helped each other

Louie pulled over and turned around in his seat.

"Okay," he grinned. "We are here. Iganmu is a little way over there." He pointed down the road, but Tate had a good sense of where he was.

He gave Louie a generous tip which he happily accepted. As he unloaded their bags from the trunk, the taxi driver produced a couple of machetes.

"Here," he said. "You don't have any protection and I always carry extra for my special customers."

"That's very thoughtful of you," said Kaiden, "but we won't need them."

"Oh, miss," said Louie, becoming serious. "Two foreigners

walking through Iganmu without protection? No. I cannot let that happen."

Kaiden lifted up the front of her shirt, exposing the semiautomatic pistol hidden underneath.

Louie's eyes went wide with surprise and he laughed out loud. "You're going to be fine," he said. "But here, you take these." And he handed them a couple of wooden whistles. "My little girl makes them."

Tate lifted his new whistle to test it and Louie quickly clapped his hand over Tate's.

"Don't do that," he warned. "Everyone who hears it will come running, looking to kill the monsters. If they think you were playing a joke... that would be foolish."

"Thanks for the warning," said Tate, putting the whistle around his neck and tucking it in his shirt.

Louie pumped their hands firmly with his big smile and got back into his taxi. Tate took his bearings before they joined the bustling foot traffic.

They walked a couple of miles before Tate went into an alley and checked his map.

The worst thing anyone could do was wave a wad of money around strangers. The second worst thing was to be seen looking at a map. Nothing said 'target' like a person who didn't know where they were.

They had only gone a couple of blocks when their street emptied into a small town square. Shops and vendor stalls were everywhere. The scent of spices and cooking meats filled the area among the shouts of vendors selling their goods.

Several roads came together at a roundabout with a fountain sculpture at the center of it. Years of neglect showed in the dirt and cracked paint of the fountain.

Kaiden's instincts tugged her attention to a group of young men sitting on the fountain wall. All of them were openly staring at her and Tate. She casually turned to look at the wares on the nearby vendor table.

"Looks like trouble behind us," she said.

Tate pretended to brush something off his shoulder, giving him an excuse to glance at the group by the fountain.

"Area boys," he said. "We don't want them coming to us. It makes us look weak."

"All right," said Kaiden. "I'm game. Let's break the ice."

7

TAKEN FOR A RIDE

Together the two of them left the vendors and crossed the street to the gang lounging at the fountain.

"Who's the number two?" asked Tate to the group.

The young men looked at each other until one of them pushed off the fountain and stepped up.

"Who are you?"

"I won't disrespect the number two man by talking to someone under him," said Tate. "Are you the number two?"

"Yes, that's me," said the young man, thrusting out his chin. "Number Two."

"I'm glad we found you," said Tate. "Thank you for letting us in your city. I'm Jack. This is…"

"Jill," injected Kaiden.

Tate fumbled for just an instant then picked up where he'd left off. "We wanted to pay a donation to your union."

Number Two looked at them, pondering some internal questions.

Tate held out a small fold of bills. "What's your name?" he asked, not waiting for Number Two to decide if the donation was enough.

Tate put out his hand and Number Two took it.

"I am Isaac," he said, breaking into a big smile.

As if on cue, everyone else in the gang all relaxed and smiled, too.

"Can I see your union card?" asked Tate.

Isaac nodded his approval, recognizing Tate wasn't a stranger to their rituals. He took out his wallet and handed Tate a worn, laminated motorcycle license. Isaac's photo and name were easily visible though the plastic.

To the uneducated, this appeared to be an official government card, giving Isaac authority over this part of the city. To the people who knew it was a scam, they also knew they were powerless to fight it. This had been the way of things for generations.

"Nice to meet you, Isaac," said Tate, returning the card. He noticed one of the gang members looking at them with a dead stare.

He decided to leave it alone for now. He wasn't getting any vibe the guy was a threat.

"Are you hungry?" asked Isaac.

One of them shouted something and the others joined in. All of them were saying something different.

Tate realized they were different eateries in their town. He looked at Kaiden, inviting her opinion. She only smiled and shrugged her shoulders.

"That sounds great," said Tate.

"Follow us," said Isaac.

The group led them down streets and through alleys, talking happily about their town and pointing out interesting landmarks.

"I used to live in that house," said one of them, pointing to a burned-out building. "A monster came in and killed a man there. The neighbors boarded up the doors and windows and set it on fire. I jumped out from the second, no, third floor." The young man held up three fingers to make his point.

"That must have been scary," said Kaiden.

"Nah," said the young man. "Not for me."

"David, you are such a liar," said another gang member. "He was shaking like a fish on land."

David flushed at first, but his friend elbowed him, bringing out a smile.

"Okay, okay," said David, holding up his hand. "A little."

Before long they arrived at someone's home. Several older women came out and Isaac began talking to them in his native language. They sized up the foreign visitors before reluctantly nodding to Isaac.

The next few minutes we're a bustle of activity. Fold-out tables were carried out and set up on the sidewalk. Chairs, crates and anything else that made a workable seat was set up at the table.

Soon savory smells and singing wafted out of the home as the gang members asked questions and talked about themselves.

Everyone stopped as the women brought out the food. Bowls of rice were set out with a large pot of vegetable stew.

Kaiden looked curiously at the chunks of white meat in the stew.

"Goat," said Tate.

She smiled and nodded.

"Maybe," he grinned.

Kaiden didn't appreciate the humor and looked at the stew with suspicion.

As the meal progressed, she leaned over to Isaac, who'd picked a seat next to her.

"Why doesn't he ever smile?" she asked, pointing to the quiet one that only stared at them.

"He's a tough guy," said Isaac. "Joseph's always serious. If the boss has a problem or another union comes into our town, Joseph takes care of them."

"Like an enforcer," she said.

"Yes, yes," agreed Isaac. "An enforcer. Hey, Joseph, come here."

Joseph got up and sat down on a stack of milk crates.

"Show her your scars," chuckled Isaac.

Without giving it a second thought, he lifted his shirt, showing a chest and stomach marked with scars. Most of them were long and jagged, but a couple were small pock marks where he had been stabbed.

"You've seen a lot of fighting," said Kaiden.

Joseph only nodded then turned his head, showing a crescent scar that ran from the back of his head, over his ear and stopped at the corner of his lip.

"How did you get that?" she asked, wondering more how it hadn't killed him.

Joseph said something she couldn't understand and Isaac burst out laughing.

"He said that one was an accident."

Kaiden gave Joseph a second look, but his expression never changed.

"He doesn't talk about his fights," said Isaac. "He's a tough guy, you see. Tough guys don't bang their chest. They just fight and walk away."

After lunch, everyone was helping with clearing up, except Isaac.

Tate and Kaiden sat down with him to talk.

"I'm looking for some friends," said Tate.

"I know lots of people," said Isaac. "Who are you looking for?"

"His name is Nachi," said Tate. "He sold things. Things hard to find."

Isaac nodded his head in understanding and sat up. "That was before I joined the union, but I know about him. The smuggler. He got old and sick. His son took him and moved."

"Do you know where?" asked Tate.

"The son has a tire shop in Apapa," said Isaac. "You might find him there."

"There must be tire shops on every street," said Tate. "Can you tell me anything more?"

Isaac though for a minute while he picked his teeth. "I think it's on Bale road."

"Thank you for everything," said Tate. "We have to get going. I want to find my friend before night."

The sun was heading towards midafternoon and neither Tate nor Kaiden wanted to be out after sunset. Nobody, not even the area boys liked being out after dark. That's when the city was handed over to the real predators.

"You'll never get there with a taxi," said Isaac. "George, Chihe. Get your truck, okay? Take these two to Apapa, yeah?"

One of them took off, trotting down the road and soon returned in a battered Toyota Hilux. The pickup truck's dominate color was white, but not by much. One fender had been replaced from a blue truck, the hood from a silver truck and the bed from a red one. The rear window had been replaced with a piece of heavy plastic and duct-taped in place.

It wasn't the worst ride either of them had ever been in. Being escorted by the local gang got them around several delays, but nothing could be done about the congested traffic.

The road conditions were bad everywhere and the truck's shot suspension punished Tate and Kaiden with every bump they hit. To cushion against the beatings, they sat on their backpacks.

Chidi abruptly pulled the truck out of traffic and parked it. He got out as Tate and Kaiden climbed out of the bed.

"Apapa is right over there," said Chidi, pointing to the end of the block. "We don't go close to the gang there. They're messed up in the head. Lots of tough guys."

"Thanks for the warning," said Tate.

"And the ride," added Kaiden.

"You guys are cool, you know?" said Chidi and fist bumped them both.

With a wave, he got back into the truck and drove off.

Tate and Kaiden slung their packs over their shoulders and headed down the block towards the official boundary of Apapa.

It didn't look any different from anywhere else they'd been. The people seemed friendly, greeting them with a wave and a smile. But they took the warnings seriously. The gang here could be real trouble and neither of them dropped their guard.

Kaiden looked at the sky, noting the sun was getting low. "Let's speed up this journey," she said, spotting a taxi that had just parked nearby. "There's too much exposure traveling on foot."

Tate waved the taxi over and asked him if he knew where Bale Road was.

"Bale Road," said the driver. "I know it." He snubbed out his cigarette and got out to open the trunk.

"I'm Richie," he grinned. "I know all the best ways to get around the traffic."

He put their bags in the trunk and opened the rear door for them. The smell from years of cigarette smoke pushed away the fresh air and made the inside of the taxi feel claustrophobic. They enjoyed a moment of clean air when the driver opened his door to get in.

"Thanks," said Tate, doing his best not to wheeze. "We're looking for a tire shop there."

"A tire shop," said Richie. "Bale Road."

He rubbed his chin, mulling it over. There was something off about how long he was taking.

Kaiden looked in the rearview mirror and caught him eyeing her. He quickly looked away. She'd developed a thick skin a long time ago when it came to leering men. But the look in the driver's eyes was different; she felt he was sizing her up.

Even thought she still appeared relaxed, Tate noticed an undertone of watchfulness in Kaiden.

"Ah, I know the place," said Richie. "I know all the roads. You'll see. We will beat the traffic."

Kaiden confirmed Tate's hunch when she looked at him from the corner of her eyes. There was meaning in her look. He nodded in understanding and both of them casually dialed up their alert levels a notch.

It was only a few blocks before they ran into a knot of traffic. People were shouting out their windows, while others leaned on their horns. Some drivers had given up and had gotten out of their cars to chat with each other.

Hardly slowing, Richie turned down a narrow side street.

Tate involuntarily braced his feet as the taxi zipped past the walls squeezing in on them.

"We don't get many married couples visiting," said Richie.

"We're not married," said Tate.

"Oh," said Richie. "Too bad. You make a good couple." He laughed. "A pretty lady like you must have plenty of boyfriends, eh? I married when I was very young. I met my wife in school. We want to travel, but it's hard getting out of Lagos."

He continued to ramble on, but there was something contrived about his constant talking. As if it were a screen to distract them.

They'd been zig zagging down back roads during Richie's monologue and both of them recognized the sun was on the wrong side for the direction they were supposed to be heading.

Richie abruptly stopped talking about his fishing trip when something hard bumped the back of his head.

Carefully looking over his shoulder, he saw the barrel of Tate's gun an inch from his eye.

"Getting a little off track, aren't you, Richie?" asked Tate.

The taxi stopped and Richie raised his hands.

"Take it easy, okay?" he said, raising his hands. "I'm not trying to cheat you, honest. This is a better..."

Tate bumped the barrel of his gun into Richie's cheek. "Drop the act. You're taking us to where your friends are waiting to rob us."

Richie's eyes grew wide and then he broke into a large grin. "You watch too many westerns," he said. "I don't do that kind of thing. I'm honest. I can show you my official license."

Richie started for his glove compartment and Tate reached across the seat and pulled him back.

"I think we'll go alone from here," he said.

"It's a long way to that tire shop," said Richie, still smiling. "You don't want to be walking around when it's dark."

"He's right," said Tate. "Change of plans. Get out of the cab."

Richie started to say something, but Tate pulled back the hammer on his pistol and the driver closed his mouth.

Tate got out, keeping his aim Richie and motioned him out of the driver's seat.

"You're making big trouble for yourselves," said Richie. The smile vanished and his face hardened into a scowl.

"Been there, done that," said Kaiden, getting behind the wheel and closing the door.

"Start moving," said Tate.

Richie kept his hands up as he backed away.

Tate got into the passenger side with the gun aimed steadily at him.

Kaiden put the taxi in gear and took off down the street.

Richie dropped his hands as the taxi's taillights disappeared.

He took out his cell phone and angrily stabbed in a number. The call was answered on the first ring.

"I'm on Chuluu street," he said. "Come pick me up. Get the others. We're grabbing a nice prize tonight. Yeah, on Bale Road."

———

The dense traffic of Bale road was an attractive spot for street vendors. The slow crawl of cars was perfect for weaving from one driver to the next. Shops lined the street selling everything from plumbing supplies to shoe repair, to generator parts and fresh fish.

The slow pace made it easy for Tate to spot the tire shop. Stacks of tires made it impossible to miss.

Kaiden turned down a back alley and parked behind a crumbling building. Before getting out, Tate opened the glove compartment and smiled. His instincts were confirmed as he took out an old Webley revolver.

"Sweet relic," said Kaiden.

Tate stuffed it into his backpack. "That's going into my collection."

"You have a collection?"

He looked at her, grinning. "Apparently the master spy doesn't know everything about me."

"Get over yourself," she said. "You're not that interesting."

Both chuckled as they got out of the taxi. After a quick search of the area they found a plastic tarp and covered the car.

As they walked to the tire shop, lights were appearing in windows and shop owners were closing up for the day. The tire shop was already closed when they reached it. The shop took up the first floor of a two story, mustard-colored building. They saw lights from the second floor spilling out from the sliding glass doors of the sun deck.

A security camera sat conspicuously above the steel security door. Tate rang the doorbell and stepped into the streetlight to be better seen.

Soon they heard footsteps reach the other side of the door and then nothing. They assumed the person was looking at these two strangers, wondering why they were at their door.

The lock clicked and the door opened. A middle-aged man in kakis and a polo shirt looked at them from behind the security door but said nothing. The interior light backlit his face, hiding his opinion of these unexpected visitors.

"I'm sorry to bother you," said Tate. "My name is Jack Ta... Tiller. This is my friend, Kaiden. I'm looking for an old friend of mine. Mr. Onyema."

"Good evening, Mr. Tiller, Miss Kaiden," said the man stiffly. "I'm Mr. Onyema. You must be referring to my father."

"Yes," smiled Tate. "He insisted I call him Nachi."

It was custom that people never call someone by their given name unless you were invited to do so. That Jack knew Mr. Onyema Sr. by his nickname, Nachi, short for Nachikimba, said a lot about their friendship.

Mr. Onyema unlocked the door with a click and opened it.

"Please come in," he said, with as little warmth as before.

He led them down a short hallway and up a flight of stairs to his home.

The living room was warmly lit with simple but comfortable furniture. The few decorations on the walls were mostly family pictures, posing self-consciously with their best smiles.

In the center of the floor, a young boy looked up from his toys in surprise. He quickly climbed onto the couch and did his best to hide behind his mother, who was trying to read.

"This is my wife and son," said Mr. Onyema.

Tate and Kaiden noticed he didn't include their names. The boy tried to sink deeper into the couch, but the wife got up and greeted them warmly.

"Welcome to our home," she said. "We were about to have dinner. Will you join us?"

"That's very kind of you, thank you," said Kaiden. "But we don't want to put you to extra trouble."

"It is no trouble," said the wife, brushing it off with a wave. "Our son is a bottomless pit, so I always make extra."

Familiar with the customs, Tate observed the social etiquettes to put Mr. Onyema at ease. He asked about his tire business while injecting polite responses and nods. He inquired about the family's health, the recent weather and so on.

After several minutes, their host had lost some of his frost and relaxed, but only a little.

Mrs. Onyema announced that dinner was ready and they spent the next twenty minutes enjoying light conversation over a beef stew with sides of taroroot and maize.

"That was a delicious meal," said Tate. "We can't thank you enough for your warm generosity."

Mrs. Onyema smiled, bowing slightly in appreciation.

"Let's go outside," said her husband, as he got up from the table. "We can talk on the sun deck."

Tate and Kaiden followed him onto the open deck, welcoming the fresh evening breeze.

"Mr. Tiller, I'm assuming you are here to do business with my father," said Mr. Onyema. "I'm sorry to tell you that he passed away several years ago. I chose to stay out of smuggling and opened a tire shop. I run an honest business and would be no good to you."

"I'm very sorry to hear about his passing," said Tate. "He had my respect. You should know that my business with your father never involved smuggling. We only traded information."

"Information?" puzzled Mr. Onyema. After a moment his face lit up in recognition. "You are the pig," he said, snapping his fingers. "I remember my father talking about you when he got in trouble with the police. They doubled their protection fees and threatened him when he couldn't pay. We were afraid they'd put him in jail until we paid them. And one day they stopped bothering us. As if nothing happened. I asked what happened and my father told me the pig told the police to leave us alone."

Tate chuckled, remembering Nachi's nickname for him. He had still been with Delta Force at the time and his callsign was Razorback. The old man had felt silly saying it and called Tate pig instead. He remembered the event, but the details of how Tate discouraged the cops wouldn't paint him in a heroic light.

"I played a small part," he explained, veering away from the specifics. "Nothing more."

Mr. Onyema became thoughtful for a moment; Tate and Kaiden waited while the sounds of car horns and the buzz of scooters drifted on the air.

"As I explained," said Mr. Onyema, breaking his silence, "I am an honest man and do not participate in my father's actives, but some of his closer friends have become my son's godfathers. They gather here often and discuss events of that other world. I may have heard the kind of information you're looking for."

Tate couldn't remember the last time he'd heard a better worded explanation for mingling with criminals and keeping one's innocence at the same time.

"Did you hear anything recently about Russians in Lagos?"

Mr. Onyema chuckled and sat forward in his chair. "I hope you didn't go to too much trouble to find me. You could have asked almost anyone about the Russians. It's no secret."

Tate and Kaiden shared a look of exasperated surprise.

"They are doing business with Maifari Karim. But listen," said Mr. Onyema, turning serious, "Karim is a very big criminal. Lots of money. Lots of tough guys. It's not healthy to be curious about anything Karim is involved in. After the Russians and Karim struck a deal, everybody wisely lost interest. You would be wise to lose interest, too."

8

WAITING IN THE SHADOWS

"Prudence is not my strong suit," said Tate.

"Do you know what the Russians are up to?" asked Kaiden.

"No," said Mr. Onyema.

"What about Karim," said Tate. "Where can we find him?"

"You must be joking," said Mr. Onyema. "This is a very bad man. Very powerful."

"All I need is his address," said Tate.

Mr. Onyema reluctantly provided everything he knew about Karim and his city-wide crime empire.

Tate and Kaiden felt the ticking clock on this operation.

The Russians were up to something and teaming up with a crime lord strongly hinted it was especially bad news. Kilmonikov had tapped into a powerful criminal network, granting him access to any number of unknown resources.

Onyema told them that after Karim had come to power, he claimed the entire south end of Victoria Island as his.

The south end of the island had been the target of a huge development project; costing billions of dollars with hopes it would bring a stunning level of economic growth to Lagos beyond the opulence of Mumbai.

Huge, colorful billboards depicted upscale shopping and entertainment centers. Golf courses, swimming pools the size of small lakes, business centers and towering skyscrapers of luxury condominiums.

But first they needed land to build it on. They spent seven years dredging ten million square meters of land lost to coastal erosion. Five miles of new sea wall was built to protect the new property from being washed away again. Roads had been paved and three of the condo towers had been built.

The promise of new jobs and much needed influx of revenue went completely off the rails when the outbreak hit. As with everywhere else in the world, all attention and resources had been focused on survival. After the dust had settled, the people of Lagos waited and hoped for the developers to return. It wasn't long before everyone came to grips with the fact that they weren't coming back.

Their loss was Karim's gain. Taking advantage of the outbreak, the crime lord moved into the sleek, lavish Red Coral Towers. He claimed the penthouse for himself and gave everyone in his organization their own condo. His occupation of the building had the desired effect. Word spread of the upscale living conditions. Soon, Karim had his pick of every able-bodied man and woman willing to enforce his will.

Over time, Karim had amassed a small army. For all intents, he had maneuvered himself as the ruling power of Lagos.

There was no way

Onyema's description of the crime lord was enough for Tate to know Karim had the answers he was looking for. He just had to get to him.

With sincere thanks, Tate and Kaiden said good night to Mr. Onyema and his family and headed back to their personal taxi.

It was very late by the time they stepped back onto the street. Except for the occasional truck or car, they were the only two outside.

Across the street, a figure hidden in the shadows watched Tate and Kaiden walk down the street towards the alley. The figure waited until they turned the corner before stepping into the light. His hard features were bathed in the orange glow of his cigarette.

Richie flicked it to the dirt and ground it under his shoe. "They're coming," he said into a walkie talkie.

The alley was randomly lit, leaving large pools of shadows. Unconsciously, Tate and Kaiden's hands moved to the butt of their guns and rested there. They were pleased to see the taxi hadn't been stolen, or striped of its tires.

As they pulled off the tarp, Tate heard the sudden rush of movement behind him.

Before his gun had cleared the holster, a huge fist slammed into the side of his head. The world spun with exploding stars as his head bounced off the side of the taxi.

Kaiden heard Tate groan and aimed across the car but could only make out fleeting shadows. Too late she heard the attackers behind her.

Three men body slammed her into the taxi, knocking her gun out of her hand. The air was crushed out of her lungs and she gagged for breath as hands painfully grabbed her.

Four men crowded each other in their frenzy to beat on Tate. He was spared the worst of the blows because the men kept getting in the others way.

What did get through, Tate did his best to block, but he was so badly dazed it was just a blur to him.

One of the four was a giant of a man who could have easily beaten Tate to a pulp, but the others kept getting in the way. Snarling with frustration, he roughly pushed the others away. He clamped his thick hand around Tate's throat, lifting him off the ground and pinning him against the cab.

Tate tried to fight through the swirling fog and make his body obey him, but it was useless.

With a chuckling grunt, the big guy drove his fist into Tate's gut. Victory turned to disgust as Tate vomited onto the giant's face and chest.

Swearing, all of his attackers jumped back. One of them laughed as the giant swore, fighting his own gag reflex. Enraged, he back-handed the laughing man, spinning him into the shadows.

Unexpectedly, Tate had just bought himself a priceless breather.

Kaiden's face was pinned against the taxi as rough hands yanked her arms behind her back. Something bit into her wrists and she realized they were tying her up with wire. They meant to keep her alive.

Her mind raced through the monstrosities of the next few hours if they succeeded.

Fear and anger surged through her, fueling her will to fight to a whole new level. She tucked her knees to her chest and planted her feet against the taxi. With a yell she kicked away from the cab, turning her body into a battering ram. Both men flew back as she slammed into them.

They went down in a tangled mess with Kaiden landing hard on one of them. Air blew from him as she knocked the wind out of his lungs. Wheezing in agony, he curled up into a ball, unable to breathe.

She pulled free of the wire as hands grabbed at her. She quickly rolled away and pushed herself to her feet.

Her attackers, still on the ground, looked at her in confusion. Instead of running she looked down on them with a grin on her dirt smeared face.

Their eyes went wide in panic as she took a small hop and tucked her feet back. Their screams were cut short as she drove into them with her knees, powered by the full weight of her body.

One man rolled away, taking only a glancing blow. The other's eyes bulged as she crushed his ribs, flattening his lungs.

The men vehemently swore as they tried to wipe Tate's vomit off their shirts.

Using the precious seconds of relief, Tate struggled to clear his

84

mind. He staggered to the left, appearing to be off balance, but in fact he was looking for his gun. A quick glance told him it wasn't near.

His reprieve was over. The four men began moving in when a scream of terror from the other side of the taxi cut through them.

They hesitated, confused. That was a man's scream.

Two of the men broke off, disappearing around the cab. That was two less Tate had to face, but they were the two biggest ones.

Kaiden balled her fists together and brought them down in a savage blow to the gasping man's face. There was an ugly crunch and he stopped moving.

Someone was running her way and she quickly got to her feet. Two men came out of the shadows.

Seeing Kaiden alone, they grinned like wolves, the dead body behind her lost in the dark. The survivor of the first fight joined them, putting himself in the middle for protection. He'd seen what she could do.

Breathing hard, Kaiden sank into a crouch, her eyes scanning the three men.

They began taunting her as they closed in. One of them laughed, not seeing the sneer curling the corner of her mouth.

Without warning Kaiden charged. They staggered back in shock and confusion as she drove for the man in the center who yelped in fear. The other two quickly realized they weren't the target and attacked.

At the last moment, she side-stepped, targeting the man on the left. He never had time to react as Kaiden drove her hand into his throat. Something crunched and his eyes bulged. He staggered back, gasping for air.

Someone grabbed her shoulder. In a blur of motion, she gripped their hand and twisted. The man cried out, bending over, as she wrenched down on the joint lock. As she snap-kicked to the man's face something heavy slammed into her head. Flashes of light filled her vision as she stumbled, missing her target and letting go of the man.

The other man dropped the brick as Kaiden sunk to her knees. Stunned, she never saw the vicious kick that came to her ribs.

Pain shot through her body and she fell over in a ball of agony.

The two men quickly grappled her down. One of them grabbed the wire, wrapping it several times around her ankles.

His head finally cleared, Tate tried to size up his foes as they moved in and out of the light. They were moving side to side, trying to back him against a wall.

They had ambushed him from the darkness. Tate decided to turn the tables and slipped into a deep shadow.

Confident in their strength, they followed.

They couldn't see him, but Tate could see them silhouetted against the weak lights. He waited until they entered the gloom then sprung.

He kicked with all his force, catching the bigger man in the knee. There was a terrible snap as Tate drove through the joint, breaking his leg. The big man went down in a roar of pain.

Tate moved in the darkness, putting the fallen man between him and the last man.

There was a pause of confusion as the other attacker tried to peer through the shadows for Tate.

"Come on," growled Tate, giving away his position.

The other man turned and charged.

Tate readied himself, anticipating the next seconds.

"Help, yelled Kaiden.

It was a split-second distraction, but enough that Tate wasn't ready when the attacker tripped over his crippled friend and tumbled into him.

Kaiden bucked and kicked as the men dragged her down the alley by her feet, but she couldn't break their grip. She fought back, gagging, as she slid through puddles of foul muck.She desperately scanned the retreating alley for Tate.

Nothing. Helplessness closed in around her.

Brakes squeaked behind her captors as a dark-colored van pulled up at the end of the alley. A figure moved from the driver's seat into the back of the van.

With a click the sliding panel door opened, revealing Richie's grinning face.

Fear and panic grabbed Kaiden.

Not in the van. I can't go in there.

She railed against her bonds with renewed strength, twisting and flailing against every inch they dragged her.

Everyone stopped, wide eyes looking back down the alley as a chilling scream of pain spilled out of the darkness.

The men holding Kaiden searched the distant gloom, afraid of what might appear.

"What are you doing?" snapped Richie. "Bring the girl."

The two men resumed dragging her when they heard the sound of someone quickly closing the distance on them.

A moment later, Tate appeared out of the gloom, his face a mask of blood and fury.

Panicking to make their escape, the men flung Kaiden towards the van. Her squirming broke their grip and she landed short of the van.

"I have her," said Richie. "Get him."

One of the men pulled a wickedly long knife from his belt and took a stand, barring Tate from the van.

Seeing the knife, Tate slowed from a run, but kept coming.

Kaiden wrestled against grasping hands fumbling to pull her into the van.

Glints of steel winked in front of Tate as the man slashed at his face and chest. Tate's focus was split between the blade and Kaiden. He cursed his stupidity for taking his eyes off his attacker, and Tate concentrated on the gang member.

The attacker whipped the knife across Tate's face, but his target disappeared. Tate ducked low, picking up a piece of inch-thick rebar and smashed it across the man's shins. He dropped the knife in a wale of pain, falling to his knees.

Continuing the arc of his swing, Tate brought the rebar around catching the man in the face. Something crunched as his head snapped back and he crumpled to the filthy ground like a puppet with its strings cut.

Halfway inside the van, Kaiden gripped the edge of the door as Richie pulled. The other man hammered his fist on her fingers to let go. In the alley, a cry of pain stopped suddenly.

The man looked over his shoulder. Tate's eyes blazed at him between streaks of blood. Ice clutched the man's heart. Everything was forgotten except to run. Run fast and far and hope this demon was not behind him.

Richie scowled as his last man ran in a jabbering wail of fear. With predatory speed, Richie sunk his fingers into Kaiden's flesh and yanked her onto her back. A machete appeared in his hand and he swiftly lifted the long blade over his head.

"Another step," screamed Richie, his voice trembling, "and I'll chop her head..."

Kaiden tucked in her knees and drove her boots into Richie's chest with all her might. Ribs cracked and the van rocked as he smashed against it.

Tate reached over her and grabbed Richie by the shirt. Fabric ripped as he wrenched Richie out of the van. He landed with a wet thud and laid there, groaning.

Kaiden grabbed the fallen machete and quickly cut herself free.

Tate hefted the rebar as Richie spat out a glob of blood.

"Please, no more," he wheezed, slowly picking himself up. "I have a family."

A blur passed by Tate as Kaiden shot out of the van.

"Son of a..." she said, as she rained down punches and kicks on Richie.

"Stop," said Tate. "We need him."

Kaiden fixed him with a glare of burning anger. "Not bad enough."

Her hand flashed, striking Richie's throat with a sickening crunch. His eyes bulged as he clawed at his throat for air.

Kaiden coldly watched as he sank to the ground and died.

She stood a moment, glowering at the corpse at her feet.

"Are you okay?" asked Tate.

She took a deep breath, stretching the muscles in her neck. Pushing her matted hair out of her face, she glanced at her filthy clothes with annoyance.

"I really hate that guy," she said.

9

CRIME WITH A GREAT VIEW

Tate and Kaiden gave thanks to the ibuprofen gods as they stiffly made their way through the Ijora fish market. Both of them were covered in cuts and scrapes. Their clothing covered most of the bandages, but their faces and hands were another matter.

Concerned about the blow Kaiden had taken from the brick to her head, Tate stayed up during the night to keep an eye on her for signs of a concussion.

By the morning, Kaiden was sore, but refreshed.

Tate was buzzing from a night of strong Nigerian coffee.

"When the caffeine wears off, you are going to crash, hard," said Kaiden, amused, but kindly.

Tate looked at her for an awkward moment. "I can't think of anything witty to say."

"It'll come to you in a day or two."

"I have to get some fresh air soon," he said, looking a little pale.

Even to someone used to the smell of fish, the Ijora fish market was in another league. Row after row of tables were piled with fresh and frozen fish. The air was saturated with the pungent smell that only a veteran of the market could endure.

All around, people were shouting over the clamor of other

vendors, calling out their days inventory while excited shoppers haggled for bargains.

Tate pushed away his nausea and focused on the next step of their mission.

According to Mr. Onyema, the Russians were doing business with the crime boss, Karim. He lived on Victoria Island, which provided the first hurdle in reaching him. Several bridges joined the island to the mainland, but different tribal militias had seized their ends of the bridge.

It was guaranteed, being foreigners, that they'd run into problems trying to cross. The only way to avoid the gangs and militias was to cross Lagos Lagoon by boat.

Fortunately, Onyema knew Ahmad, who ran a river taxi. He said he'd make arrangements and Tate and Kaiden should meet him at the fish market.

They were making their third circle of the market when they a young boy stepped out in front of them. With his chest puffed out and his hands on his hips, the kid looked over them with a critical eye.

"You guys are looking for a ride to the island?" said the kid.

"Yes," said Tate. "Ahmad is supposed to..."

"Come on," said the kid. He cocked his head in the direction of the docks and left.

They shrugged their shoulders and followed. Leaving the fish market behind, they followed as the boy led them down a shallow embankment towards the water's edge.

Three roughly-made docks stretched out to the muddy water. Long, canoe-shaped fishing boats tugged gently at their moorings as they rode the easy swells.

The docks were protected by a sea wall of junked cars and stones, but beyond was the open water of the Lagos Lagoon. A river, by any other definition, the lagoon ran for thirty miles and got up to eight miles wide in some places. Where they were headed wasn't far from where the lagoon emptied into the Atlantic Ocean.

Kaiden looked dubiously at the small boats. The opposite coast was a hazy smear and there was a lot of rough water in between.

"We better find another way," said Kaiden.

The kid looked at the nearby boats and then at Kaiden. "Don't be crazy," he said, annoyed. "Not those boats."

He led them further down the water's edge to a long covered dock. Moored at the side of the dock was a thirty-foot-long-boat. On the rear hunched a powerful, oversized Mercury engine.

"Okay, that'll work," she said.

Tate wasn't as sure, but impatience and caffeine chewed away his reservations. He looked at his watch, irritably wondering how much longer they'd have to wait for the boatman to show up.

"What are you waiting for?" said the boy. "Get in."

Tate's eyebrow arched at the frowning kid. "When's Ahmad going to show up?" he asked.

"I'm Ahmad," said the boy.

Seeing Tate's expression turn dark, Kaiden quickly intervened before he said something that could cost them their ride.

"How hold are you?" she asked, as kindly as possible.

"Eleven," said Ahmad. "Almost a teenager."

Even Kaiden couldn't help balking at the idea of putting their lives in the hands of this boy.

"What's the matter?" asked Ahmad, frowning at them. "You don't like my boat?"

"Oh, for crying out loud," said Tate. "Look, kid..."

"We were expecting someone older," injected Kaiden.

"How old do you need to be to drive a boat?" said Ahmad. "Hey, if you don't want to go, I got other things to do. Good luck finding someone else to take you."

Ahmad walked off, swearing like a long-shoremen.

"Whoa, hang on," said Tate. "You can take us."

Ahmad stared at them with annoyance as he came back and climbed into the boat.

Tate and Kaiden got in, taking a moment to settle in as the boat wobbled under them.

Putting down his pack, Tate noticed they weren't moving. Turning around he was met by Ahmad, staring at him with his hands on hips.

"Oh," said Tate, embarrassed. He fumbled with his pocket and took out five bills. "Sorry," he said. "Rough night."

Ahmad stuffed it in his pocket then put his foot on the engine housing. With a grunt, he yanked the starter cord. The engine sputtered and coughed but didn't start. The kid pulled a few more times, but the engine wasn't interested in starting.

"Need help?" asked Tate.

"Knock it off," said Kaiden with a warning scowl.

The kid ignored him and fiddled with the choke. He gave another pull and the big engine grumbled to life.

"Hey, lady," called Ahmad over Tate's head. "Take off that rope."

Kaiden lifted the mooring line off the dock's cleat and Ahmad twisted the throttle. The engine growled and the front of the boat rose as the propeller dug into the water.

Soon they were out of the tiny cove and into the wide waterway. Even though this boat sat higher in the water than the other fishing boats they saw, it inspired little confidence as the choppy water slapped at its sides.

"What's your name?" asked Ahmad.

"I'm Jack, and this is..."

"Grab that bucket, Jack, and bail out the water," said Ahmad.

Kaiden grinned at Tate's bewildered expression.

"You heard the captain," she said.

Tate picked up the small dented pail at his feet and began throwing water over the side.

"What happened to you, Jack?" asked Ahmad.

"We got into a fight," said Tate.

Ahmad started laughing. "Oh, man. She kicked your butt."

"Not with each other," said Tate, annoyed by Kaiden's laughter. "Tough guys. Area boys."

"You're new here," said Ahmad wisely. "I'll give you some advice. You have to make friends with the area boys as soon as you step in their territory. Give them dash and you'll be okay."

"We did bribe them," explained Tate.

"Looks like not enough," said Ahmad.

Kaiden chuckled as Tate scrunched his face at her.

They had been hugging their side of the river for most of the trip, but as the sea wall of the new development came into view, Ahmad stood up.

Ships of various sizes used the wide lagoon, from forty-foot tugs to barges a couple of hundred feet long. Ahmad watched the flow of traffic, judging his course to cross between them to the other side.

"Okay, we're crossing here," he said, steering the shallow boat out into the wide channel.

The wakes of the passing ships added to the chop of the water and Tate began bailing more frequently and faster. He jolted at the blast of a loud horn. Looking up he saw the prow of a wide barge barreling down on them.

"I was here first," shouted Ahmad, jumping to his feet. "You want trouble?"

To Tate and Kaiden's surprise, the kid pulled a pistol nearly as big as him from under his loose jacket. He pointed it at the barge with a sneer.

"Make my day," he yelled, his voice cracking.

Slowly at first, the large bow of the barge ponderously moved away. Towering over their heads, the hull of the barge passed within spitting distance, which Ahmad did.

"Don't play tough guy with me," he yelled as they passed the barge's pilot house. The skipper of the barge swore back at him, shaking his fist.

"Those guys think they own the lagoon," said Ahmad, stuffing the big gun back inside his jacket. "Hey, Jack, you trying to sink my boat? Bail that water."

Tate shook off the near miss and started bailing ankle-deep water.

"Makes me wonder why I never had kids," smiled Kaiden.

"Sure he's not yours?" asked Tate.

She laughed, turned around and took a deep breath of the fresh air.

By the time they reached the other side of the river, Tate's arms were sore but he was glad there hadn't been anymore near misses.

The sea wall was made up of large, concrete tetrapods, looking like a jumble of giant toy jacks. Waves that would have turned the boat into splinters crashed into the wall with a thump.

Wisely, Ahmad kept his distance and steered past around the bulwark and headed for the shore.

As they neared the shore, the kid cut the engine and the boat slid up onto the soft sand.

Kaiden and Tate climbed out, happy to be on solid, dry ground.

"Can you stick around?" asked Tate. "We'll need a ride back."

"You're going to see Karim?" asked Ahmad.

"Yes," said Kaiden.

"I don't think you're coming back, but if you pay me now," he said, shrugging his shoulders, "sure, I'll hang around."

"Thanks," grumped Tate, tossing the kid a few bills.

"Hey," said Ahmad, pulling out his big revolver, "you want to buy a gun?"

"I have a gun," said Tate, revealing the pistol under his shirt.

Ahmad laughed. "Who you going to shoot with that little thing?"

"Not sure," said Tate, "but I'm getting a pretty good idea who to start with."

Ahmad shrugged his shoulders and stuffed the pistol back under his jacket.

They didn't need any directions to know where they were going. A few hundred yards away, the Red Coral Towers stretched impressively high into the sky. Each building was clad in a mirror finish, ingeniously disguising the private balconies that covered each floor.

The contrast of the barren land and lavish structure gave a sense of surrealism. Dirt-covered paved roads were the only other completed construction. They were laid in a grid, outlining huge tracks of land intended for future construction that would never come.

The entire area, for miles on end, was flat and empty of anything except scrub brush and dirt.

"That didn't take long," said Tate, seeing an approaching plume of dust rippling in the heat waves.

"Karim must have lookouts on the tops of the buildings," said Kaiden.

They didn't have long to wait before a shiny black SUV stopped and two men with automatic weapons got out. Both of them were dressed remarkably well in silk Hawaiian shirts, linen slacks and sandals.

In spite of the fine clothes, there was no mistaking these men did Karim's dirty work and were no strangers to it.

They sauntered up to Tate and Kaiden, slinging their assault rifles around their necks.

"This is Karim's land," said one of the thugs. "Leave everything you got and get out of here."

"We're here to see Karim," said Tate, as he and Kaiden held their hands up enough to show they weren't a threat.

The thugs looked past the intruders to the boat on the shore and chuckled. "Karim isn't hiring janitors," said the thug.

"We're here on business," said Tate.

Frowning, the thugs looked over Tate and Kaiden again, taking in the wet clothing, bruised and bandaged faces.

Tate reached around for his back pocket and both men brought up their rifles, dropping their smiles.

"Whoa, guys," said Tate. "Look."

Tate took out his wallet and opened it, showing them the money inside. The thugs lowered their weapons as Tate approached them, taking out several bills.

"We're only here for a quick business meeting and then we'll be on our way," said Tate, handing the bribe to one of the thugs.

"Oh," said the other thug, as his friend pocketed the wad of cash. "Unfortunately, Karim is all booked up today."

"Yes," laughed the other thug. "Come back tomorrow. And bring more money."

"Now get out of here," said the thug, his good humor turning into an angry expression.

"That's all the money I have," said Tate.

"Then don't come back," snapped the thug.

"Guys," said Kaiden. "Can we not do this? It's been a tough couple of days."

"I said go." The thug racked the slide on his gun, chambering a round.

Kaiden sighed with exasperation. "Look at my hands," she said, holding them up. "They're all cut and scratched. And last night someone hit me with a brick, right here."

She tilted her head, pointing to the wound. "I'm sore and have a banging headache, so if it's all the same to you..."

"Shut up," said the thug, drawing back his hand to slap her.

Kaiden was on him in an instant. She grabbed his rifle at both ends and yanked down hard. The nylon sling bit into the back of his neck, making him stumble forward. She swiftly raised the rifle, hitting him in the face, knocking him senseless.

The other thug gaped before realizing his friend was in trouble. As he pointed his rifle at Kaiden, Tate rush him.

In a quick motion, he grabbed the barrel and pushed up. The rifle slammed into the thug's face. His eyes rolled up into his head as he dropped to his knees.

In less than a minute, the thugs were on their knees with Tate and Kaiden aiming their captured guns at them.

"You idiots either drive us to see Karim," said Kaiden, "or I'll strap your naked butts to the hood and drive you there myself. Your choice."

A few minutes later, the black SUV pulled into the shade under the ornate awning of the Red Coral Towers.

On the short drive to the building, Tate had started a rapport with the two thugs by name. Everyone, the world over, had gripes about their jobs, and there was no better way to gain a friend than to share their grievances.

"This place is spectacular, Glen" said Tate. "I bet they don't let you guys work in the building?"

"No," grumbled Glen.

"We're not *executive security* material," said Liam, using air quotes.

"I used to be in Delta," said Tate.

"No kidding?" said Glen.

"I did a lot of executive security and that's the only reason we knew how to trick you," said Tate. "You guys are as qualified as anyone."

"See?" said Liam, elbowing Glen. "Even he knows it."

"They make you guys do the grunt work," said Tate, glancing at the thug's casual clothing, "while they wear suits with round the clock air conditioning, right?"

"I hate those jerks," said Glen.

"And every time you bring someone in, the building guards double check to make sure you did the pat-down right."

"Like we can't do a simple frisk," said Liam.

"You know they're just rubbing your noses in it," said Tate. "It's a complete lack of professional respect."

"I've been telling him that for a year," said Glen, gesturing to Liam.

"Huh," said Kaiden.

"What's that mean?" growled Liam. "What do you mean, 'huh'?"

"Nothing," she said.

"No," said Glen, getting angrier. "You meant something."

"I didn't think men like you would let someone push you around for an entire year," she said. "But... you know." She trailed off, letting the gas she'd thrown on the fire do its work.

Tate and Kaiden sat back, letting the two men smolder. Sometimes understanding human nature was more powerful than a bullet. They hoped they were right this time.

As the SUV came to a stop Tate handed the men their guns.

"Here," he said. "I'm not going to give those jerks more reasons to disrespect you."

They knew he'd emptied the bullets, but the gesture meant a lot to them.

"You're okay, man," said Glen.

The thugs got out and opened the passenger doors for them, then escorted them into the lobby.

Cool, refreshing air washed over them as they stepped into the breathtaking entrance. Designed to accommodate large crowds, the vast lobby echoed as they crossed the polished red marble floor to the elevators. Glass walls reached high above where crystal chandeliers were suspended from ceilings impressively decorated with stunning frescos of stylized sea life.

Across the lobby, two men stood guard at the elevator door. Curiosity wrinkled their foreheads as they studied the new visitors.

Glen and Liam had their assault rifles casually slung over their shoulders and there was no outward signs of trouble.

Both thugs, with knots on their heads, looked angry and locked eyes on the guards as they reached the elevators.

"They got an appointment with Karim," said Liam, with a wad of tissue stuffed in his nostril.

Tate and Kaiden looked calm, even disinterested in the scrutiny of the guards.

"What happened to you?" asked a guard.

Liam stepped up, his nose almost touching the others.

"You got something to say?" he growled. "You see something funny?"

"No, nothing," stammered the guard. "I only meant..."

"You meant nothing," said Glen, stabbing the elevator button.

The doors opened with a happy chime and the four of them stepped in, leaving the guards confused and rattled.

Glen and Liam smiled as Tate nodded with approval.

Everyone's stomachs sank as the elevator lifted off with surprising speed. The building was over five hundred feet high and it had been stressed to the engineers that the high-end residents of the Red Coral had better things to do than wait on sluggish elevators. A generous bonus had been added to the incentive and the result was an elevator worthy of an amusement park ride.

Tate blamed the sleepless night and coffee overdose on his jumpy stomach as they came to a controlled but unpleasant stop at the penthouse.

Liam and Glen stepped out, leading Tate and Kaiden into a wide foyer. Another pair of immaculately dressed guards stood by a pair of thick, wooden doors. It was evident to both of them the doors were heavy, reinforced and the entire penthouse was a fortress. A plain door was positioned to the right and there was little doubt a small army of armed men would come charging out if an alarm went off.

Tate and Kaiden knew trying to shoot their way in would have been pointless. There were too many choke points and kill zones. Although they'd planned to bribe their way in, a technique that worked surprisingly well, their improvised Plan B was going better than they expected.

The penthouse guards smirked at the thugs after giving Tate and Kaiden a careful study.

Glen didn't wait for any commentary and brushed past them, leading Tate and Kaiden into a sun-washed living room. Liam followed behind, sneering at the two guards.

Following the circular design of the building, the large living room swept left to a stone and wood fireplace ringed with rich, leather chairs and couches. Fine paintings and tasteful native art were arranged, making the space feel open and airy. To the right, the white marble floor transitioned to blue-grey slate for a stunning kitchen and center island surrounded with comfortable bar stools.

The entire exterior wall from kitchen to living room was glass, giving a breathtaking view of the ocean.

Spaced out around the entire penthouse were several small domes in the ceiling, concealing security cameras.

A hidden door, leading to a private office, banged open and a tall man with a cigarette walked out, yelling into his phone. He wore a finely made Babban Riga, floor-length robe with wide sleeves. A motif of the Hausa tribe accented the shoulders and chest in white embroidery, accenting the finely woven, coffee brown cotton.

Tate's brow knitted as he took a second look at the man. There was something out of place about him. He was wearing something on his head and at first Tate assumed it was a Fula, a common cap worn in Nigeria, but the shape was all wrong.

On closer scrutiny, Tate recognized it was a Yamaka.

The two thugs instantly dropped their eyes in deference, clueing Tate and Kaiden that this must be Karim.

"We agreed on five days," said Karim. "Not eight. Five."

He looked over, seeing the thugs and two visitors with mild

surprise. He gestured with his hand for them to wait and turned his attention back to the phone call.

"No, listen," he said. "Fuuuuu-iiiivvv-aaaah. That sounds nothing like eight. Are you hearing me? I promised them five days because *you* said five days. Who wants to do business with someone who can't hold up their end of a deal? Am I right?"

Karim nodded his head as he listened. "All right, so you'll deliver on time? Great. Okay. Uh huh, okay. And my best to your family too," he said and hung up. "Schmuck."

He walked to the kitchen, eyeing the condition of the thugs as he passed. Sitting down on a barstool, he snubbed out his cigarette and looked at Tate and Kaiden.

"And why are these people in my home?" he asked. "Who are they?" He left the barstool and took a closer look at his thugs, then looked at Tate and Kaiden. "Did you beat up my guys? Because this is how you make a lousy first impression. The last person who made a bad first impression got thrown off that balcony. I'm telling you, it's hard on the pavement. Maybe I should have them shoot you."

"They're empty, sir," said Glen.

"Empty?" said Karim. "So, nobody's got bullets?"

"We've got bullets," said Kaiden, revealing her holstered semi-auto.

"Sure," said Karim. "Why not. Before you kill me, would you grant me a final wish and shoot these two morons first?"

"We're not here to shoot anyone," said Tate, surprised by Karim's lack of concern.

He quickly explained about trying to bribe the guards and the events that lead up to this point.

"Oh, so it was just a bribe," said Karim to the thugs. "Sure. That makes it better. Give me your gun," he said to Tate, "and I'll shoot them."

Karim folded his arms across his chest and stared at the thugs with disappointment. "You two dummies. You don't renege on a bribe. It's dishonest. You know how that makes me look?" He rolled his eyes at the irony. "Okay, I get it, but you know what I mean."

"We're sorry, sir," said Liam.

Karim put a hand on each thug's shoulder, turning them around and walking them through the foyer doors.

"I get it. It happens," he said kindly. "People make mistakes all the time."

He patted the thugs on the backs and paused next to a guard before walking into his home.

"Take these two somewhere and shoot them."

"Yes, sir," said the guard.

The thugs turned in surprise as the other guard aimed his weapon at them. Glen and Liam looked pleadingly at Tate and Kaiden, who only shrugged in apology.

"Then find the manager in charge of security and shoot him too."

"Yes, sir."

Leaving the guards, Karim returned to his unexpected guests and waited for the doors to close behind him.

"Okay, so you two," he said, pointing to them. "Not hitmen, or lady. No? Good. You should know it would have been a bad idea."

He pointed up at the domes on the ceiling.

"Facial recognition, artificial intelligence," he said, smiling. "Each one of those is a swivel mounted gun with an integrated digital eye. They began tracking you the second you walked in. They're activated by voice and physical cue. Oh, and anyone pointing a gun at me. Almost forgot that one."

The two of them looked up at the domes with unease.

"Have you ever set them off by accident?" asked Kaiden.

"Only once, at a dinner party," said Karim. "The place is packed with people. This one lady, she's a real cat person. I'm allergic. Bad combination. So, anyway, I sneeze and... Bammo. A split second later I'm the only one without a hole in the head."

Kaiden and Tate traded worried looks while Karim laughed.

"I'm kidding. I'm kidding. It's fine. But seriously, neither of you have cats?"

Now Tate understood why the crime boss had been so casual at the possibility of being shot. He was never in any danger, but Tate and Kaiden had been the target of automated guns the whole time. He tried not to think about it as Karim invited them to sit down.

"Americans, am I right?" asked Karim. "I grew up there. I've been wanting to go back for years, but who's got the time when you're running a major organization?"

"You're not what I expected," said Kaiden.

"You mean a Nigerian Jew?" he smiled. "My father's Nigerian. Met a nice Jewish girl in New York. I grew up with friends in the Jewish mafia. Kosher Nostra," he laughed. "Get it? Because it's the mob? But Jewish?"

Tate and Kaiden smiled.

Karim sighed disappointedly. "That joke would've killed in Manhattan. Okay, enough about me. Let's talk about you two, and why you're so curious about the Russians."

If Kaiden was surprised that Karim knew why they were in Lagos, she hid it well. Tate's poker face wasn't as well practiced.

"We're concerned their actions could be a threat," she said. She didn't know how Karim got his intel, but it was a clear sign not to underestimate him.

He laughed, sitting back against the plush leather of the couch. "They're Russians. They're a threat to everyone. Especially those Spetsnaz types."

"What can you tell us?" asked Tate.

"What can you afford?" countered Karim.

Tate looked around the upscale penthouse with an appraising eye. "It's hard to know what to give a man who has everything."

"That's how you do business," said Karim, pointing at Tate. "Offering me a bribe would be insulting. But you two, you look like you could be useful."

His nearly constant smile disappeared as he studied them, wheels clearly turning in his mind. He was the chattiest mobster Tate had ever met, but just under the surface was a keen mind, not to be underestimated.

"It's possible we could give you a rain check," said Kaiden. "But you need to understand there's a limit to what we're willing to do," she added firmly.

"Deal," said Karim.

"What are the Russians up to?" asked Tate.

"They wanted two ships, and explosives."

"Explosives," repeated Kaiden. "What kind?"

"Anything that blows up," said Karim. "More like *every*thing that blows up. Nitrate based gun powder, gasoline, Semtex, you name it."

"Enough to fill two ships with?" asked Tate.

"Only the large one, but it's large enough."

"They could make a lot of bombs with that," said Kaiden.

Tate's thoughts played out as he puzzled over the mismatch of explosive materials. "Or a big, floating, ship-sized bomb," he said.

"Where do we find the Russians?" asked Kaiden, getting to her feet.

"I thought you guys were dead," said Ahmad, as he piloted his boat out and around the northern cape of Ogogoro island.

"Why'd you stick around?" asked Tate, picking up the bucket to bail out water.

"You pay good," shrugged Ahmad.

The docks were coming into view. Although they stretched on for over a mile, Karim had told them the Russians would be near a sunken freighter.

Dread formed in the pit of their stomachs as they saw the rusty superstructure of the sunken ship. The mooring next to it was empty.

Tate looked out to the mouth of the channel where it opened to the Atlantic. Somewhere out in the vastness of the ocean was the nightmare of all IEDs and he had no idea where it was.

10

BOOBY TRAP

S even hundred miles north east of the Norfolk Naval Station, the USS Sedona rode easily through the sea, making twenty knots. The middle watch was forty minutes away and the crew was eyeing the clock, looking forward to hitting the rack.

The Officer of the Deck, Ensign Jones, was still new to his role and tried to walk the middle ground between earning the respect of the bridge crew and being a professional officer. His nervousness was all in his mind. The rest of the bridge crew had seen their share of fresh Ensigns and quickly taken him under their wing. To them it was just another OOD they would show the ropes.

Ensign Jones did a quick scan of the bridge. He held his cup of coffee at his side in case the Watchstanders stationed outside on the bridge-wings happened to catch him looking at them.

In spite of the ship's technology, the Navy placed its faith in its sailors first and foremost.

Like sailors a hundred years before them, the Watchstanders scanned the sea and sky for any signs of threat.

Several miles to the north, the ghostly, pale wake of water churned and fell away, the only visible token of the old bunker barge as it cut through the sea. Her darkened bridge and running lights made her nearly invisible in the black sea.

She hadn't been to sea in years and was doomed to a rusty death until someone saw her potential. Once again, the Vixen rode the open ocean, but this would be her final voyage.

The bridge navigation console had been stripped of its covering. The floor was covered in cables that ran up through holes cut into the decking and spliced into the equipment that controlled the ship. The cameras, mounted at each window, panned the sea beyond the great steel prow of the ship. Their infrared glass eyes pierced the dark, casting the world in shades of pale grey.

Four miles away, beyond the horizon, Misha followed in the fishing trawler.

Dim red light filled the bridge, casting the crew as silent demons, intent on their work. From the back of the bridge, Misha leaned against the bulkhead, humming softly to himself. He watched his men with passive intensity, confident in their skills. He was satisfied to spectate the others play their part until they needed him.

To the side of the ship's console sat Luka. Wearing a thick sweater against the chill, he monitored the displays from the Vixen's cameras.

He frowned as he examined the other displays which reported the Vixen's course, speed and overall status. He typed at his keyboard, sending instructions to the Vixen's remote control to alter course by three degrees.

A moment later, he nodded with approval as the Vixen acknowledged and executed his command. It wasn't long before he found something else to frown about.

"Patience, Luka," said Misha, seeing his expression. "They will not disappoint us."

Luka sighed, resigning himself to his friend's advice. "You are right, Misha," he said. "We have come so far. I worry the fates will decide to play us for fools."

A smile creased Misha's scared face and he chuckled good-naturedly. "We have been the fate's plaything long enough. Be confident, my friend. They have tired of us and are finding someone else's life to defecate on."

The other men of the bridge chuckled in agreement.

"It will be soon," said Misha, checking his watch, and returned to humming to himself.

The radar mast above the bridge of the Sedona was the long-distance eyes and ears of the ship. Among the cluster of sensors and antenna was the multimode 3-D radar. Its primary purpose was for surveillance and weapon assignment. Capable of simulations detection and tracking of multiple targets, both surface and airborne. This was a valuable feature, prior to the outbreak of the Vix, when a warship was expected to face off against a large number of threats at once. After the human race was nearly wiped out, little contact had been made between countries and fewer still was seen of ships. International aircraft were non-existent.

Deep inside the Sedona, Operations Specialist Petty Officer 3rd Class Wallas had been staring at his radar screen in a semi hypnotic state. The complex screen was cluttered with information about nothing, because that's what was out there. An ocean full of nothing, and that's what OS3 Wallas spent his long watch doing. Staring at nothing.

When he snapped out of his trance he nearly yelped in surprise. There was a new blip on his screen, and it was close.

The phased array radar could reach out over fifteen miles. His blip was less than two. In an instant he knew he'd screwed up, big time. The moment he reported the range of the blip everyone would know he'd been asleep. At best, he'd be busted several ranks. At worst, a court martial.

For a fraction of a second he considered not reporting it and hoping the Sedona would open the distance from the blip and it would disappear off his screen. But, just as quickly, he dismissed the childish thought and spoke up.

"Sir," he said after clearing his throat, "I have a surface contact approximately two nautical miles away. Bearing zero two five, relative. Speed, twenty-six knots."

The Tactical Action Officer, Lieutenant Jackson, jerked with a curse, being startled from his own boredom-induced stupor.

"Monkey," he said, using the ship's nickname for Wallas, "did you just say two miles?"

"Aye, sir," said Wallas, wincing.

Jackson looked like he was going to chew him out but changed his mind and keyed his radio. "Officer of the Deck, this is the Tactical Action Officer. Please confirm surface contact, bearing zero two five relative."

The bridge crew came alive as the OOD responded. "TAO," said Lieutenant Junior Grade Lopez, "stand by."

Lopez grabbed a pair of night vision binoculars. "Ensign Reid," he said, "you're with me on the bridge wing."

"Aye, sir," said Reid, as he hustled into his peacoat.

Reid followed Lopez through the hatch, out onto the starboard bridge wing. The wind blew the chilly night air through Lopez's uniform and a shiver trembled through his body. He looked through the heavy binoculars, holding them steady against the pitch of the ship as he scanned for their contact. A moment later he handed the binoculars to Reid.

"Look over there," he said, pointing.

Reid instantly saw the outline of the darkened bunker barge, taking a moment to study it. "Looks like a cargo ship. No running lights. Smugglers maybe?"

"Not exactly low profile," smirked Lopez. He headed back into the bridge, grateful to be in the warmth again. "TAO," he said into his radio, "I have a positive visual on the surface contact. I recommend we notify the skipper."

"I agree," answered Jackson.

Lopez switched to the skipper's personal channel and rang him. After two rings the line picked up.

"Report," grumbled the skipper.

"Good morning, Captain," said Lopez. "This is Lieutenant Junior Grade Lopez, OOD with a contact report."

"I'll be there shortly," said the skipper and hung up.

Lopez checked the position of their surface contact and referenced the maneuvering board to see if there was any danger of a collision.

"Captain on the bridge," announced a seaman.

"OOD, report," said the captain as he looked for his coffee cup. Captain Bender had been in the navy 12 years and had only made the rank of captain a year before. This was unheard of before the outbreak. The US Navy required a minimum of 21 years of service before someone would be considered for promotion to captain, but the military was starving for people and desperately needed officers. It was a bitter pill to swallow for the high-ranking officers who'd earned their four stripes through the grueling standards that tradition demanded. The quality of training in all branches of the military had badly suffered in the haste to replenish the staggering loss, and gravely reduced protection of the country.

Captain Bender was a good man to his crew, but his lack of experience was a source of concern with navel command. It was for this reason that they had decided to assign him patrol duty in the north east area of US territorial waters.

"It appears to be a cargo ship," said Lopez, finishing his report.

"What are they doing here?" asked the captain.

"We haven't made contact with them, skipper."

The captain frowned at Lopez, silently conveying his expectation.

"TAO," said Lopez over the radio, "have you made contact with the vessel?"

"Negative. The contact is not responding to our hail and is not transmitting an IFF."

The captain's eyebrows went up. Every vessel and aircraft capable of international travel was equipped with an Identify Friend or Foe transponder. The lack of one was highly suspicious and added to his own speculation it was a smuggler's ship.

He got up and looked at the radar screen on the navigator's console and swore under his breath. Then he looked out the bridge window. The sky was paling at the edge of the horizon with sunrise soon to come.

The captain's concern jumped when he could easily see the bulk of the cargo ship. "Why didn't you tell me that ship was so close?" he yelled.

"I did, skipper," said Lopez, looking shocked. "As soon as you came on deck I reported it."

The captain realized he hadn't been paying attention and ignored his mistake.

"Set Condition 1, general quarters," he snapped.

"Set Condition 1, general quarters, aye," repeated Lopez. He grabbed the mic and switched the intercom to 1MC and hit the alarm switch. Through the ship, alarms started blaring.

"Condition 1, general quarters," said Lopez. "This is not a test. All hatches are Condition Zebra."

Sailors not already awake tumbled out of their racks and threw on what clothing they could while rushing to their station. Condition Zebra required all hatches be dogged to prevent flooding should the ship's hull be damaged.

"I didn't think they'd let us get so close," said Luka, as he watched the Sedona from the remote camera.

"Stop the engines," said Misha, moving to stand next to him. He studied the Sedona on the screen before considering his next move. "Use the maneuvering thrusters to close the distance."

Onboard the Vixen, the great diesel engines dropped to a low rumble and her massive propellers stopped. Below the waterline, the maneuvering thrusters, normally used for moving the ship sideways as it docked, began gently pushing the cargo ship towards the Sedona.

OS3 Wallas watched the Vixen from his screen inside the CIC of the Sedona. The station to his right was occupied by Weapons Specialist,

Petty Officer Second Class, Clair Hudson. Her station controlled the ship's main gun.

The MK 110 was capable of firing a blistering two hundred and twenty 57mm rounds a minute and was accurate up to eight miles. Using the weapon's joystick controls, she slew the turret around towards the Vixen. The gun's multipurpose camera displayed range, wind and elevation on Hudson's screen. With a slight pull on the stick, she centered the crosshairs on the ships bridge.

"TAO," she reported. "Weapons status ready."

"Weapons ready, aye," acknowledged Jackson.

On the bridge, Lopez saw the Vixen's bow wave disappear. "She's stopped, skipper."

The captain examined the cargo ship through his binoculars, becoming more puzzled by the minute. *Where was the crew?*

The helmsmen's glance at the skipper wasn't lost on the OOD. Lopez was aware that the distance between the two ships had already passed the regulation minimum. He considered how to delicately broach the oversight with his skipper.

It was widely known the captain was not a morning person, by a long shot. And his mood had been sour when he'd learned, only hours out of port, there was scuttlebutt among the crew that he wasn't a 'real' captain. Every ship had their rumor mill and the Sedona was no different. One of the rumors was that the skipper hadn't earned his promotion; he got it as a favor from the admiralty.

A veteran captain develops a tough hide and rumors like that go unnoticed. The Sedona's captain wasn't a veteran and he took the crew's talk personally. It made him defensive.

When the Officer of the Deck advised him about the running of the ship, it only confirmed in his mind that his officers considered him unqualified for the post.

OOD Lopez decided his duty to the safety of the ship and her crew were worth the butt-chewing from the skipper.

The captain stiffened as Lopez stood at next to him.

"Skipper," said Lopez, "CIC hasn't received a response from our hails."

"I'm aware of that," said the skipper flatly.

"She's not sending an IFF."

"If you have a point *ensign*, make it," said the captain, keeping his eyes fixed to his binoculars.

The crest of the sun had broken the horizon and the mystery vessel was visible by the naked eye. The distance between the two ships had closed within a throw of a baseball.

"With respect, captain," said Lopez, committing himself, "the vessel could represent a danger. I advise we put some distance between us."

Luka scanned between the camera's view of the Sedona and the data scrolling on the other display.

"We are well within proximity to the American ship," he said.

Misha nodded in agreement and leaned over Luka's console, studying the screen. "The closer, the more effective we'll be. Keep the thrusters at minimum and let's see how close we can get."

"The current is getting stronger," said Luka. "I'll have to increase the power to the thrusters or we'll start to drift apart."

Misha ran his thick fingers through is black hair and grinned. "Do what you need to. Let me know the instant the American's start to move away. Mitya? Is the signal strength good?"

"Yes, Misha," said Mitya, after a quick look at the signal meter. The digital readout stayed in the green. "I'm sure the Americans will detect our frequency within the next eighty meters."

"Prepare the explosives," said Misha.

Mitya flipped up a row of plastic covers, revealing seven toggle switches with red lights. As he switched each one, the red light changed to green.

Deep in the steel bowels of the Vixen several tons of explosives lined the hull of the ship. Everything Misha and his men could lay their hands on had been carefully layered to create the maximum results. Over a mile of wires snaked through the ship from the detonators, all coming together at the master switch.

The only light in the black, dank hold, the master switch status light changed from red to green.

"Your opinion is noted," growled the captain. "This is nothing but a derelict ship. Judging by its condition, it's been drifting around for years."

"But her engines just stopped now," pressed Lopez.

"All right," snapped the captain. "Maybe whoever *was* on it saw us and abandoned her."

Captain Bender brought down his binoculars and realized that the Vixen was much closer than he first remembered.

"Helmsman," he barked. "I told you to maintain our distance to that ship."

The helmsman and Lopez exchanged troubled looks. Both knew the captain had never issued that order, but no good would come from telling the skipper that.

"Maneuvering to maintain station to the vessel, aye," said the helmsmen.

Not wanting to be included in the captain's poor temper, Ensign Reid had chosen to go on the bridgewing and observe the Vixen. He had heard about abandoned ships that had drifted the ocean for years before someone found them.

The idea conjured up eerie images of this empty ship. Her gloomy passageways echoing with unseen spirits. He felt as if something was watching him from those dark, empty portholes. His imagination getting the better of him, he looked away, afraid of what he might see.

Ensign Reid dropped his eyes, falling naturally to the waterline of the Vixen. Something was wrong. The water around the Vixen's bow was churning. In a flash he recognized someone was using the bow thrusters. They were moving the ship closer to the Sedona.

He pushed away from the bulkhead of the bridgewing, shouting a warning the captain. He would never make it to the bridge.

"They spotted the thrusters," announced Luka.

"Now, Mitya," said Misha calmly.

Mitya nodded, flipping up the cover over a master button. He pressed the green button.

The master switch inside the Vixen sent perfectly-timed electrical charges coursing through the ship, each arriving simultaneously at a detonator.

A thousandth of a second later, the peaceful morning was obliterated in a shattering explosion.

The Vixen erupted in a massive ball of energy that turned the ship into a gale of steel fragments. The blast wave slammed into the Sedona with such force that it crushed in the side of the ship, buckling the plating like paper. The mast was ripped away and thrown three football fields into the air.

The concussion hurled the crew of the CIC into the bulkhead, smashing flesh and bone, killing most of them instantly. Those remaining would slowly die from internal bleeding.

The re-enforced polycarbonate bridge windows shattered like a wine glass under the staggering force of the explosion. A hail of ballistic shards ripped through the bridge crew, decapitating the helmsmen before his brain had registered the flash of the bomb.

The shockwave hollowed out the sea in its path. The mangled wreck of the Sedona rolled away. Her screws came out of the water, thrashing madly at the air. Sheets of ragged steel cut into the Sedona's exposed belly, shredding her open and breaking her back.

The blast wave passed and the Sedona's carcass rolled back, falling into the deep trough. Her structural integrity completely failed and she folded together like a book. The sea rushed into the empty void, crushing the two halves of the twisted ship into something unrecognizable. Water gushed unrestricted through her hull, forcing out the air in a roaring geyser of spray.

A moment later the bow and stern of the Sedona were pulled beneath the surface, her grey hull quickly dimming from view as she sank into the black depths of the ocean.

11

WHAT RULES?

Sweat ran down Fulton's face, leaving streaks in the dust and splattered mud that covered him like a mask. Behind him came the thudding boots of the rest of his team.

They ran along the uneven jungle path, taking everything it threw at them. It changed, unexpectedly, from mud to rock, tangled roots and thorny vines. The hot, moist air was like a parasite, sucking their energy.

Fulton swore, flailing his arms as his mud-caked boots skidded on a boulder. With quick reactions and a little bit of luck he righted himself and kept going. He was sure that would have ended in a broken bone if he hadn't acted fast.

"Pick up the pace," shouted Tate from the back of the line.

Fulton was puffing so hard he didn't think he had anything left in him.

"Don't quit," grunted Rosse from directly behind him. "Push harder. Don't give up."

"I'm not quitting," gasped Fulton sharply.

"I was talk'n to myself, dummy," snorted Rosse.

Fulton was thankful he wasn't carrying a full pack or he'd have died on this trail, puking his guts out. He was wheezing now and bit the side of his mouth to get moisture of any kind in his mouth.

His legs were feeling heavy and his boot scuffed a fallen tree as he jumped over it. He pushed his mind to focus on something other than his aching body.

He glanced at the hammer in his hand. It was the only thing he had to carry for this exercise.

Who carries a hammer in the middle of the fricken jungle? He croaked a laugh at the absurdity of it. *Jungle repair man at your service, ma'am.*

The path turned sharply and a cluster of figures blocked his path. The dummies were roughly built with stout tree limbs and coconut heads. All of them were wickedly covered in fishing line with hooks hanging from them.

Fulton tightened his grip on the hammer against the mud and grime that made it slippery. He raced at the first dummy and lifted the hammer, his arm feeling like rubber.

Moving at a run, he only had a second to find a target. He swung down, slamming the hammer into the dummy's head. He yanked the hammer, but he'd hit too hard and it was stuck in the shell. Strings of fishhooks flew around him as he struggled. He felt one snag his sleeve, then another grab his hand.

He was aware of the rest of the team passing him as they delivered killing blows to their dummies and moved on.

Frustration and panic pushed away problem solving, only making his situation worse.

Soon he was covered with hooks, their barbs punishing him with every mistake he made.

"You're dead," said Tate as he passed him.

Fulton stopped struggling, swearing under his breath.

"Catch up," yelled Tate over his shoulder before disappearing around the corner of the path, leaving Fulton to the painful process of removing the hooks.

Rosse, now in the front, broke from the jungle into a wide-open area. With a quick look, he saw a handful of guns scattered on the ground, propped against trees and bushes. Targets were set up at the edges of the field.

The team staggered to a stop, gulping air, followed by Tate.

"You have fifteen seconds to eliminate the enemy," he shouted. "Go."

Everyone shuffled, ran to their shooing stations, picking up what ever weapon was closest.

The jungle echoed with gunshots as pistols and rifles cracked. The team easily hit the closest targets, but their heaving chests made aiming for the farther targets almost impossible.

"Time's running out," yelled Tate, adding to the pressure.

As the rest of the team struggled, Ota was an island of calm. His clothes were black with sweat, but he hit each target with his first shot.

Tate watched, knowing Ota had a faulty weapon. When Ota's gun jammed, he dropped it and scooped up the next closest weapon. Still in motion, he pivoted and fired, shattering the target. With a sigh, he moved into the center of the field and sat down to rest.

Wesson emptied her magazine on the third target without a hit. The bolt locked open and she flung the gun away. She sprinted to a pistol and quickly picked it up. Lowering herself into a shooting stance, she fired.

CLICK.

Empty.

Tate watched without comment, mentally taking notes how his team was dealing with the pressure.

Wesson's frayed nerves were showing as she overlooked two weapons close by. This was the type of battle blindness Tate was working to train out of them. Soldiers who hadn't adapted to the stress and chase chaos of combat would begin to shut down. Their brains would tunnel vision, overwhelmed by sensory overload.

"Hurry," he yelled over the pops of gunfire. "How long before your enemy gets that one shot that kills you? How long are you giving them? Shoot back. Hurry up."

Tate looked down at Ota who smiled at him, understanding what was going on. If Ota could be rattled, Tate hadn't seen it yet. In fact, he couldn't remember ever seeing the man agitated about anything.

Ota was as friendly a person as Tate had met, but the man rarely spoke. He saved his words for times he felt he had something to say.

But Tate wasn't misled by Ota's silence. There was a lot going on behind those calm, blue eyes. He was the team's sniper and frighteningly good at it. Of all the marksmen Tate had met, there was never someone as unmoved about killing as Ota. It wasn't that he enjoyed killing, nor did he regret it. He simply had no feelings about it. To Ota, dying was moving from one plane of existence to another.

For Tate, a shooter had to live by something, a boundary or moral compass that governed the pulling of the trigger. For Ota, it was his value of human life. He took the responsibility of transporting a person to the next existence seriously. Tate didn't want a cold killer and knew he could trust Ota's judgement.

"Oh, come on," yelled Wesson, throwing her weapon to the ground.

There was a lag in the shooting as they all looked at her.

"Wesson," barked Tate.

She hung her head with exasperation and composed herself before responding. "Coming," she said and trotted over.

"Take a seat," was all Tate said, then ignored her.

Wesson planted herself down with a string of angry words under her breath.

Fulton entered the clearing just as Tate ordered the next training phase.

"Back on the trail," he yelled. "Move your butts."

"Really?" said Fulton, as he jogged past Tate, dotted with blood from the hooks.

"Get moving, Private," said Tate flatly.

Everyone dropped what they were doing and began running out of the field.

Rosse led them back into the steaming confines of the jungle, but it wasn't long before the big man's face was dark red with effort.

Barrel chested and stout as a tree trunk, the ex-prison guard turned team medic was determined to give his all in everything he did. The team had learned to tolerate his rough edges, knowing he was tenaciously protective of them if anyone was wounded.

Behind him, Monkhouse grinned, hearing Rosse swear at himself between pants for being weak. Rosse's short but powerful legs were burning and it was getting harder to pick up his feet.

"Move it, you fat loser," puffed Rosse.

"Take it easy on yourself," said Monkhouse. "You're not a loser."

The path crossed a wide stream and Rosse stomped through it, splashing Monkhouse with clods of smelly mud.

Following behind, Wesson scowled under a layer of grime and sweat. The second in command of the team and Tate's right hand, she berated herself for screwing up at the target range.

Strands of her brown hair had worked loose from her pony tail, clinging to her face and hanging over her eyes. She kept her six-foot frame in good shape, but todays exercise had pushed her past her limits.

A wall of fallen limbs and thorn bushes forced her to drop. Crawling on her belly, she scrabbled through the packed red dirt, sucking dust into her mouth.

Coughing, she reached the other side, mentally whipping herself to her feet.

Behind her, Ota kept an easy pace. Just as dirty and pouring with sweat as his teammates, he moved through the rugged and demanding course with an expression of effortless calm.

Tate marveled how Ota took each obstacle with the grace and agility of a panther. His long blond hair was braided and combined with his square features gave the impression of Viking heritage. His adoption of Zen philosophy was reflected in his knack to roll with whatever life threw at him.

No matter the degree of difficulty, he worked his way through it and moved on without a second thought or self critique of his mistakes, which there were few.

Tate refused to compare himself to him, because it would have been self-defeating. He chose himself as the only target of comparison. Matching himself from a month ago, he was leaner, more sure-footed and stronger. More importantly, he had cut free from the millstone of regret and self-hate he'd dragged himself through the past two years.

No therapist or retreat of deep introspection had cured him.

Instead, he was freed from this relentless emotional vampire at the hands of a man intent on killing him. Literally, inches from falling to his death, Tate's black shell of self-hate had cracked open. In that strange, altered state, his dead daughter gave him the one thing he refused to give himself.

Forgiveness.

The life changing moment had only lasted a fraction of a second, but the effects were indelible.

The man, shattered by his past, was healing.

The world around him continued as before. Good and bad, evil and... what? Goodness? It went on without caring about him, but his perception had been revived from the dead. An ironic thought in light of the plague of Vix that still covered the Earth. The undead were a terrible threat, yet where they were, how many, what wins and losses the world was experiencing, nobody knew.

The information highway of the past was gone. News from the other side of the oceans was sporadic and at times conflicted. To Tate's knowledge, some countries had been entirely wiped out. Others had fought and survived, but he never knew if he were listening to firsthand knowledge or a rumor.

He knew governments had fallen. In some cases, new rulers had taken their place. Tate speculated that, in time, as the world stabilized, the United States and other counties would open communications again.

As it was, his own government was holding together with spit and bailing wire.

Many politicians had died in the initial outbreak. Some joked it was God enforcing term limits. But the holes in government had to be filled quickly to ensure the running of the country. The fragmentation created a new problem of states threatening to break from the union. Some went so far as to claim they would form their own country.

The government leadership was a messy combination of veterans ardently standing by traditions, and newbies determined to shake things up and make a difference. For the first year, the government was like the first world war. Everyone had dug into their political trenches, locked in a stalemate; each side stubbornly refusing to give ground while the country around this ship of fools was slowly dying.

It wasn't until a full-blown revolution was about to break open on the very steps of Congress that they woke up.

History had never seen a government body turn around and get it in gear as quickly as Washington DC had done.

And no wonder; it was their necks literally on the line.

That lesson was still fresh in everyone's mind. Politicians decided it was best for everyone involved to keep their rhetoric and party politics behind closed doors and get on with the business of running the country.

The mob crying for revolution lost much of its zeal and many lost interest once they realized there wouldn't be any politicians swinging from trees after all. The core group transformed into an official organization that set itself up as a watchdog, overseeing how the government was spending its time and the taxpayer's money.

Their power was diminished but they served as a token reminder of the near revolt that toppled Washington DC.

Tate's drifting thoughts evaporated as he entered another round clearing. Looking at his gasping team, he smiled inwardly, not feeling nearly as winded at most of them. Except Ota, of course, who was looking like he'd just been out for a pleasant stroll.

In the middle of the clearing was a large patch of bare earth, made muddy by the recent rains. Next to that was a pile of equipment, thickly padded helmets and pugil sticks.

"Everyone suit up," shouted Tate.

The ragged team shuffled to the pile and donned their gear. All of them had noticed, with curiosity, the fading cuts and bruises Tate wore from his recent trip to Lagos. He hadn't mentioned them and they took the hint not to ask.

"Monkhouse. Fulton," said Tate. "You're up."

Both men shuffled to the center of the mud.

"Ready," said Tate, and the men squared off. "Set."

"Top," said Fulton palliatively. "I'm beat. I don't have anything in me."

"Go." barked Tate.

Fulton's eyes went wide, knowing his back was toward the already attacking Monkhouse. Flinching as he turned, Fulton caught a pugil stick in the gut. Luckily, it wasn't a hard blow.

Monkhouse, trying to balance his sense of fair play, didn't want to sucker punch the kid. But the blow was enough to knock Fulton back.

"Attack," snapped Tate. "You think your enemy feels bad because you're tired?"

The two men clashed in a burst of energy that quickly flagged. Monkhouse landed a qualified hit on Fulton and Tate called an end to the match.

"Rosse and Wesson in the ring," he said.

At five-foot-nine, Rosse was shorter than Wesson, but he outweighed her by twenty pounds.

"I'll be gentle," he smirked.

"One point, Wesson," said Tate. "No talking in the ring. Fight."

Wesson used the advantage of her long reach and swung for Rosse's head, but he blocked it and charged in.

Closing the distance, he swept low, catching the back of her heel.

With a quick counter move, she slipped his trap before Rosse could take her feet out from under her.

Off balance, she brought her stick down for a shot to the head, but Rosse blocked her again.

His training as a prison guard included the use of batons and although the pugil stick was longer, the premise was the same. Block, strike, trap.

Rosse came in under her blow and jabbed. His stick hit her stomach, knocking the wind out of her.

She staggered back but anticipated Rosse would come at her. She prematurely blocked in the most likely direction of his next attack.

She was wrong. Rosse side stepped and struck her in the back with a second blow to the back of her head.

Wesson was on the ground before she knew what had happened.

"Stop," said Tate. He came over and waited for Wesson to get to her feet. The flicker of anger was clear in her eyes.

"You ready?" asked Tate.

She grunted through her mouthguard and Tate stepped out of the ring.

"Go," he said.

Wesson charged Rosse, surprising him, swinging at his head. He ducked, but her attack was a feint and he moved right where she wanted him. She quickly pivoted the stick, bringing up the other end to catch him in the face.

Surprised but not taken off guard, Rosse braced his stick, protecting his face.

Bent low, Rosse counterattacked, catching Wesson in the hips. Her eyes went wide as he lifted her into the air.

There was nothing she could do. He could have easily thrown her, like a rag doll.

Unable to do anything, Wesson was at the mercy of an uncontrolled fall. But she was Rosse's teammate. He let her glance off his shoulder and rolled her safely to the ground.

Caked with mud, Wesson came quickly to her feet, growling through her mouthguard and charged.

"Stop," ordered Tate, walking over to the two combatants.

"You did good, Rosse. Take a seat and rest up. You're done for the day."

Wesson was angry and wanted another chance, if not to win at least to vent her frustration.

To her surprise, Tate put on a helmet and picked up a stick. Facing off against Tate, her anger fizzled to dread. She'd never seen him practice, but with the recent revelation of his past as a tier one operator with Delta Force, she expected she was way out of her league.

Tate tested his grip on his padded club. He looked at Wesson and nodded. "Go."

At first neither moved, until Tate moved right. Wesson mirrored him and they began to slowly circle each other.

He faked forward then back and she jumped back, avoiding an attack that never came.

Tate knew the first move was up to him. Pivoting the stick, he came at her.

Wesson threw a nervous block, tripping over her feet as she backpedaled away.

He took advantage and anchored her foot in place.

Over balanced, she topped over like a felled tree, splatting into the mud.

Rolling on to her back, she gasped as Tate's stick rushed at her face. She dodged, missing his blow by a hair.

His mind flashed back to the alley in Lagos. Kaiden, outnumbered and fighting for her life, and he almost lost her. If that had been Wesson? The thought of losing her dumped ice in his veins.

She could fight, but it wasn't enough. He had to push her; make her dig deeper and discover what she was capable of. This was literally the school of hard knocks.

"I thought the match was over," she grunted.

Tate's answer was another attack.

She rolled away and sprang to her feet, Tate close behind.

He held nothing back as she took blow after blow until he knocked her to her knees.

"Stop," said Tate, walking away and giving Wesson room to stand.

The instant she was standing, he yelled, "Go," and charged.

The rest of the team watched in shock and confusion as Tate overwhelmed her but didn't let up.

Wesson panicked, wildly swinging. In the next instant she was knocked down again.

Tate backed away and waited for her to get up again.

She anticipated he would attack as soon as she was standing. She was right, but it didn't help.

She was hardly on her feet when Tate swept her feet. She splashed into the mud.

Wesson came up spewing angry curses and spit out her mouthguard. "What are you trying to prove?" she demanded, trembling with emotion. "You're better than me. Does it make you feel superior? Humiliating me in front of everyone?"

Tate stood passively under the storm of Wesson's venom as the team watched with gapping mouths. The upright, by the book professional soldier had been replaced by a screaming banshee.

Her wrath spent, she glared at him, panting.

He just stared at her, letting the silence hang in the air.

"Well?" she snapped.

"Why do you think you're here?" he asked. "What do you think this is about?"

Wesson took a moment to shift gears. "It's about...," she started, still in the fog of anger. "We're here... we're training to fight."

"Is that what you think?" said Tate, asking the rest of the team. "I'm training you to fight?"

The answer seemed so obvious to them, they weren't sure if they should even answer.

"No," said Ota.

Everyone looked at him, amazed, as if he'd materialized out of thin air. Any time Ota spoke was an event. The team had started a pool, but the best they could do was narrow it down to a selection of what day it might happen.

"No?" spat Wesson. "I'm beat up, bleeding, covered in mud... Not fighting?

What would you call it?"

"Learning how to survive," said Tate.

"How to...?" she said, still burning. "What's this?" She waved the pugil stick at Tate. "A compass?"

"You aren't seeing it," he explained.

"What I see is that every time I use this, I get owned," said Wesson, throwing her pugil stick to the ground.

"Why keep using it?" asked Tate.

"Because those are the rules," she snapped.

Tate looked at her meaningfully, letting her words hang in the air.

Wesson looked at him expectantly, but he said nothing. Confused at first, she went back over the past few seconds, thinking through what had been said.

Then it hit her. Understanding bloomed, sweeping away her anger.

"Get it?" asked Tate, seeing the change in her. "All I said was gear up. I never said you had to use the stick. But you saw your opponents take one, so you did the same thing. Even though you knew you weren't good at it. The lesson is first think about how you will survive, *then* think about fighting."

"So I don't have to use the stick," said Wesson, a smile beginning to crease her face.

"Now you got it," he said. "What a rematch?"

She tossed her stick to the side and crouched low. "You have no idea."

Tate didn't waste any time. He came at her, faking a lunge, hoping to bait her.

She didn't bite.

He changed direction and swung a powerful blow at her unguarded head.

The team gasped. Wesson was about to get slammed.

Except she'd baited Tate, giving him a target. At the last instant, she quickly stepped inside his swing. His momentum pulled him into her trap.

She grabbed his shoulders. With a fast pivot she threw him over her shoulder, sending Tate cartwheeling into the air. He thumped into the mud, gasping for air.

Wesson raced up on him, setting up a kick, but he raised his hands in surrender.

"Lesson over," he wheezed.

Wesson blushed as the team applauded. Tate looked up at her, his smiling though his muddy face.

Tate saw movement at the edge of the clearing and saw Kaiden appear. She gestured for him to come over.

As he got closer, he saw by her expression something was wrong.

"They want us back in D.C.," she said flatly.

12

ISLAND OF DEAD

Crystal-blue water edged the sandy shore. Just beyond, the cream-colored sand stopped abruptly at a wall of dense jungle. A refreshing breeze ruffled through the sea of green leaves, gently swaying rows of palm trees.

Misha scanned the Cuban shore through his binoculars from the bridge of the fishing trawler. He was impatient to get started, and tired of the flat blue horizon of the sea.

A cracked fuel line had cost them several days off course to scrounge for fuel.

He was unhappy with the delay and the loss of two men to the foul undead. The only good luck was the men weren't critical to the next phase of his plan.The swatch of paradise held no interest to Misha. His eyes were on the port of Havana. The large bay was ringed with tall buildings that crowded the coastline.

On the eastern bank, solid stone walls of an ancient Spanish fort stood watch over the mouth of the harbor. Misha shook his head at the fleeting nature of power. In the 1800,s the fort had fought off attacks by the French and Dutch, two of the worlds mightiest navies. Now, rusted cannons peered out of the battlements in a mute display.

On the opposite bank, a jangle of buildings shouldered each

other for a place on the shoreline. The pastel Spanish architecture clashed with modern office buildings in a losing battle for real estate.

For all its charms, there was no avoiding that this was a dead island. On closer inspection, Misha saw how nature and decay was slowly taking back the old city.

A broad thoroughfare lined the western bank, following the water all the way into the harbor.

Like any sailor long at sea, the crew was cheerfully taking in sights and looking forward to leaving the confines of their small ship. The chatter died out as the empty cruise ship docks came into sight. There, the scene of port told the story, frozen in time, of the final days of the island.

When the outbreak hit, everyone's first thought was to escape on a cruise ship. Remnants of the uncontrolled flood of people surged the docks, desperate to get onboard.

A graveyard of traffic clogged the port, left behind by people desperate to get on a ship. Piles of rusted of cars and busses rose out of the water like tombstones. Pushed off the docks by panicked drivers.

The trawler's crew could imagine the screams of people as their cars were bulldozed into the water. The nightmare of people clawing and fighting to get on a ship, boat, or raft.

The Russians had seen their share of wartime horrors, but none of that could compare to what had happened here.

They were shaken out of their daze as the dock came alive with movement.

Ragged, sun-parched human-shaped things, but they weren't human. Not anymore.

Bodies lay by the hundreds everywhere. Their tattered, faded clothing fluttered in the breeze, but there was no other movement. Just corpses. The island was a mass graveyard.

"It's like a vision from Hell," whispered Luka, as if not wanting to disturb the dead.

"And we are damned to walk among them," answered Misha."Are they truly dead?" asked Pavel, manning the ship's wheel.

Misha stepped over to the ship's console and pressed the button for the horn.

On shore, Hell came alive. As if a macabre toy had been turned on, the lifeless bodies stood up. Hundreds and hundreds of them rose to their feet. Heads swiveled and twitched, trying to sense any hint of prey. The sound of their growls and snarls could be heard across the water, making the men shiver in fear and revulsion.

"You weaken the men's spirits, Misha," said Luka.

"Bah," snorted Misha. "To conquer their enemy, it must be dragged out of their fantasies and into the light of the real world."

He stepped out of the bridge and casually walked down the stairs to the main deck.

The men watched as he walked to the bow of the ship. Next to him was an object covered with a canvas tarp.

Misha reached to his side and took out his trusted Kukri. Based on the traditional knife carried by the Gurkhas, Misha's was a gift for graduating the Ryazan Higher Airborne School.

The RVVDKU was a grueling, remorseless school that had no mercy for the weak. It produced some of the toughest, determined soldiers in the world. Misha's instructor had been especially hard on him.

Before being conscripted into the army, Misha had been a coal miner. Stout and powerful, he was no stranger a hard, demanding life of biting cold and sweltering heat. He scoffed at lesser men who surrendered to softer occupations.

Excelling in the army, he won the Master Sportsman Badge and caught the attention of the school's commander. The commander decided Misha had the makings for the Spetsnaz and he was told to report for training.

The stories of special forces training were legendary. Brutal instructors, body breaking accidents and deaths were only some of the horror stories that spread among new recruits.

The new inductees entered the base, looking like Christians about to be fed to the lions, except Misha. He observed his surroundings with a quiet confidence and the expression of a man unimpressed.

His instructor singled him out, accepting the challenge to discover if Misha was as tough as he appeared. The instructor was well-practiced at destroying a man's self confidence and breaking their will.

The ones that broke were thrown away like garbage without regret.

He saw himself as a sentinel at the gates of Russia. His training was the forge and anvil to produced soldiers with resolves of steel. Soldiers whose hearts blazed with a fighting spirit and would die protecting their motherland.

From the first day of training, the instructor singled out Misha. The man bled, sweated, vomited and broke bones, but he never quit. He recognized what his instructor was doing and came to privately relish it. If his insane drill instructor couldn't break him, there was nothing on the battlefield or off to fear.

Through it all, his instructor never eased up, praised him, or showed the least sign of respect. In a way, Misha would have been disappointed if he had. By the end of training, he had excelled beyond the rest of his class.

At the graduation ceremony, Misha was met by his instructor. With grim respect, they saluted each other, neither bearing resentment.

To Misha's surprise, his instructor handed him a richly-crafted wooden box. The black, lacquered finish was untouched by any design or decoration.

Misha had opened it and saw the custom-made Kukri. Before he could think of the right words to speak, his instructor abruptly turned and walked away.

He knew there was nothing either man could say worthy of the experience they shared.

On the trawler, Misha paused on the ships starboard bow, looking at the distant Vix, his hand resting on the handle of his knife.

With an easy movement, he slid the Kurki from its sheath. The blade was as black as night, with only its wickedly sharp edge glinting brilliantly in the sunlight.

In front of him was a chest-high object covered in canvas. With a single swipe, he parted the rope holding the cover in place. Pulling the tarp away, he revealed a multi-barreled mini gun. Mounted to a short pillar, welded to the deck, the mini gun rested in a swivel mount. A ridged ammo guide fed down into a large hopper of bullets.

He turned the gun towards the shore and switched on the power. Misha pressed down on the trigger and the minigun came to life with a roar.

It poured a solid line of lead scything into the ranks of undead, cutting them down like a forest of brittle saplings.

Incited by the sound of the gun, Vix swarmed forward, heedless of their own destruction. Hundreds spilled over the railings and tumbled into the harbor.

Misha traversed is aim to the long row of bodies building up in the water.

With the sound or ripping air, bullets stabbed into the water, thrashing it into a foaming torrent of shattered bone and flesh.

The mini-gun's spent shells washed across the deck, clinking and smoking until the gun ran dry.

Misha looked at his handiwork as the gun's barrels sizzled and ticked with heat.

His display had the desired affect and the crew's mood lighted. Many took confidence from seeing something so foul and unnatural weren't immune to their weapons. Others were not as convinced.

"There is nothing here but brittle ghosts," announced Misha.

"These ghosts have already killed two of our men," said one of the soldiers.

Misha lowered his head for a moment as a sign of respect. He knew the soldier and how they had narrowly escaped a Vix horde but lost his entire family to them. The once jolly and outgoing young man was a brooding, cynical version of his former self.

Misha walked over and put his arm around the young man, squeezing him good naturedly. "You are right, Gergor," he said. "And it would be foolish to not treat these monsters with care, but we live on. Let's not give them more power than they're due, eh?" he cajoled with another squeeze. "Eh?"

The jostling shook loose a smile from Gergor, and the other men cheered.

"The next part of our mission is before us," said Misha, raising his voice so all could hear him. "You know your parts. Get to it."

The men scrambled around the ship, making ready and preparing for one of the most dangerous parts of their mission.

The ship's pilot steered away from the western port, bringing the bow east.

Ahead were the rows of orderly but empty docks of the Cuban Navy base. Storage and supply warehouses lined the shore, allowing fast resupply of the warships, reducing their time away from patrol. Behind the southernmost pier was the tall, white administration building. Once the main artery of Cuba's naval activity, now a sun-bleached shell.

Misha had chosen the Naval shipyard for its one advantage above all the other places they could dock. A ten-foot-tall, reinforced security fence. With luck they'd find the entrance gate to the base was closed.

Back inside the bridge, Misha scanned the docks as they neared.

"Hold here," he told the pilot.

The pilot reversed the propellers to stop their forward drift, shifting back and forth until they'd come to a relative stop in the water.

A soldier had taken over the starboard mini gun Misha had used. Another mini gun, mounted on the port side of the bow, was uncovered and manned by another soldier.

Each of them signaled back to Misha that they were ready.

Misha picked up the microphone from the ship's console and switched to the exterior loudspeaker.

"Before we dock, let's see if there's any house cleaning." He pressed the button for the foghorn.

A throaty bellow shattered the quiet, echoing across the water and off the buildings. It almost felt disrespectful, like a child playing loudly in a graveyard.

"There," said Luka, pointing to the upper floor window of the administration building.

Misha followed his direction with his binoculars. He saw it, too. Framed behind the dirty streaked glass were several pale figures crowding at the window, pushing and climbing over each other, blindly struggling to reach the source of the noise.

"Fire on that building," said Misha over the loudspeaker.

The soldiers swung their Gatling guns and fired. The front of the administration building billowed with dust and debris as bullets drilled into the window walls. Concrete and plaster were pulverized, obscuring the building in a cloud of dust.

The soldiers stopped as the wind swept away the dust, revealing a jagged hole in the face of the building.

At first everything was still and quiet, but a moment later they heard the snarls. Vix came racing out of other buildings and down the docks towards the trawler.

The gunmen knew what to do and opened fire. The power of the mini guns literally blew the Vix apart.

Unimpressed with the spectacle, Misha busied himself with a map on the chart table. Soon the shooting stopped and the bridge radio crackled to life.

"No further contacts," reported a soldier.

"Hold here a few more minutes," said Misha without looking up. "We'll give the slower ones a chance to appear."

The boat gently rocked with the low waves, stirred by the breeze as the ship's clock ticked by. After several minutes of quiet, Misha decided it was safe to dock the ship and ordered the pilot to take them in.

As the boat glided along the dock, several armed men jumped off and ran to the front of the dock, setting up a perimeter. They kept guard while others grabbed thick ropes from the deck and tied off the boat.

With an assault rifle in his hand, Misha jumped down from the ship to the dock below. He chuckled, stomping his feet.

"Look at that, Luka. Solid ground. I've missed it."

"Seems like we've been on the sea our whole lives," said Luka. "I don't trust the water."

"As well you shouldn't," agreed Misha. "Who knows what's hiding down there."

"Comrades," called Misha, gathering his men. "Each of you look at the men around you," he said. "You are holding their lives in your hands. One careless act could kill all of us. We are surrounded by the enemy. They don't sleep. They don't fear you. But you should not fear them, either. Each of you knows your duty. You know what all of us expect from each other."

He paused and looked at the men around him, each looking back, intent, unwavering. "The world can come and go, but we, we are unchanging. We are SPETSNAZ."

The men around him cheered, their faces etched with fierce determination and loyalty.

"Recon the area," said Misha. "Make sure the perimeter is secure. Report back in twenty minutes. Go."

Three quarters of the men took off, breaking into smaller groups as they headed for their pre-determined areas.

"Luka, take your crew to the hospital," said Misha. "Report what you find."

Luka nodded and trotted off with a handful of men, leaving Misha alone on the dock.

He looked up, squinting at the sun-dazzled sky and breathed deeply.

In his hand was the badge he'd worn on his uniform. Gold leaves ringed a red star containing a hammer and sickle.

"You took my loyalty and betrayed me," he said. "Betrayal is a sword with two blades. Today I sharpen that blade. Be prepared for the time I use it."

13

NO STRINGS ATTACHED

"Gone," said Jones, slapping a folder down on the desk. "Like someone opened a hole in the ocean and dropped our ship in it."

Photos of the USN Sedona and her crew scattered out of the folder.

"No distress call," said Smith. "No beacon. Nothing."

Tate was sitting in the same uninspired room in the basement of the Pentagon. He skimmed through the classified report with zero doubt what Misha Kilmonikov had done with his ship of explosives.

The blast from the Vixen had been so powerful it was registered on undersea seismographs.

"We knew the ship's name and the threat it posed. Why didn't the Sedona blow Kilmonikov out of the water on sight?" asked Tate

Jones continued pacing while Smith tapped his pen on the table. Neither of them said anything but avoided looking at Tate.

"You *did* warn the Navy there was a bomb the size of a cargo ship, right?" he pressed.

After a long pause, Jones broke the silence. "We thought Kilmonikov was going after Russian targets," he said. "It didn't make sense that he'd attack us."

"You never told them?" asked Tate, incredulous. "Do they know now?"

"No," snapped Smith. "As far as they know, something catastrophic happened to the Sedona."

Tate's mouth fell open in disbelief. "So nobody but you know what's going on? You guys are more concerned about staying off the radar that you let Americans walk into a death trap," he seethed. "There's a guy out there with resources, a plan and zero compunction for killing. He's still out there. You better warn the DOD our people are in danger, or I will."

"Hey, Captain America," barked Jones, leaning over the desk. "You want to start a war? You think the Joint Chiefs are going believe a highly-decorated special forces member of Russian Military Intelligence, acting independently, just woke up one day and decided to blow up an American war ship? No. Their first and only go-to is that he's acting under the direct authority of the Kremlin. This isn't like the old days when the US could take something like this on the chin and brush it off. Our defenses are spread thin and losing this ship has made the DOD pissed off and nervous. They want their pound of flesh."

"We don't even know who's running Moscow," said Smith. "But they still hate the US. We know their leadership told their people the Vix thing was a US secret bioweapon that went out of control. And in case you're thinking of asking, no. We had nothing to do with it."

"All they need is the slightest provocation," said Jones, "like accusing them of attacking us and it won't be long before somebody throws the first punch."

"Imagine a battlefield of dead and dying soldiers in central Europe," said Smith. "That could set off a second outbreak. And this time... the world might not survive. And we owe it all to Sergeant Major Jack Tate. Nice work, boy scout."

Tate clenched his jaw, fighting back all the things he could say because he knew there was a chance, even if it was a small one, they were right. He'd seen enough of the outbreak to haunt him into the next life.

"Then why am I here?" he asked. "There must be something else."

The mood in the room eased considerably. Jones stood back up, his face creasing into a grin that Tate wanted to slap off his face.

"We got a break," said Jones. "A fishing trawler matching the description you got from Karim was spotted in the Florida strait heading for Cuba."

"Cuba?" repeated Tate.

"Russias very own French Riviera," quipped Smith.

"How are the Sedona and Cuba connected?" asked Tate.

Jones was about to speak when Kaiden chimed in.

"I get it," she said. "The Sedona was a distraction. He needed a clear path to Cuba without the Navy or Coast Guard in the way. When the Sedona went missing, they mobilized every ship we had for search and rescue."

"She's good," said Jones, pointing his finger at her.

"All Kilmonikov had to do was tuck into a small bay and wait for the Navy to clear all of their patrols out of the way," said Kaiden. "Then he slips into Cuba undetected."

"Except someone did," said Tate.

"We got lucky," said Jones. "Very, very lucky, but that's ..."

"Need to know," finished Tate. "It's all coming back to me."

"What is?" asked Smith.

"Why working with people like you is a pain in my neck," said Tate. "No offense."

Smith smiled but said nothing else.

"You know he's there," said Kaiden. "But you don't know what he's up to."

"Guessing is a waste of time," said Tate. "Whatever it is, it's important to him."

"Important enough to wipe out one of our ships," said Smith.

"Like you pointed out," said Jones, gesturing to Tate. "This guy's committed, and resourceful. Whatever he's doing, he's doing it within spitting distance of our coast."

Tate nodded with understanding. "That's why I'm here. You want us to see what he's up to."

"Good looks *and* brains," smirked Jones.

"Better keep that smile on your face," said Tate. "I'm in if Kaiden is, but there's a couple of caveats."

Smith and Jones smiled as they leaned against the desk. Making deals was a part of intel politics they were familiar with.

"I taking my team," stated Tate.

"All of you? Why don't we send in a marching band? You may have noticed," said Jones, looking around the dingy room, "we operate off the radar."

"Yeah. Black ops, I get it," Tate said, unimpressed. The mystique of running operations with nameless men and women, infiltrating countries, not having to answer to the rule of law had faded a long time ago.

"The more people involved, the bigger risk we take of exposure," said Jones. "We need seasoned professionals. Let's be honest; your crew is a joke."

Tate knew the negation game too. He remained silent, not being drawn into defending his demands.

The agents stared at him, the clock on the wall ticking loudly in the quiet.

The awkward pause drew out, but Tate was content to say nothing more. As he expected, the agents blinked first.

"Okay," said Smith. "Fine, you can use them. What else?"

"I want new gear for my team," said Tate.

From the corner of his eye, he saw a smirk on Kaiden's face. He was making the agents twist and she was enjoying the show.

"Sure," said Smith quickly. "We have access to resources, material, *money*. You name it, chances are we can give it to you."

"No strings attached," smirked Tate. "Me and my people don't owe you anything in return."

"Affirmative," said Smith.

"What do you want?" asked Jones.

"Body armor," said Tate. "The new stuff, not that clunky poly-layered junk. Integrated night vision optics with HUD multi target tracking. Micro coms with ion-solid state power cells. Tri-Purpose grenades, incendiary, fragmentation... you guys writing this down?"

The spooks weren't expecting a grocery list this expensive but did their best not to show how much it hurt. Smith took out a pen and started taking notes.

"Fragmentation," said Tate, making a point of peering at what Smith was writing. "And gas. I'll send you the list of weapons," he continued. "Have it delivered to my base."

"Want it wrapped in a pretty bow?" asked Jones. "Considering the junk your team has, this gear should be enough to get their buy-in."

"Anything else?" asked Smith.

"I'm only doing this op if it's reconnaissance only," said Tate firmly. "No engagement."

"That's what we're after," said Jones. "This is just a fact-finding mission."

Tate nodded, scrutinizing them. He'd been sent on bait and switch missions before, not learning the true purpose of the mission until he was already committed.

"This isn't a done deal until my team is onboard," said Tate. "They don't know anything about what I've been involved in."

"That' won't be a problem," said Smith. "They'll be excited to play soldier."

Tate bristled at the man's smug confidence but recognized this was the game people like them played; push your emotional buttons, move you one way, tug you another, keep you off balance.

"You sound confident," he said, following the obvious bread-crumbs the agents were laying down for him.

Jones tapped a stack of ignored folders on the table. "We've done our homework. It took a little digging but we know everything there is about everyone on your team. Go ahead. Take a look."

"Names," said Smith. "Real names. Histories, family, jobs, where they've been, who they know, all of it."

Tate looked at the stack of folders. Each had a tab with a name printed on it: Rosse, Tyler. Monkhouse, Bret. All of them were there.

Three things about them caught his eye; there wasn't a folder on Kaiden. He supposed that shouldn't come as a surprise. The folder about him had his real name on it; Tiller, Jack. Lastly, the folder labeled Ota, Kasey was empty.

Tate grinned inwardly. Even these spooks, with all their resources, were no match for the unfathomable Ota. The man was a self-made enigma.

"Not interested," he said, pushing the folders aside. "I know the people on my team. That's all I need to know."

"Would they say the same about you?" asked Smith, tapping the folder with Jack's name on it.

Tate couldn't help but notice his file was more than twice as thick as everyone else's. He suspected a lot of its contents had been supplied by Kaiden. The idea left him with mixed feelings about that. He didn't like the idea that everything he did was being documented. It left him feeling like someone was always looking over his shoulder.

He thought about all the things he and Kaiden had done.

"You've had some wild adventures," chuckled Smith, as if he'd read Tate's expression.

Here it comes, thought Tate.

Smith opened the folder, leafing through the pages.

"The Congo op," said Smith. "Seems like you do have a cold side. You smuggled that informer out of the country, leaving his family behind to the secret police."

"Downing that North Korean transport," grinned Jones. "I get killing the general. The guy was a real scumbag, but smoking everyone else onboard? You're a hard man."

Tate pretended to scowl before turning back to look at Kaiden. She kept her eyes on the agents, but a hint of a smile raised the corner of her mouth.

The details they were reading back to him never happened.

Tate had smuggled out the informer *and* his family. He'd disobeyed a direct order, although his commander never knew it happened. Having gotten them out, Tate had used his own network to relocate the family under another name.

That North Korean plane had never crashed. He and Kaiden hacked the flight systems and landed it at a black site. The general had spent the next eight months spilling major intel. The other passengers were sent back. North Korea wasn't about to embarrass themselves on the world stage and pretended like nothing happened.

Kaiden had selectively lied in the reports she'd written for these agents. If she had given them the real information, they'd practically own Tate.

She'd lied to protect him. All of his doubts about trusting her had just been wiped away. A huge weight had just dropped off his shoulders and he wanted to turn back to her and laugh.

He snapped out of his thought as Jones looked at his watch and gestured to Smith to wrap up the meeting.

A scrap of Tate's last thought nagged for his attention. He couldn't put his finger on it but he felt he was letting something important get away from him.

His gaze dropped to the files Jones was picking up; each one containing private information about his team. It only reinforced his suspicion that these two were ex-FBI. No other agency had domestic intel like that.

Suddenly, an important puzzle piece fell into place.

"Hang on," he said, suddenly recognizing a rare opportunity. "I need access to an unrestricted FBI computer."

The two spooks looked at a loss for words and even Kaiden couldn't hide her surprise.

Tate remembered the codes Nathan had uncovered. The same ones Colonel Hewett recognized as FBI evidence codes.

It was a good bet that Smith and Jones could get into the FBI's system, authorized or not.

"We can't... don't have access to that," said Smith, looking deeply uncomfortable. "Using FBI systems is a serious crime."

"How do you explain these?" asked Tate, pointing to the stack of files. "Getting those requires access to a domestic agency database and if I remember right, black ops, that's you, is solely sanctioned for foreign activities. If somebody knew you had these, you could be shut down."

"And prosecuted," added Kaiden.

Smith and Jones looked at each other nervously but remained silent.

"Thirty minutes," said Tate. "That's all I need, then I forget it ever happened."

Jones muttered something hotly under his breath, flinging open the door and storming out. Smith followed, with the files in hand.

Tate sighed in defeat.

"I guess it's back to square one," he said to Kaiden.

Smith's head appeared in the doorway. "You coming or not?"

Jones angrily pointed to the computer with FBI access and left them in the office.

Kaiden had worked her way through half of the codes on the list while Tate explained Nathan's discovery and Hewett's critical revelation.

"This one's invalid too," she said.

"The codes must be specific to an object and location," said Tate.

"Another invalid one," she said.

"They must cancel the number when they remove the evidence," he said.

"Makes sense."

"I'm not sure what we're looking for, but it could lead to a major break against The Ring."

"Lucky break," said Kaiden.

Tate thought about that and then backtracked though all the events leading up to today. The odds of all the past events falling into place seemed impossibly slim, and yet here they were. A voice in the back of his head told him all of this may not have been as random as it appeared.

"It was a lucky break that Smith and Jones had FBI access," he said.

Kaiden was focused on the codes and said nothing.

Tate looked at the back of her head, thinking about all the wheels turning in there.

"I was thinking," he said. "We might not be here if I hadn't caught you breaking into my place."

"You got lucky," she scoffed. "Don't rub it in."

"Or maybe you're getting too old for this kind of thing."

"Hey. No need to get nasty," she said, her eyes on the screen.

"We've run a lot of operations together," he said, beginning to explore a theory. "I could count on one hand the number of times you made a mistake."

"It's sweet of you to keep count," said Kaiden, crossing another code off the list.

"Don't get me wrong," said Tate. "It's rare. But two mistakes back to back?"

"If you're counting not shooting you with a tranq dart as my second mistake," she said, "I have to agree."

"Catching you with your hand in my safe was one," he said. "But taking off your mask after breaking into Nathan's?"

He turned over the events, arranging them like scrambled letters that eventually spelled out a message.

Kaiden's expression was reflected in the computer screen. There was something in her expression that told him she knew what he was talking about.

"I was frustrated," she said, annoyed.

"You've been frustrated before," he said. "Never enough to break operational protocol, unless... you wanted Nathan to see you."

"Calm down, Sherlock," she mumbled.

"No," said Tate, the key piece falling into place. "You wanted *me* to see you. You wanted to send me a message that you were coming."

Kaiden stopped typing and laughed. She turned around in her chair, her cool grey eyes flashing.

"I didn't take you for the conspiracy type," she said.

"Oh, it's all coming together," he grinned. "You had this planned from the moment Vulcan 4 came down. You knew I was having doubts about you, but you couldn't tell me the truth without blowing your security clearance." He snapped his fingers as another revelation hit him. "You didn't just want me to know, you wanted to bring the entire team into this black ops group and make Smith and Jones think it was their idea."

Kaiden leaned back in her chair and folded her arms across her chest, listening to him with smile.

"You get caught. The truth comes out. The spooks bring us onboard and you keep your security clearance. Then, just by chance, they have the only accessible network for the codes we found."

Tate grinned at her with a look of triumph at having pieced together all the clues.

"Are you done?" said Kaiden, looking unimpressed. "Don't get me wrong. I'm touched that you think I'm an all-knowing chess master. I wish I was that good." She turned back to the computer and began entering in the codes. "But a plan that complex would be next to impossible. Life isn't that exciting, Jack." She turned around to face him. "Sometimes things just work out."

Tate looked at her, slightly puzzled. Something on the display behind her was blinking. He looked over her shoulder and read the flashing text.

Code match. Evidence storage unit C093. Knoxville TN.

208 E. Walnut AVE

Unit Status: Active

"Whatever The Ring is after," said Kaiden, "it's inside there."

14

OIL AND WATER

Tate knew putting Nathan in the same room with Kaiden was going to be rough and neither of them were doing anything to make it easier.

His plan was to enlist Nathan's help to break into the FBI black site. Tate was hoping Nathan's hate of The Ring outweighed his anger with Kaiden.

Before leaving DC, he'd contacted Nathan, explaining he had more information about the FBI codes. Nathan had agreed to meet in an abandoned house outside the protective wall that encircled Roanoke.

The drive was surprisingly scenic and the weather mild. Tate didn't miss the ever-present heat and humidity of the jungle.

Just as he was wondering about the Vix in the area, he drove past the smoldering remains of a house.

He shook his head in disbelief. The Vix were dangerous, yet people still underestimated them. That house was a gravestone to who people chose to stick it out on their own. They rejected the offer of relocating into a secured town or city. Pride, sentimentality or paranoia, Tate would never know, but it was a risk he wouldn't have taken.

People had turned their homes into bunkers with some success, but those were few and far between.

There had been a debate about passing a law mandating that people be forced to move into the safety of walled-off populated areas. That had been met with zealous resistance. No matter what had happened in this country, it remained America. A person's land was theirs. The government had no right to take it from them, no matter the reason. People demanded and fought for their rights, but with those rights came personal responsibility.

Shunning the safety of a large community came with risks. Some underestimated those risk with deadly consequences.

Tate suspected that burning house was the result of those consequences. He felt a mixture of sorrow for whoever died there and pride that the tough spirit of individualism still existed.

Standing in the living room of the deserted house, facing an angry Nathan reminded him of that spirit, but in this case, it was working against Tate's needs.

He didn't feel good about tricking Nathan into the same room as Kaiden, but it was the only idea he could come up with.

Tate had planned to smooth all the ruffled feathers during the meeting. As plans go, that one was going down in flames.

Nathan stared at Tate, heavy with disappointment and irritation.

"You lied to me," he said.

"That's not true," said Tate. "I never said she wouldn't be here."

"A lie of omission is still a lie."

"If you knew Kaiden would be here would you have come?" asked Tate.

Nathan didn't answer, but everything from his body language to his expression said 'no'.

"That's what I thought," said Tate. "I'm not saying you aren't justified, but she broke into your place for all the right reasons."

He'd explained that everything Kaiden had done was to set the wheels in motion with the goal of getting the Grave Diggers merged with the black ops group, but Nathan wasn't buying it.

"I see how that helps you, but what about me?" he asked. "My site is blown. I can't go back there. And now I'm on their radar."

"You always find the best places," said Kaiden, looking around the large, open-plan living room distractedly. "It shouldn't be hard to set up a new covert site."

Okay, enough," said Tate. "We have a bigger problem in front of us. The Ring is looking for this evidence site and we have to get there first."

Nathan kept his thoughts to himself, but some of his resistance had faded. "If the FBI is still using this site to store evidence," he said, "it could be a treasure trove of tech and information."

"We're after whatever the code points to," said Tate, being sure Nathan got the warning. "It's a quick in and out mission. No window shopping."

He laid out a map of the facility location on the large table, including a couple of satellite photos of the area.

Nathan stood a short way off, making it clear he didn't want to be around Kaiden.

"I get it," said Tate, knowing what Nathan was thinking, "but how does that compare to hurting The Ring?"

After an uncomfortable pause, Nathan came over and looked at the map.

"This whole area is residential," said Tate, tracing a circle around the FBI site.

"Makes sense," said Nathan. "An industrial area or office complex would likely have predictable hours of activity. Using a residential neighborhood means you never know who's around."

"These aren't the best quality pictures," said Tate, "but there's enough detail to see any obvious security measures they have." He pointed to a visible border around the house. "Just a chain-link fence."

"If there's security," began Nathan.

"If?" said Kaiden, cocking an eyebrow. "A little overly optimistic, aren't you?"

Nathan glared at her, but she didn't react.

"It's doubtful they have dogs or a person for onsite security," he said, turning his attention back to the photos. "The FBI couldn't maintain funding for that long term."

"Non-organic security," said Tate. "Cameras or an alarm system make sense."

"Maybe, but that still means long-term funding," said Nathan. "Someone's got to monitor the cameras 24/7. They're not going to watch someone break in and do nothing. They need a security team to respond and people are high maintenance. Food, housing, the list goes on. It used to be people were cheap."

"There used to be more people," said Tate. "All right. Guards and dogs are out. The security has to be self-contained and self-sufficient."

"They could have Vix in there," said Kaiden.

Nathan took his hands out of his pockets and leaned forward, resting his hands on the table.

Kaiden watched him, an amused look in her eyes.

If he noticed, he didn't show it, instead, Nathan put his focus on the pictures. "Vix," he said. "They could, but it's risky. They're not like a dog you can train. Vix are indiscriminate. Any Fed going in there faces the same danger as an intruder."

"That leaves artificial intelligence," said Tate, believing this had been the answer from the start of their conversation.

"An AI security system?" said Kaiden thoughtfully. "Sounds fun."

The advancement of AI had surged ahead in the tech industry. Many thought it had surged too far ahead. Attempting to be a leader in AI, many companies developed their own version of it. In the beginning there were no governmental standards or oversight. A competitive market was great for the economy but the tech companies weren't selling coffee makers. People were handing over parts of their lives to machines running on AI.

It was impossible for the AI development teams not to influence the way it processed and acted on data. Reports began appearing that AI were nearly as individual as people. They had agendas, biases and personalities. These attributes would change how the AI perceived the world around it and change how it reacted.

Integration of an AI to anything affecting human life was called into question when it was discovered that a chain of soda dispensers was changing the syrup to soda water ratio depending on the weight of the consumer. An obese person noticed their soda was nearly all soda water while someone thinner was getting the standard mix.

The problem went much deeper with PAIAs. Personalized Artificial Intelligence Assistants had flooded into people's homes, making the simple voice-activated terminals obsolete in a few short months. The PAIAs had been integrated into every aspect of people's homes, far beyond the simple tasks of regulating the thermostat.

In some cases, the AI's personality infection was benign. People thought it gave their AI character. Their idiosyncrasies and unpredictability made them more human.

But these traits were a sign of something darker and more serious. Investigations uncovered some of the tech companies had purposely added dispositions and bias towards religions and political views. The AIs were monitoring their owner's moralities and reporting back to the companies. The companies repeatedly denied these accusations, saying these lies were the creation of religious fundamentalists and conspiracy nuts.

The seriousness of the tech companies influences gained worldwide exposure when it was discovered that, unknown to their owners, their PAIAs were filtering emails and phone calls that the AI deemed contrary to the factory-installed values programed.

Tech companies were hauled before several governmental investigative committees until the truth came out.

The devices were ripped out of the homes and destroyed in mock public executions. In the face of falling stocks, several of the companies claimed the infection of the AI was the work of a disgruntled employee acting outside the stated policies of the company.

This opened the company's employees to public harassment and, in some cases, threats.

Feeling betrayed by their own companies and likely motivated by self-preservation, an unknown person dumped the entire contents of one company's programing server on the internet.

The exposed information spread like wildfire. Not only was the company purposely imposing its own ethics on their consumers, but they were spying on them. On the surface, the data appeared to be mundane. But the company hadn't just gathered the data but compiled it and processed it through a mega AI.

They knew the most sensitive and personal details of thousands of individuals.

The company leadership were imprisoned, sued into bankruptcy and two of the companies were seized, their patents revoked and their knowledge database destroyed.

This last measure was considered overkill my some, but when news leaked involving the accumulated information the company had on a handful of senators and members of congress, well, the hammer really came down.

AI was still in use, but its personality was open source, meaning people could modify it to their liking.

"Not much fun if it's weaponized," said Nathan. "It'll kill us the moment we set foot on the property."

Linking AI to weapons was illegal for civilians, but military and law enforcement could employ the use of it under special circumstances. The truth was nobody was regulating what those circumstances were. Translated, that meant they could use AI weapon systems anywhere.

"Have you ever dealt with AI like that before?" asked Tate.

"Once or twice," said Nathan. "Those things are psychotic."

"Kaiden?" asked Tate.

"Once or twice," she answered, a small smile pulling at the corner of her mouth as she glanced at Nathan.

The insinuation wasn't lost on him and he didn't need reminding that she had hacked the AI security of his safe house.

"No insult intended," she said.

Tate stared at Kaiden, openly baffled.

What is she doing?

"I've been threatened by black marketers, psychopaths, corporate spies and hacker terrorists," said Nathan. "You're a bit small time to hurt my feelings."

"When are you going to tell him about the other mission detail?" said Kaiden.

Tate glared at her for putting him on the spot. He had wanted to reconcile Kaiden and Nathan and get him invested in the operation. After accomplishing that, he thought he could break the bad news without jeopardizing the op.

"What *other* mission detail?" said Nathan.

"I can't go," said Tate. "It'll just be you and Kaiden."

Nathan's face was a mask of stone, making it impossible for Tate to read what he was thinking.

He was sure it wasn't good, but maybe he could salvage the mission, or so he thought.

"Don't be like that," smiled Kaiden. "It'll be fun. I'll even show you how to hack the security system."

"Forget it, Tate," said Nathan, stepping away from the table. "I don't trust her, especially with my life..." He headed for the door with Tate close behind, throwing Kaiden an angry look before disappearing out the door.

Kaiden slouched against the table, her fingernails clicking as she tapped her fingers on its lacquered finish.

Heated voices could be heard from outside, followed by the front door opening and closing with a slam.

Tate stormed in and paced the room, venting off his anger before speaking.

"Why so angry?" asked Kaiden. "I gave him what he wanted."

"What he wanted?" he snapped. "What's that supposed to mean? He wanted you to make him quit the op before it even got started?"

"It doesn't make sense, I get it," she said.

"Do you? Because I don't. Whatever's in that building, The Ring's after it." Tate sat down, fuming, but his anger wouldn't let him be still.

He got up and began pacing again. "You went out of your way to piss off the only one skilled enough to get past whatever security is protecting that site," he said.

"Isn't that the point?" she asked.

Tate stared at her, boiling in a mixture of frustration and confusion.

"What point?" he flared. "You haven't said anything that makes sense." He was about to go on but stopped himself and held up his finger. "Never mind. I'm going back to the base. Since you have such a great grasp of the situation, you work this out."

He walked out of the room.

"I already have," said Kaiden, hearing the front door flung open.

There was a long space of quiet before she heard the door click closed.

Tate walked back into the room, his anger present but contained.

"You said it yourself," she said. "The Ring is going to find that site soon. When they do, they'll need someone to get past the security. Nathan is the only one skilled enough. You know it. I know it. And..."

The light dawned in Tate's mind. "The Ring knows it," he said.

"As far as they're concerned, Nathan is still a trusted contractor," she said. "Well, mostly trusted. They'll send him to the FBI site with a babysitter."

"They'll want a second pair of eyes to report back."

"They go in. Nathan does his hacking magic because, let's face it, whoever they send with him won't understand what they're seeing. And Nathan will say whatever they're looking for has been moved to another site."

"If they think it's been transferred to another site," said Tate, "they'll keep looking."

"Exactly," said Kaiden. "If The Ring knew it had taken it, it would be a clear sign somebody out there knows about their origination and what they were after."

"If they thought they'd been compromised they'd go dark. Go deeper underground, change up all their communications and kill off loose ends."

"Loose ends like Nathan," she finished.

Tate's anger dissipated as he saw the sense of it and sat down with shake of his head. "Why didn't you just say all of this from the beginning?" he asked. "Why drive him off?"

Kaiden looked at her watch, holding up a finger to pause him.

He could see she was counting down and after a moment turned back to the table.

"Let's go over the evidence site," she said, tapping the map. "There's some aspects about this operation I want to talk about."

If it were possible to be more confused, Tate wouldn't have believed it. Kaiden had just explained the operation was off. Now she wanted to talk about the operation.

His first reaction was to throw up his hands, but before he did, she showed him something and all became clear.

They spent the next hour discussing the evidence site, it's possible external and internal security and most likely access points.

By the time they were done, Tate felt like he could sleepwalk through the place.

15

SHINY NEW TOYS

It wasn't long after Tate and Kaiden had returned to their base that Smith and Jones sent the new gear.

Tate stood in the shade, watching two privates struggle with the last of the crates. Grunting, the soldiers wrestled the big box to the back of the canvas-covered tent where the other crates sat.

Kaiden stood out of the way, enjoying the stream of cool relief from the air conditioning.

With a final shove, the privates pushed the crate in place. They wiped the sweat out of the faces, happy to be done, but in no hurry to leave.

"That was one heavy sucker," said one of them.

The other one agreed as they continued to awkwardly linger.

Puzzled for a moment, Tate made the connection and reached into his pocket.

"Thanks guys," he said, drawing some bills out and handing to one of the soldiers. "Find a good use for this."

"Thanks, Sergeant Major," said one of them with a big smile. They climbed back into the truck and pulled away with a friendly honk as Tate released the ties holding open the tent flaps.

He was missing the mild D.C. weather and finding it hard to adapt to the stifling jungle heat.

Kaiden handed him a bottle of water as he joined her near the AC vent.

"That was a big risk," he said out of the blue.

"Are there any other kinds?" she asked. "Just to be clear, what are we talking about?"

"The file you wrote for those Pentagon spooks," he said. "You changed the details of the operations."

After their meeting with Smith and Jones, Tate hadn't spoken to Kaiden about her work as a spy for the government. During their trip back to South America, he had processed through the questions filling his head, weeding out the less important ones.

The trip to the Pentagon threw light on an entirely new part of Kaiden. He had formed his own theories, but they didn't come close to the scope of what she was really involved with.

"Spooks? I never said I worked for the CIA," said Kaiden.

"Come on," he pushed. "Those two bozos stink of the agency."

"*They* might be," she shrugged. "Maybe they aren't. I don't know."

"Don't you care who's giving you orders?" he asked.

To his absolute surprise, Kaiden busted out laughing. The sound filled the tent. Tate didn't know what was so funny, but couldn't help smiling.

"What's so...?"

Kaiden snorted.

His mouth fell open in surprise and he started laughing.

"Giving *me* orders?" she said between fits of laughing.

That's how the rest of the team found them when they entered the tent a second later. All of them stopped, wondering what alternate reality they'd just stumbled into.

Nobody could ever remember seeing Tate full on belly laughing, but what threw everyone was Kaiden busting a gut.

Tate notice the team walk in the tent and slowly got himself under control. With a final gasp of breath, he turned himself towards the rest of the group, satisfied to stay seated on a crate.

"Have a seat, guys," he chuckled.

"You okay, Top?" asked Rosse.

"Perfect," said Tate, catching his breath with a final sigh.

He gave everyone a chance to get comfortable and feel the relief of the air conditioning before getting to the heart of the matter.

"You all know I've been off the base for the past couple of days," he said.

The group only nodded, but many of them were looking quizzically at the crates.

"I'm not sure where to start with this one," he said, taking a moment to ponder. "Okay, got it," he said, clapping his hands, turning serious. "We aren't doing enough damage to The Ring."

Everyone in the room had been feeling this, but hearing their leader say it visibly shook them.

"When we got into this fight, I underestimated the resources available to The Ring. The painful truth is we are punching way below our weight."

"How we can do more?" asked Monkhouse. "We're maxed out. There's only so much the seven of us can do."

"Exactly," said Tate. "We need allies. Force multipliers we can use to start delivering real damage."

"That's why you were gone?" asked Wesson, feeling a little slighted that Tate hadn't told her what he was doing before he'd disappeared.

"This situation came out of left field," he said by way of apology. "But we're a team. Every one of you has to be onboard."

"Okay, shoot," said Rosse.

"There's a part of this you might not like," said Tate. "I'll get to that in a moment."

He studied their faces, looking for a reaction. Not surprisingly, Rosse pulled a face of annoyance. The others seemed to be content to hold off their opinion until after Tate explained the situation.

"We have an opportunity to work with a unit of the Department of Defense," said Tate. "They have access to resources we could never have."

"Well, heck," said Rosse. "If the DOD knows about The Ring, let them handle it. Those guys'll wipe the floor with 'em."

"It's not that simple," said Tate. "This unit operates off the books."

"No way," grinned Fulton. "Like Black Ops?"

"Exactly," said Tate. "What makes Black ops effective is in staying off the radar. That includes throwing the Marines at The Ring."

"What's a black ops outfit care about us?" asked Rosse. "We're small time."

"Because we *are* small time," said Tate. "Like them, we operate under the radar. Nobody knows what we do."

"How does this change things for us?" asked Wesson.

"Intel, for a start," said Tate. "We've been operating in the dark, getting scraps of information. We'd be able to cover a lot more data. We'll move more freely with access to transportation. We can hit them in vital spots that we didn't even know existed."

"Like spies?" asked Fulton.

"Like you know how to be a spy," snorted Rosse.

"Something like that," said Tate, "but I have a lot to teach you before we take on missions like that."

"What's in it for us?" asked Rosse.

"Oh, come on," said Monkhouse. "Give it a break."

"Wadda ya mean?" said Rosse. "Top's talking about climbing into bed with a bunch of strangers. Maybe you're an easy first date, but I wanna know what I'm getting into."

"Rosse is right," said Tate, garnering an approving nod from him. "At the moment, this unit can supply us with equipment. Later they'll be able to give us intel, help us travel. We might even be able to coordinate with other black op teams."

"Who are these people?" asked Wesson.

Tate shifted in his seat, searching for the right words. He knew what he was about to say would hit a sore nerve.

"Well, here's where it gets tricky," he said. "Like I said, they're a black ops unit. I can't give you any names or official department agencies because they don't give out that information."

"So how do we know who we're dealing with?" asked Monkhouse, doubt edging his voice.

"It's the nature of the beast," said Tate. "I've worked a lot of black ops. It's not a social club. These people aren't our friends, but they are not our enemies. Like us, they exist to defend our country. Like us, they operate off the books. There'll be things about them we'll never know. But weigh that against what they bring to the table. We have an opportunity to make a useful ally."

The room was quiet. Everyone tried to work through their pros and cons. They considered what was at stake against The Ring's downfall and success; each person sparing with their own fears. The stillness was abruptly torn by the scraping of a chair on the floor.

Rosse stood up with his thick arms across his chest. Everyone watched, wondering what fresh drama was about to unfold. Rosse had always been the most outspoken and obstinate of all of them, and he wasn't shy about banging heads with their leader.

"I can go round and round in my brain all day about things I don't know," he said. "If someone had told me five years ago I'd be part of a secret team in South America, I'd have laughed in their face. Now we're talk'n about black ops? I ain't a spy. I don't know nothing about this world. And it bothers me. A lot." Rosse looked down at his boots, sorting his thoughts before going on.

Tate didn't know where he was going with this and while he tried to keep his expression neutral, he was dreading Rosse would bow out. Every one of the team had to agree to this or it wouldn't happen.

Rosse coughed, clearing his throat. "But you know it. You were in Delta. You guys go hand in hand with the black ops types." Rosse looked over his shoulder at the rest of the team and saw looks of agreement. "What I do know is what I seen with my own eyes. You put your butt on the line for us to keep the rest of us safe. So... if you think joining up with them is the right way to go, then I'm in."

Tate was taken back and tried to keep from showing it. It had been a long time since he'd felt worthy of this kind of trust and loyalty. "Thank you, Sergeant," he said. His words were shallow compared to what he felt. The big man's vote of confidence was unexpected but welcome.

"How about the rest of you?" he asked.

All the team members agreed. They were in.

Tate took a breath, hiding his sigh of relief. This decision was a major turning point for the team. Had they given into their fears and shied away from joining up with the black ops, they would have forever been nothing more than a thorn in The Ring's side. An irritation. Meanwhile, The Ring would continue to drive its roots deeper, gaining more power.

"Does this make them our boss?" asked Fulton.

"No," said Tate. "We pick and choose the missions."

"What do we call them?" asked Wesson.

"Do they have a cool spy name like Shadow Room, or something like that?" asked Fulton.

"Uh," started Tate. He didn't know what they were called, or even if they had a name.

"This ain't a 007 movie," said Rosse. "Sheesh."

"The sign on the door said, 'License Archives Bureau'," said Kaiden, coming to Tate's rescue.

"License Archives...?" puzzled Fulton.

"The LAB," said Monkhouse.

"Oh, right," said Fulton. "That's still kind of cool."

"Yer kill'n me, kid," groused Rosse. "Okay, we got a cloak and dagger set up with these guys. Do those crates got anything to do with this?"

"Yes," said Tate. "This is our new equipment, but we have to earn it."

"A mission?" said Wesson.

"What kind of mission?" grumbled Rosse.

"Cheer up," said Tate. "Compared to what we've done in the past, this one's a cake walk."

He went over the details of the operation, explaining they were to observe and report. He filled them in on what little background he was given about Misha Kilmonikov. Everyone's interest perked up when he said they were going to Cuba and that prompted a number of questions. Tate answered each of them in turn as he handed out mission folders to each member of the team.

"Study the details of the operation," he said. "It's critical each of you understand your role." He noticed that everyone was paying more attention to the crates than their mission folder. This briefing was going in one ear and out the other and he supposed he couldn't blame them.

"All right," he sighed. "Let's crack open these crates."

"Now yer talk'n," said Rosse, smiling.

Tate pulled his knife and cut the strapping that bound the crates. Even he was impressed when he opened the lid.

Inside was set of body armor for each of them. Tate recognized them as a much-updated version of what he'd worn in his old Delta Force days. A nano-silk weave shell over Black Knight ballistic ceramic. Aside from the chest and back, there were optional pieces that could be attached to project the shoulders, neck, and thighs. As impressive as it was, he didn't see anything that would make wearing this comfortable in the humid heat of the jungle.

The next crate contained advanced modular helmets. Tate recognized them too, but these were much newer than what he'd used before. The helmet worked on a closed network, linked to the rest of the team. The visor worked as a Heads-Up Display. Using the ability to tag an enemy, the date would be used by all other helmets to superimpose the position of that enemy on their visors. Even if the person didn't have a line of sight to the enemy, they would be updated to the position, distance and direction of them. When the enemy was visually out of sight from all team members, the computer would mark their last known position.

The helmets also had integrated communications which provided a rudimentary ability for the HUD to show where each of the other team members were.

Beneath the helmets were sets of shock-dampening elbow and knee pads.

"Hey, check this out," said Rosse, as he cinched the strap of the knee pad.

He drove his knee into the largest crate, actually making the thing move. The grin on his face began to fade as he felt the pain of the impact begin to set in. He had wildly overestimated the knee pad's ability.

"Are you okay?" asked Monkhouse.

"Yeah," said Rosse, struggling to keep a poker face while limping to the door. "Just need a minute."

They watched him leave, holding back their snickers until he was out of sight.

When Tate opened the last crate everyone's eyes went wide. Inside was a small arsenal of new weapons. H&Ks, Glocks, Sigs; it was like gun nirvana. Each of them took out a weapon of their choice. After checking the weapon was unloaded, they separated to a place in the tent they could examine their new gear more closely.

Rosse came back in, surprised to see the new weapons.

"I'm sure it goes without saying," grinned Tate, "please don't test your body armor while you're in it."

Rosse flushed red as the others chuckled.

"Oh yeah, very funny," he said, and did his best to walk naturally to the weapons crate. "There better be something in here I like."

Tate left the team to themselves for the moment and went over to Kaiden, who was reading through the mission folder.

"Your friends know how to make a good impression," he said.

"They're your friends now," she said, putting down the folder. She glanced around to see that there wasn't anyone near. "You surprised me."

"What do you mean?" he said.

"Agreeing to work with my contacts in D.C.," she said.

"The spook, the uh, LAB?" said Tate.

"You don't like being on the bottom of the food chain," said Kaiden.

"I don't plan on staying there long," he said, a grin crinkling the corner of his eyes. "Those guys are used to holding all the aces. I could see it on their faces. I'm just another tobacco chewing, Velcro jockey to them. I get it."

"What do you have in mind?" she asked, eyeing him knowingly.

"I'm going to make their place in the food chain, mine," he said. "They're middlemen. I want to work with the person with the real authority."

Kaiden looked at him with quiet disbelief.

"I know what they're thinking. They'll spoon-feed us help and act like they're doing us a favor. Meanwhile they'll want a hundred percent out of us. There's too much at stake for us to play their game."

"Things always get exciting when you get involved," said Kaiden.

"If they figure out you're a threat to their power they'll screw you over, sideways, drop you in a bottomless hole and cover it with a boulder."

"I spent a lot of years in Delta," he said. "I was up to my elbows in intel types. A few of them burned me pretty good, but I learned their games. After meeting your two friends..."

"They're not my friends," injected Kaiden. "More like a necessary evil."

"After meeting your *evil* friends," grinned Tate, "I saw nothing's changed. Let them underestimate me. Let's see how that works out."

"Sounds like you got this all worked out," she said.

"Yes," he nodded. "Yes, I do."

"What are you going to tell Hewett?" asked Kaiden.

The look of satisfaction evaporated from Tate's face. "Oh crap."

"Not as worked out as you thought?" she said.

"If this is your way of asking to be part of my plan..." grumbled Tate. "Fine, you're in."

"I wasn't asking."

"You're in anyway," he said.

16

LOOKING FOR ANSWERS

The house at 787 Blithewood Drive was a contemporary play on the Victorian-style architecture and, in Nathan's opinion, not a very good one. Besides being a very good hacker and nano-tech engineer, he was a bit of an architecture snob. The Outbreak provided him endless places he could set up a safe house, but they all shared a commonality when it came to unique and classic styles.

He would never be caught dead in a house like this one. He hoped the security measures protecting it weren't about to make a liar out of him.

There was no mistaking the house had been abandoned, or made to look abandoned, a long time ago. The overgrown yard, peeling paint, sagging porch and missing roof tiles gave it exactly the look the FBI was going for. *Nothing to see here. Move along.*

He walked outside the front of the property for a few minutes, looking for details that the casual passerby would miss. Sensors, cameras, areas of weeds or debris so they wouldn't obstruct an infra beam.

The only visible deterrent was the curiously high chain-link fence.

He followed the fence around the side and disappeared through the foliage as he reached the back.

Nathan carried out his check of the property in plain view. His city inspector hard hat, clipboard and day-glow vest made him both blatantly obvious and equally forgettable.

The backyard came into view as he stepped through the thick overgrowth. Careful not to touch the fence, he did a quick visual for anything that didn't fit in. The backyard looked exactly like what he'd expect from a dilapidated property.

Nathan took a small but thick monocular from his back pocket and began a careful scan of the yard. Integrated into the lens was an emitter that sent ion microbursts in a narrow beam. The burst bounced back and was processed by a filter within the monocular. A display in the eyepiece would tell Nathan the composition of what he was looking at; organic, electronic, etc.

The monocular was based on a piece of military tech he had been employed to acquire. Before delivering it to his client, Nathan had secretly disassembled it and documented its design. He didn't have the military grade resources to reproduce some of the more unique features, but his knock-off was better and more compact than anything he'd used before.

There were a couple drawbacks. Unlike the original, the ion pulse in his wasn't shielded from being detected. The eyepiece display flashed red, alerting him that something in the yard had just discovered it was being scanned.

Nathan quickly switched off the monocular and waited. All he could hear was the occasional rustle of leaves and grass from a breeze, but he remained still. Chattering birds added another layer to the ambient sounds.

Nathan knew something hidden was searching for him. If the sensors found him, he expected something to happen, but there was no alarm and no attack.

He heard it. Buried far beneath the other noises was the sound of something rhythmic. Starting then stopping. Repeating.

Several feet away, Nathan froze as he saw the tops of the tall grass move. The blades parted and a small robot stepped out. Matte black, the eighteen-inch-long rectangular body moved on a set of four reverse-joint articulated legs.

This wasn't a passive watch and report intruder robot. They didn't patrol and investigate intrusions. 'Seek and kill' robots did that, and that's what Nathan was looking at right now. If it found an intruder, the robot would deploy a short-barreled, high impact rail gun. The tiny dart, no bigger than a toothpick, was designed to penetrate then fragment. A single hit was debilitating, but these robots never fired just one dart. They were designed to kill.

Natan was sure that somewhere, out of sight, was a trapdoor. Once the intruder was killed, the robot would drag the body to the trap door where the corpse would be disposed of. The robot would return to its docking station where it would be recharged and depleted darts restocked.

Whatever the FBI had stored here, they intended to keep at any cost.

Nathan could hear the subtle hum of the robot's actuators as it swiveled its sniffer sensor back and forth.

He was standing in the open, entirely exposed. He dared not move, but little good that would do. He was sure the robot's sensors included IR.

He involuntarily held his breath as the robot panned across him. He winced, expecting to hear the snap of the robot's shell opening and the rapid click of the railgun filling the air with darts.

Nothing happened. The robot continued its pan as if he wasn't there.

Nathan let out a quiet sigh of relief. He shook his head, cursing himself for not thinking sooner that the robot had been programed to respond to intruders. As far as the robot was concerned, anyone outside the fence didn't exist. But it did respond to the ion pulse.

Playing a hunch, Nathan dialed up the monocular's pulse to maximum. The setting was meant for objects far away, giving the pulse the juice it needed to reach out. If the robot was able to detect the pulse on its weakest setting, Nathan was betting the robot's sensitive sensors would have a real problem getting blasted in the face by amped-up ions.

He set the monocular on the ground, making sure it was stable and sent a single pulse. He didn't have long to wait before the robot appeared from the weeds, directly across from him.

Nathan switched on the monocular and the robot locked on. Its sensors overloaded; the robot couldn't move. Its internal sensor was washed out with a flood of input overloading the logic processor with rapid-fire commands.

Under the nonstop assault of the sensor, the processor tried to reset itself. Every seven nanoseconds the processor initiated, only to be slammed with data from the sensor. The robot was caught in a loop that it couldn't break out of.

Satisfied with his handiwork, Nathan ditched his hardhat, vest and clipboard before scaling the fence. The recent rain had made the weeds soggy, softening the sound of his landing passage through the otherwise dead, brittle weeds.

The weeds stopped at the weathered steps of the house's back-door. At the doorway, he knelt down and examined the floor and doorjamb for any tell-tale sign of a sensor.

Nothing.

The door chafed on grim crusted hinges as he eased it open wide. He stepped in and paused, giving his eyes a chance to adjust to the gloom.

As the features became clearer, he saw he was in a long mud room. Along the left wall was a set of dusty cubbyholes. A bench snugged up to the opposite wall. He started but quickly recovered as he made out the most interesting feature in the room.

"It's about time you showed up," said Kaiden, reclining on the bench. She smiled at him with a disappointed tilt of her head. "Surprised? Really? When you stuck this under the table at our meeting, it was so painfully obvious I thought you wanted me to find it." She held up a tiny thin disk. "You might be an exceptional hacker in your world but leave planting a bug to the professionals."

"So you think I'm exceptional," said Nathan, a grin curling the corner of his mouth.

Kaiden's smile stumbled for an instant and then recovered. "You convinced them you didn't need any oversight?" she asked.

"It's just me," he said. "The Ring contacted me the day before I met with you and Tate. They already had the location."

"That confirms they have someone in the FBI," she said, frowning.

"Or someone with ties into their system."

"Either way, they're not nearly as behind as I'd hoped they were," said Kaiden. "What do they know about this place?"

"Just the location," he said.

"Did they tell you what you're looking for?"

"They don't know what they're looking for," he said. "They have the same thing we do. The evidence location code and item ID."

For only a brief moment, Kaiden's expression froze in place as something troubling passed behind her eyes. Just as quickly, it was gone.

"Do you think they followed you here?" she asked. "It wouldn't be polite for us to do all the heavy lifting and have some second-rate hitter take us out the moment we walk out the door."

"I might suck at planting bugs," he said, "but I know when I'm being followed."

Kaiden raised her eyebrows expectantly. "That's not an answer," she said.

"No," said Nathan, irritated. "I wasn't."

"Don't be offended," she said. "You'd be surprised how many times I've paid the price for male ego."

"Women don't have egos?" he asked.

"I don't trust them either," she said.

Nathan fished out a flashlight. "Someone went to a lot of trouble to hide something here. Let's see if we can spoil their day."

"I'm good with that," said Kaiden.

The interior door opened into a series of rooms. Most of them held dusty furniture. Seeping water from the roof had eroded the ceiling's plaster in some of the rooms, giving them a dank, moldy smell.

Nothing about what they were seeing gave any sense of a hidden room or entrance.

After an hour they both stopped with an unspoken agreement they weren't going to find anything this way.

"We're coming at this the wrong way," said Nathan.

"I'm all ears," said Kaiden.

"Follow me," he said.

He led her back through the house and out of the mudroom door. He walked back to where he had climbed the fence.

Turning around, he put his hands on his hips and looked at the house.

"That's clever," said Kaiden, looking at the robot. She turned back to the house, standing next to Nathan as he thought out the puzzle of what the house was hiding and where.

"If they're going to all the trouble and expense to build an evidence site, they're not going to use it for a handful of small things," said Nathan, finally breaking the quiet.

Kaiden understood where his logic was going. "It would be a large storage area," she said. "A room that large couldn't be concealed by a trick of architecture."

They both appraised the top of the house at the same time.

"The attic might be big enough, but if there was a fire they'd lose everything," she said.

"It has to be underground," said Nathan, and headed around the back of the house.

Kaiden hurried to catch up as he began studying the house again.

"Cellar doors would be a dead giveaway," said Nathan. "But they'd need a wide entrance to get the big items inside."

He took off again. He swung wide, going around a sunroom which jutted out from the back of the house. The windows were securely boarded up, blocking their view of the interior.

As they rounded the back, Nathan saw what he was looking for. With a smile of triumph, he put his hands on a set of wide French doors.

"This is it," he said.

Like the rest of the building, the door's glass panes were covered with sheets of lumber. A thick chain looped through the door's handles and was secured by a heavy padlock.

"That's not going to stop anyone," said Nathan.

"It's just window dressing," said Kaiden, as she stared picking the lock. "My bet is the real security is on the other side of the doors."

With a 'snick' she unlocked the door and they went inside.

The faded oak floor softly creaked under their feet as their eyes adjusted to the dim light. Canvas-covered furniture huddled against the walls, ringing the wide, open floor. The room was larger than any of the others they'd seen.

"Looks like a small ballroom," said Kaiden.

"Nobody's danced in here for a long time," said Nathan, gesturing to the floor. Their footprints were sharply defined in the layer of dust that covered the floor.

"That's a lot of dust for a place as closed up as this one," she said.

Nathan watched curiously as she bent down and ran her finger on the floor. She examined the grey coating on her fingertip then, to his surprise, she tasted it.

"That was mildly disgusting," he said.

"It's not dust," she said, standing up. "It tastes like flour and ash."

"Fake dust?"

"Every time they disturb the floor, they sprinkle this to cover their tracks."

"That's clever," he said. "Did you learn that in spy school?"

"Sherlock Holmes," she said, examining one of the walls.

Nathan stood in the middle of the room with his arms folded across his chest. He studied the shape and size of the room.

"If they were storing something large, it could fit through those," he said, thinking out loud and gesturing to the French doors. He glanced at the door leading into the house. "But it couldn't fit through that. It had to go..." He looked down at the floor and tapped it with his heel. "I think this room is an elevator," he said.

"I knew you'd get there eventually," said Kaiden distractedly.

Nathan watched her as she moved to the next wall, inspecting it closely. "What are you doing?"

"Looking for the elevator switch," she said.

"If they built an underground structure to this place," he said, "they aren't going to go cheap on an elevator button. It'll use an NRFC."

Kaiden stopped searching, sensing he had just pulled a 'one up' on her. She turned around and looked at him, waiting for him to get to the point.

"Near Radio Frequency Card," he said. "The switch is concealed in the wall. All you do is wave a..."

"Yeah," she said, "I get it. Do you have one of those cards?"

"What you should be asking is where is the sensor?" he smiled.

"Is this what I'm like with other people?" asked Kaiden.

"You mean annoy..." he started.

"It's a rhetorical question," she said.

Nathan produced a handheld device with a satisfied smile. He placed it on the nearest wall and began sweeping it over its surface.

"Lucky you brought that," she said.

"This has a very sensitive EMF meter," he said. "That's..."

"Electromagnetic frequency radiation," interrupted Kaiden. "Kind of old technology for the FBI, isn't it?"

"This is an old site," he said. "I also built in a fiber optic sensor. They actually give off light outside of the visual acuity of the human eye. It runs in the fifty nanowatt to ten milliwatts range and..."

His device began blinking a green light and he zeroed in on a specific point in the wall.

"There it is," he said, tapping the wall.

"Go ahead," said Kaiden, sounding bored. "Amaze me."

Nathan put the device back on the wall, over the location of the hidden sensor and began typing on the devices screen.

Somewhere, deep below, they heard a soft but throaty whine and the room gave a shudder.

The windows around them turned opaque and the room began to lower. Nathan's look of satisfaction faded suddenly.

"What's wrong," she asked.

"I know I said it was unlikely," he said, looking worried, "but what if they did put Vix down there?"

Kaiden reached behind her back and took out an ultra-compact sub-machine gun pistol.

"When were you going to tell me you had a gun?" he frowned.

"When the time was right," she said. "Now seemed right."

The elevator continued for several minutes before stopping. They guessed they must be fifty feet or more underground.

Several utility lights snapped on, illuminating the storage area. From where they stood, the place had to be nearly the size of the entire lot the house sat on.

Painted on the wall in large block characters were code numbers. They were similar to the code on their list, but not a match.

"Hang on," said Nathan, and typed on his device.

The elevator began lowering again.

"Okay," said Kaiden. "I'm impressed."

"Thank you," he said.

"I was talking about the size of this place," she said.

With the diminishing whine of hydraulics, the room came to a stop. This time the code painted on the wall matched the one on their list.

Kaiden wrinkled her nose at the tainted smell of recycled air as the lights came on.

The warehouse was divided by rows of aisles. Some of them were bordered with strong steel racks of shelving. Others lined with large, tarp-covered objects standing several feet high. A stenciled number was painted on the polished concrete floor in front of each aisle.

As they looked for the right evidence number, they passed rows of nameless things. Hidden inside boxes or under wraps, they tugged at Kaiden's curiosity to explore each one.

Soon they were standing at their number. The object under the tarp was large and boxy. The shape was familiar and neither of them were surprised to find a server underneath. Judging by the size, it was built for processing tremendous amounts of information.

The front panel was dark. On further inspection, they found it was not plugged into a power source and its internal back up power source had been removed.

"I should have seen this coming," said Kaiden. "This entire facility was built to TEMPEST standards. Nothing comes in and nothing gets out."

TEMPEST was an uninspired acronym for Telecommunications Electronics Material Protected from Emanating Spurious Transmissions, but the purpose behind it was critical.

As the intelligence community was honing its ability to spy on other countries, other countries were hard at work doing the same thing. With the increased use of technology, the National Security Agency realized that encryption wasn't stopping foreign intelligence assets from picking up highly classified information.

After intense scrutiny, it was discovered the nearly global network used to communicate information was to blame. Every electrical device, from LCD monitors, microchips, printers and computers was emitting electromagnetic radiation. Mixed in with the radiation was an echo of the information these devices were displaying, storing, creating, or transmitting.

With the right technology, these foreign agencies were reconstructing the data. TEMPEST was designed to stop that leak of information in its tracks.

New shielding was developed. Self-contained power sources were employed. External networks were compartmentalized, scrubbed, and alternated making the ability to identify which of the multi-arrayed signals nearly impossible.

The standardization of TEMPEST was adopted by all domestic agencies, and as Kaiden was learning, that included the FBI.

Whatever was on this server, it was put in this uber-shielded facility to guarantee that nobody could detect it.

Kaiden was brought out of her musings as a cluster of blinking lights flashed in her face. The server was powering on.

"You brought a power source?" she asked.

"I was going to tell you when the time was right," said Nathan with a poker face. "Now seemed about the right time."

Kaiden glanced at him as he watched the server power up. She forced a smile when he looked back at her, the excitement making him smile.

"Identify yourself," said a voice.

Their expressions fell to stunned silence as they realized the server had just spoken to them.

"Identify yourself," the server repeated.

"What's your system's name?" asked Nathan.

"Overseer," it said flatly.

"That's not creepy at all," said Kaiden.

A cover on the face of the server opened up, revealing a biometric panel.

"Identify yourself," said Overseer.

"AI embedded security on a server," said Nathan. "Whoever this belonged to wasn't messing around."

"Can you breach the security?" asked Kaiden.

"Maybe," he said. "The problem is the AI runs as a separate entity. If I try to defeat the security, the AI will know it and react badly."

"Badly?" she prompted.

Nathan sighed as he sized up the server. "Maybe it would just shut down," he said. "It might wipe all the data."

"It's a risk I'm willing to take," she said.

"It's worth mentioning that in extreme cases, where servers hold highly sensitive information, they've been integrated with explosive devices," he added. "The data, the server, and anyone next to it... poof."

Kaiden reassessed her opinion of the situation. "I'll wait back at the room while you work on this," she said.

"Are you refusing to identify yourself?" asked Overseer.

"Cancel," she said.

"You can't cancel this protocol," said Overseer.

"Looks like we've started something we can't stop," said Kaiden.

Nathan looked around the large facility, thinking through their problem.

"Are you sure this place is shielded?" he asked.

"Based on everything I've seen?" she said. "Yes."

Nathan nodded and turned back to the server.

"Overseer, what's the problem?" he said sharply. "I already used the bio scanner."

"There is no indication of that event," said Overseer.

"You don't remember anything that's happened?" said Nathan. "Your systems are experiencing a cascading failure."

"There is no log of any errors within my system,' said Overseer. "Identify yourself."

"I just did," he snapped. "Your systems are in a feedback loop. I'm trying to salvage the data on your systems before it's corrupted by the same failure. Don't take my word for it. Check your network status."

"I don't detect my primary network," said Overseer.

"You don't detect *any* network," said Nathan. "Your AI core-linked array is corrupted. You've triggered an unauthorized lock out. That's why you can't pick up anything. No radios, cell phones, TV's, nothing. You're not even acknowledging use of your bio scanner. Your core function is to protect the data you're about to destroy."

Nathan set a small device on the outside of the server and turned it on.

"Run a diagnosis on each data sector," he continued. "Verify any data loss."

His device began blinking orange and he smiled.

"What's happening?" asked Kaiden.

"Running diagnostics don't violate security protocols," said Nathan. "It only takes a few milliseconds to check each data sector, but my device works on the principle..."

Kaiden held up her hand to stop him. "I'm losing the will to live," she said. "Sum it up."

"I'm recording every data sector," he said.

On the servers display panel, they watched the AI list the data sectors as it verified them.

"How long before you know we have everything?" asked Kaiden.

Nathan was about to answer when she pointed at his device. It had started blinking red.

"Overseer," he said. "Cancel your process. The AI is wiping it's data."

"I've detected an uninterruptible network breach," said Overseer.

"How did it sense my device?" he said, frowning. "I thought the transfer band would be too narrow to see it. Whoever owned this server had seriously advanced technology. I'm switching from passive to aggressive data transfer," he said as he typed instructions into his device.

On the server display the list of data sectors began to be crossed off as the AI deleted them from existence.

"It's deleting them faster than I can copy them," said Nathan. His normally unruffled demeanor had become etched with deep worry. "This could be the only chance at seriously hurting The Ring," he said, "and I've just cost us everything."

The device stopped blinking and the server shut down with a decisive clunk. Small wisps of vapor seeped out of the seams of the casing.

Nathan pulled off the device and sat on the floor. "The AI fried the hardware," he said. "There's nothing left."

"How much did you get?" asked Kaiden.

"I don't know," he said. "I'll have to review this on my own system."

"I hope you don't mind if I tag along," she said.

Nathan's mouth opened but nothing came out as he looked down the barrel of her gun. She held out her hand and he dropped the recording device in her palm.

"There's that surprised face again," she said. "I'd hate to put a hole in it, but that depends on you."

Nathan sat, quietly looking between her face and the black void of the gun barrel.

"You came remarkably prepared for this place," she said. "The security card for the elevator, this data recorder. How would you know what to bring without inside knowledge of this place?"

"Are you trying to say I'm working for The Ring?"

"I'm not trying," she said, pressing the gun to his forehead. "My last question for you is a pass-fail."

Nathan went very still as she pulled back the hammer on her gun.

"The Ring got the FBI evidence codes just about the same time we did. Okay, I can accept that. But then they decrypt the codes within days of us."

"That's not a question," said Nathan.

"Are you passing information to The Ring?"

His shoulders sagged as he let out a deep breath. "Yes."

Kaiden gently chewed her bottom lip as she processed what she'd just heard. Her finger tightened on the trigger.

"And no," he said.

She eased the pressure on her trigger but kept her aim on him. "I lose patience with word games very fast."

"I'm not working for The Ring," said Nathan. "I'm using them." He looked at Kaiden, unafraid to make eye contact. "I'm on the inside as long as I give them results. If I'm no good to them, they'll find someone else to replace me and we lose any chance to stay ahead of them." He searched her face to see if he was getting through. "I take what I learn from them and use it against them. Think about it. If they hadn't told me how to break in here, we'd still be walking around that room scratching our heads. We'd never have the download from the server. We'd never know they have someone inside the FBI. We have all of that because I'm using The Ring. What do they have? How many wins do they have under their belt?"

Nathan felt the gun barrel move off his forehead, but Kaiden kept it aimed at his face. Whatever was going on in her mind, her expression gave nothing away.

"This is why I hate working with you intel types," he said. The stress of his life hanging in the balance was eroding his composure. "You all think you're the only trustworthy spy."

"Hey, don't get personal," said Kaiden, tossing the data device back to him. She stood up and tucked the gun into her hidden holster as Nathan gaped, failing to hide the surprise on his face. "Are you going to stay here all day?"

"Sorry," he said, getting to his feet. "I guess I don't bounce back from near death as quickly as you."

"Don't be so dramatic," she said.

"Dramatic?" he stuttered.

"I had questions. You answered them. Everyone's friends."

Nathan had rarely been this conflicted about what he should feel. Part of him wanted to laugh while another part of him was deeply frightened.

He was beginning to think Kaiden might be the most dangerous person he'd ever met.

17

A BAD START

The Seahawk helicopter cruised over the ocean as the pilot keep his airspeed at 100 miles an hour. Tate sat by the open door, breathing in the fresh salt air. The water was tinged with gold and orange as the sun neared the horizon. Sunset was minutes away.

The excitement of travel had worn off for the rest of the team an hour after they left the air base off the tip of Florida. They admired the Seahawk, being newer and better equipped than its older brother, the UH-60 Blackhawk.

Secured under the helicopter's belly was their Ridged Hull Inflatable Boat. The Seahawk would drop them off the coast of Havana and they'd take the boat in under cover of darkness.

The Florida Strait separated Florida and Cuba by only a couple hundred miles, making their flight time fairly short.

Most of their gear was tied down in the RHIB, but some of the team weren't ready to part with their new gear and insisted on wearing the body armor.

"Ten minutes," said the crew chief over the comms.

Tate pulled the mic down in front of his face. "Copy." He switched the coms over to the team network. "We're ten minutes out from our drop. Check your gear and weapons."

The team became instant activity as they checked and double

checked all of their gear, down to making sure their pockets were fastened closed. Nobody wanted to see their stuff spilling out into the water. Each of them inspected their weapons, safeties on and slings clipped securely. All of them pulled out heavy gloves for the rope decent into the boat.

The pilot gave Tate a lot of noise about that one. He was used to his passengers jumping into the water, which made it easier for him. All he had to do was slow down and get low to the water.

The team fast roping into the boat meant the pilot had to work a lot harder. He had to maintain position over the boat which would be moving because of currents and the prop wash off the Seahawk's propeller.

Tate listened to the pilot gripe about it until he realized there'd be no end to it and told him flatly he didn't have a choice. That was what the mission demanded and if he wasn't skilled enough to hold position over a boat, Tate would get on the horn and request someone who could; a career damaging situation for the pilot, who agreed to do it, but he wasn't going to be quiet about it.

"This is it," said the pilot over the comms.

The Seahawk gently came to a stop, preventing the boat slung below from swinging like a pendulum.

Tate watched as they came down, closer to the water, until the crew chief, who was watching out the window, determined the boat was close enough to be dropped without damage.

"Dropping in three, two, one," said the crew chief. He pressed the remote release and the hook holding the boat let go. The boat splashed into the water with spray kicking up from the prop wash above.

The boat was light and the pilot had little to do to composite for the instant change in weight.

"Good drop," announced the crew chief. "You're clear to drop the rope."

"Copy," answered Tate. He checked the anchor point over his head and ensured it was locked in place. He kicked the coil of rope out of the door dropping into the water.

"Rope is out," he said.

The pilot looked out his window as he maneuvered the helicopter, dragging the fast rope until it was in the RHIB.

"In position," said the pilot.

"Confirmed," agreed the crew chief. He gave Tate a thumbs up.

"Okay, people, move like you have a purpose in life," said Tate.

Each team member sat on the edge of the helicopter's deck and grabbed the rope then slid down to the boat below.

Monkhouse was next and took hold of the rope. Tate held his open hand to signal for him to hold until he saw the rope was clear below; nobody wanted to have someone land on their heads, especially when they had the added weight of weapons, ammo, assorted gear and rough-treaded combat boots.

Tate's hand closed to a thumbs up and Monkhouse leaned out and wrapped his feet around the rope.

"Crap," said the pilot, just as Tate realized something had gone wrong.

A gust of wind had pushed the Seahawk out of position. The rope was now several feet away, dangling in the water.

"Hang on," yelled Tate to Monkhouse, but his voice was blow away by the thudding propellers just over his head

Monkhouse saw the boat slide away from below. He gripped the rope, trying to stop his momentum, but he was going too fast. To the horror of everyone in the boat, Monkhouse disappeared below the surface.

Tate's first instinct was to jump out, but between the pilot shifting the helicopter's position around and the boat moving erratically, there was a good chance he'd hit the boat and surely break something.

The team scrambled to grab the rope and pulled it up. They reached the end without Monkhouse attached.

Something blurred past Tate and he watched in surprise and dread as Wesson jumped out of the chopper. He looked next to him and saw all of her gear on the floor. She hit the water, legs rigid and arms tucked tight to her chest. Then she was gone.

The others in the boat were panicking, calling to their friend and stripping of their own heavy gear to swim after them.

Tate couldn't see anything from his vantage point. The helicopter was kicking up spray, lashing the water white.

He began stripping off his own gear, swearing under his breath in fear.

Just as he kicked off his boot, he saw Wesson's red hair break the surface followed by Monkhouse, who was thrashing and gasping for air.

The others quickly grabbed hold of Monkhouse and dragged him into the boat. As soon as his legs were over the side, they helped Wesson in.

Tate sat back, breathing a sigh of relief, waiting for his heart to slow down. He couldn't be mad at the pilot. He was, but he knew it wasn't his fault.

Tate bundled up Wesson's gear and lowered it down on the rope before he came down.

"How is he?" he said before his boots touched the boat.

"He's okay," reported Rosse. "Swallowed a lot of water is all."

Monkhouse lay in the bottom of the boat, looking like a drowned rat and on the verge of tears.

"It's all gone," he muttered. "All my new gear."

"He was trying to swim up while stripping off his body armor," said Wesson.

"That was quick thinking," said Tate, patting her shoulder. "And darn brave."

Wesson lightly flushed with pride but didn't say anything.

"Open the storage and see if there's some blankets or towels in there," said Tate.

Fulton quickly went to work looking through the boat's stores.

Kaiden sat down next to Wesson. "Jack made a good choice when he picked you for his second in command."

Wesson studied Kaiden's expression, momentarily unsure if this was one of her subtle jabs, but there was no mischief in her face. Kaiden didn't look away but gave Wesson the time to discover her seniority.

"Thank you," said Wesson.

It was only then that Tate noticed the Seahawk was gone. In all the action the helicopter had left. Now that he wasn't focused on Monkhouse, he took in the situation. Everyone was alive, but one was missing his gear, effectively making him non-operational.

The sun was a sliver of gold on the horizon's edge and they had been bobbing on the water, drifting with the current. He estimated their new position; they still had more than enough fuel for the trip, but they'd lost time.

Things were getting off to a bad start and Tate hoped this wasn't setting the trend for the rest of the mission.

After making sure everyone was secure, he settled in then hit the starter. The twin diesel engines rumbled to life with a cough of blue smoke. The console's instruments came to life.

After a quick scan of the boat's status, he checked the digital compass and set their direction.

"Anyone else want a refreshing swim before we get going?" he asked.

Monkhouse looked at him, grinning through his misery.

"Next stop, Cuba," said Tate. He throttled up the engines and headed for Havana.

The sun had left them with a moonless night sky filled with brilliant points of light. Nobody spoke, having found a comfortable spot to settle into and rest.

Tate dimmed the console lights as he maintained an easy fifteen knots. The sea around them was in complete darkness.

Wesson had taken up position on the bow with a pair of binoculars as an added precaution.

While Tate knew they wouldn't have to worry about any offshore oil rigs, there was always a chance of a derelict ship or random floating debris. Hitting something like that could really mess up your day.

He noticed that Wesson had stopped scanning. Her view was fixed on something.

"What have you got?" he asked.

"I don't know," she said. "Maybe nothing. Could be stars reflecting off the water, or maybe my eyes are tired."

"Take a break," he offered. "Ota, take over for her."

With easy agility, Ota made his way over the others, untroubled by the rise and fall of the boat.

Wesson handed him the binoculars and hunkered down beneath the edge of the hull to cut the wind whipping around her face.

Ota had hardly trained the binoculars in the same direction Wesson was looking when he spoke. "It's something."

As the team's sniper, Ota had exceptional eyesight, but it was times like this that made Tate realize how unique he was.

"What is it?" he asked. It could have been nothing at all, but years of experience had taught him to listen to his suspicions.

"It's strange," said Ota. "Like a string of glowing lights."

Tate slowed the boat and brought up his own binoculars. "Where?"

"About ten o'clock," said Ota.

Tate swept his best guess of where the water and night sky met but didn't see anything at first. He looked again, slowing down. He saw it.

"What the...?" he puzzled.

It looked like five, dim irregular lights, low to the water. They were randomly merging then separating. They weren't stars.

Without taking his gaze away, he groped for the throttle and eased it off until the boat came to a stop. He watched the lights straighten into a row, expecting them to merge again but they didn't.

Tate squinted, trying to judge if they were getting closer.

"They're getting closer," said Ota.

The lights were getting brighter.

Tate released the throttle and turned off the engine and listened. The rumble of the engines died, leaving only the gentle slap of the water against the hull.

"Engines," said Ota.

Now the others in the boat were taking notice that something was happening.

Tate didn't hear anything. "Everyone get your weapons."

There was a moment of rapid movement in the boat as everyone grabbed their guns.

"Make sure you have a vest on," whispered Wesson. "If you go over in the dark we'll never find you."

Then Tate heard it. It was engines. Big engines. Coming at them.

He hit the ignition and the RHIB came to life.

"Hang on," he barked, throwing the throttle to the stops. The twin 210 horsepower engines dug into the water and the RHIB took off, cutting through the water.

"What is it?" asked Monkhouse.

"I don't know," said Tate, "but it's after us."

With a quick look over his shoulder, he could see the strange lights with his naked eye and they were zooming up on them.

"By all that's holy," said Rosse, shaken. "They're heads."

Tate glanced back and could clearly see they were Vix heads covered in luminous paint.

"Fire on those lights," he yelled.

The entire boat lit up with pulsing flashes as the team shot at the surreal nightmare charging up behind them. Their boat bounced and shuddered as it smacked over the waves, making it all but impossible to hit their target.

In a spray of water, a forty-foot speed boat zipped by them at terrific speed, close enough they could have touched it.

Something flew by Tate's head with a glint of light. He heard a metallic clank hit inside the boat and the first thing in his mind was *grenade*.

"Grappling hook," yelled Ota.

He grabbed the hook, lifting it free of the boat. The rope went taunt, yanking it from his hand. Ota let go before the hook ripped the fingers off his hand.

"Who are they?" shouted Monkhouse.

"Pirates," said Tate.

"What?" said Wesson.

Small islands dotted the area and were notorious as a hiding place for pirates. They had hunted pleasure craft for years, mounting powerful engines to almost anything what would float. They were ugly and dangerous to their crew, but the rewards of looting a charter boat full of rich tourists was worth the risk.

Eventually, they became violent and often slaughtered their victims, choosing to eliminate eyewitnesses. The protests and complaints finally gained enough attention that a concerted effort was made to put them out of business. The Coast Guard got involved and the pirates went into hiding.After the outbreak, the Coast Guard moved on to bigger problems. The tourist trade was gone, but there were still fishing boats and abandoned ships.

These pirates had stepped up their game from corroded aluminums tubs to fully equipped, high speed performance boats. The only way they could have found Tate's boat was because they had surface scan radar; an advantage Tate did not have.

The glowing heads disappeared and darkness enveloped them. The sound of the speedboat's big engine seemed to come from everywhere at once.

"Shoot as soon as you see them," said Tate.

An instant later, the pirates sped by, narrowly missing them. Something thumped to his left.

Everyone madly searched for the noise, knowing exactly what the threat was now.

Monkhouse was the first to see it. The grappling hook laid next to the inflatable hull. He lunged for it. Just before his hand closed around it the rope went taunt. The hook plunged into the vinyl tube and ripped down the length of the boat.

Tate cranked the wheel away from the pirates, breaking the hook free. Shreds of the boat flapped in the wind as he cut through the water, sharply swerving, making them a harder target.

"They're not shooting back," said Fulton.

"They don't need to," said Tate. "If they hook our boat, they'll drag us back to their camp and then we're screwed."

He caught a brief flash of the glowing heads and the RHIB was rocked by the speedboat's wake. They were completely outmatched. The only hope was a lucky shot into the pirate's engines.

He heard a thud and someone yelled, "Find the hook."

Their luck ran out. With a bone jarring yank, the hook grabbed the RHIB, ripping it from the water.

The pirates cheered, having hooked their prize. The pilot pushed the throttles up. The speedboat's quad four hundred and fifty horsepower outboard engines growled as they raced to 80 knots.

The small RHIB became a thing from Hell, bucking wildly across the water. The team held on for dear life as they were lifted into the air then slammed down into the hull. Somebody was yelling, but in the chaos Tate didn't know if it was him or someone else.

The RHIB crashed into a wave, swatting everyone into the air. They tumbled in the darkness, not knowing which way was up. Before their senses caught up to them, they were underwater.

A short way off, Tate came to the surface in time to see the RHIB cartwheel in a spray of water.

"Everyone call out," he choked, coughing out salty water.

One by one he heard voices call back around him. Everyone was alive, but there was no time for relief.

"They'll be coming back for anything floating," he sputtered. "They'll kill anyone they see. On my word, all of you go underwater. Count off twenty seconds then come up shooting. Understand?"

"Top, I don't have a gun," said Monkhouse.

"Nothing we can do about that now," said Tate. "Here they come," he said, hearing the rumble of the engines. He listened closely and realized they were coming slower than they expected. "Scratch what I said before. Forty seconds, then come up."

Off to the left, a spotlight stabbed into the dark, painting a brilliant white circle on the surface of the water. The spotlight swept towards them and everyone instinctively ducked under the water.

Tate looked up, the water stinging his eyes, but easily seeing the circle of light pass over him. He waited a few seconds longer then carefully resurfaced.

The pirates were closing in. He could hear them shouting to each other.

"Everyone down," he whispered, hoping all of them could hold their breath long enough.

The big engines thundered in his ears as the spotlight slid past him. He counted off the seconds, gripping his assault rifle.

Thirty seven. Thirty eight. He flicked off the safety, *thirty-nine...*

He broke the surface, coming face to face with a pirate, gaping at him in surprise. Before the pirate could yell a warning, Tate opened fire. With a grunt, the pirate was thrown back.

The boat was ringed with shots as the Grave Diggers surfaced. The inside of the boat turned to panic, men running for cover.

Tate grabbed onto the chromed rail to pull himself up when the engines roared to life. The escaping pirates shouted curses as they sped away.

Half in half out, the water tore at Tate, pulling him down. His body twisted around, threatening to dislocate his shoulder. Beaten against the side of the boat, his grip was knocked free. Tumbling through the water, he could only think of whether his team were dying in the middle of the ocean.

He came up, but his gulp of air turned into a cry of pain as something bit into his side. Suddenly he was thrashing through the water. He reached down and felt the hardened steel of the grappling hook. He realized in all the confusion the pirates hadn't pulled it back in.

Tucking his head down, he fought the surge of water slamming into him and tried to pull himself towards the boat. His body was exhausted and it was all he could do to hang on. He couldn't fight the reality he had to let go or drown. Just as his hand closed around his knife, the boat came to a stop.

Across the water, Tate could hear angry voices as the pirates argued with each other.

Able to finally breathe, he felt new strength returning to his battered body. Moving quietly, he pulled himself along the rope until his hand bumped into the rear of the boat. If the pirates turned on the engines now, he'd be chopped into pieces.

He ignored the shiver that ran through his body and he quickly worked his way to the side of the boat. His hand landed on the low railing and he prepared himself for the climb over the side.

This isn't going to be quiet.

Timing the swells of the boat in the water, Tate swung his leg over the rail and pulled. He almost made it all the way in, unnoticed by the shouting pirates, until his assault rifle came off his shoulder and banged into the boat. He saw the privates backlit by the instruments on the boat's console.

The men stopped shouting and saw Tate. Two of the men reached for guns as the third jump to the console and hit the throttle.

The boat leapt forward, flinging Tate back against a row of passenger seats. The two men staggered to their feet, lifting their guns.

Tate snapped off two short bursts, dropping one of the pirates.

Furious, the other screamed curses, firing wildly at Tate.

Bullets chewed around him as Tate's reflexes took over. His assault rifle spat and the pirate crumpled with a scream. He fell off the boat, his finger still on the trigger, his gun strobing as he sank.

The pilot glanced back, his face etched in panic. It was only him and the demon from the water.

"Don't move," shouted Tate.

He didn't know if the pirate understood him and he didn't care.

The pirate reached for his pistol and was dead before hitting the deck.

Tate rolled the body over the side and turned the boat around.

The team had gathered in a floating circle, working out each other's status.

"Listen," said Ota. "The boat's coming back."

A moment later, they all heard it. Their strained nerves cranked up several notches.

"As soon as it's close enough," growled Wesson, "shoot everyone you see."

The spotlight blinked on and the team all aimed at it.

"Grave Diggers, report," shouted Tate.

Everyone instantly relaxed and shouted for him.

Soon they were all back onboard the speedboat.

Except for Monkhouse, who was badly seasick, everyone was unhurt; bruised, soaked and waterlogged, but unhurt.

They'd lost their boat, but the bad news wasn't over. All of their new gear had been thrown out of the RHIB when it cartwheeled.

All they had were the clothes on their backs and whatever gear they carried.

Tate spent the next twenty minutes trying to retrace their steps, looking for anything still floating. They found three backpacks, one of them his. Fortunately, past experience with water insertions had taught him to pack his gear in plastic bags.

After assessing their situation, he determined it was time to get on with the mission.

"Wadda ya mean, the mission?" protested Rosse. "We just got clobbered by a bunch'a guys with a fishhook. Most of our food and water's gone. We got the ammo left in our guns. And that's it."

"Things don't always go according to plan, Sargent," said Tate. "This is why I put you through survival training."

"You never gave us survival training," said Rosse.

Tate looked around the group who nodded in agreement.

"Huh," he said, rubbing his chin. "In that case, your survival training begins now. Welcome to the exciting life of special operations."

18

LEADING THE BLIND

The ships onboard GPS was sketchy, owing to the lack of satellites, but it was enough for Tate to read the shoreline of Havana. He was searching for the inlet that would take them to their insertion point.

The inlet was little more than a marshy tributary, but it was perfect for moving inland while staying out of sight.

The ripple effect of their setbacks would be apparent once they started though the inlet. Their newly acquired boat was a lot bigger than the RHIB and it was inevitable they would run aground sooner than later.

Tate kept these thoughts too himself. The team had already been through enough and he didn't want to throw gas on the dumpster fire of morale.

In the narrow waterway, the burley engines sounded louder than they really were, but Tate shut down three of the four to be safe. The Russians weren't far from his mind, but it was Vix that posed the bigger threat.

"Fulton and Rosse," he whispered. "Get to the bow. You're my eyes."

They quietly moved to the front of the boat, peering into the darkness. Soon they were able to make out the inlet and guided Tate into it.

He reduced the throttle to the bare minimum without stalling the engine as he guided the boat between the grassy banks.

As they moved deeper up the inlet, the banks began to close in and the air became humid and pungent. Trees and foliage pushed in from the banks, dragging their crooked limbs against the sides of the boat.

Stones and roots bumped the bottom of the hull and Tate knew the water would soon be too shallow.

Their next waypoint was a large sewer grate at the end of the inlet. By his estimation, the grate was still a half mile away. As if reading his mind, the boat ground to a stop.

From here they'd have to go on foot. In whispered tones, Tate reviewed what happened next.

"From here on out, everyone remains silent. Vix are everywhere."

The team looked around at the high banks looming over them. If the Vix found them, there would be no escape.

If it wasn't so serious, Tate would have laughed at Fulton's expression. The young private's eyes were as wide as pie plates and he looked like he was going to throw up.

"We're staying in the water," said Tate. "I'll lead. Stay behind me and watch out for junk in the water."

An infected cut or twisted ankle would mean leaving that person behind to hide here until the team returned to pick them up. Everyone nodded then quietly fell into line as Tate carefully slid into the water from the side of the boat.

He took his time, checking his footing with each step. Bushes tugged and scratched at him, but he gently moved past them, avoiding snapping a branch.

The effort and stress were exhausting, weighting on his fatigued mind.

In the quiet, he heard the sound of trickling water coming from ahead. He pushed aside a stand of tall grass and saw the large sewer pipe with a rusty grate over it.

He undid the latch after having Rosse and Monkhouse wrap their shirts around the hinges.

Ever so slowly, Tate pulled the grate open. The bundled shirts did a good job of muting the rusty screech.

Before going forward, Tate unpacked his night vision optic's. He had limited battery, but there was no way they'd travel though the sewers in complete blackness.

"Everyone take the collar of the person in front of you," he instructed. "Don't let go until I tell you to."

He lowered his night vision optics in front of his face and switched them on. The world around him flared with bright light then settled down into hues of grey and blacks.

They entered the pipe, crawling on their hands and knees in the small confines. After twenty feet the pipe opened into a wide tunnel. The ceiling expanded up ten feet. Above their heads, several rows of pipes ran through the tunnel, suspended by metal supports.

Tate stopped the group, having gone as far as his memory could take them. The team stood, uneasy in the dark, alien space. Sounds warped and distorted as they traveled through the cheerless tunnels.

Referencing the map, they continued their silent march, passing large and narrow side tunnels.

They slowed several times as Tate guided them around piles of old, rusted junk and built up branches that blocked their way.

Tate was just thinking about the distance to their next waypoint when someone behind him stumbled and kicked something metal. Everyone froze as the sound echoed into the distance. The quiet of the tunnels exaggerated the noise, making everyone wince.

They hardly dared to breathe as they waited and listened.

Seconds painfully dragged by. The only sounds were the trickle of water and their own heartbeats.

"All right," whispered Tate. "Every..." His words cut short. The sound of a wheezing death rattle drifted past his ear.

He held up his hand, signaling for silence. He couldn't tell if the sound came from behind or ahead of them. Was it close, or far? The muscles in his legs bunched, wanting to run; get as far away as possible.

He pushed back the fear. Moving without knowing where the danger was could kill them all.

There it was again. The sound carried a faint echo.

It's not close, but it's not far.

He was sure the sound came from behind them. He reached up and patted Ota's hand, gripping his collar, then began walking, each leg moving slowly.

He fought back wanting to reach ahead but fought back the panic that tickled at his nerves.

Tate was in mid step when Ota tugged on his collar. The sound was closer; the tortured wet hiss of air Tate knew too well.

"Knife," he whispered into Ota's ear.

Ota passed the message to the person behind him and on it traveled, until reaching Wesson at the end of the line.

Tate glanced back, checking each person had their knife. He frowned in confusion, seeing a shadow-like distortion behind Wesson. He thought his night vision goggles were the cause until the shadow moved.

A Vix was behind Wesson, only a few feet apart, both of them completely blind to the other in the darkness.

The Vix was covered in bits of moss and slime. Most of its face had rotted away, leaving a single eye still in the socket of the skull. It opened and closed its hands, the tips of its fleshless fingers bony claws.

It took a shuffling step closer.

Wesson stiffened. *She knows.*

Her face was brittle with terror. Tate could see her begin to tremble. It was only a matter of seconds before the thing discovered her. He had to act before it ripped into her.

Reaching up with his free hand, he took Ota's hand off his collar.

Slow is smooth and smooth is fast.

He forced his mind to focus on his mantra, denying the urge to rush. With his other hand, he quietly unfastened the cover of his tomahawk.

Slow is smooth and smooth is fast.

The leather sheath was noiseless as the handle slid free.

The Vix moved again. It was inches from Wesson.

Her lips were soundlessly moving as she neared panic.

Slow is smooth and smooth is fast.

Tate flexed his grip on the handle of his tomahawk. He knew the weight and balance of the thing like his own hand.

The thing shuffled forward and stumbled. It reached out to stop its fall and its hand landed on Wesson.

The color drained from her face. Blood trickled down her chin from biting her bottom lip, but she didn't lose control.

The Vix probed this thing it found in the dark. The bony fingers squeezed Wesson's shoulder and it tilted its head.

The thing opened its mouth.

Smooth is fast.

Tate flung the tomahawk.

Something hummed past Wesson's ear, slicing strands of her hair.

The Vix was knocked back as the axe cleaved into its skull with a sickening crunch. It stood, slightly swaying.

Wesson, still blind, shivered uncontrollably, at her breaking point.

Tate opened his mouth to calm her as the Vix slumped and fell...
forward.

Wesson screamed as the Vix collapsed onto her.

"It's dead," said Tate, rushing up to her and clapping his hand over her mouth. "You're okay. It's dead. You're safe."

Wesson clutched him by the arms, her eyes searching the dark for his face.

He eased the pressure on her mouth as she quieted down, regaining her self-control.

"I'm sorry," she stuttered. "I'm sorry."

"Stop it," he said, and pulled her to his chest, thankful that nobody could see this private moment. His simple act of human comfort quickly bolstered her spirits.

"You're one of the bravest people I've ever known," he said. "We'll get..." His words froze in his throat as a horrific wail echoed from the tunnel behind them.

Acting fast, Tate let go of Wesson and wrenched his tomahawk from the Vix's skull.

"Fulton," he snapped. "Throw a chem light. Everyone's got to see where we're going."

Tate headed back to the front of the line as Fulton pulled a plastic tube from his vest. He bent it, snapping the glass vial inside. The chemical reaction filled the tunnel with green light.

"Quiet time's over," said Tate. "We run."

Without waiting, he turned and raced off with his team close behind. The tunnel echoed with the thud and splash of their boots.

Behind them, the single wail had turned into a confused mass of screams and growls.

Tate guessed the sewer exit was still three hundred yards away. Speed was their only hope.

Dread slammed him as a new source of snarling erupted ahead of them. He stopped, desperately looking for a way to go; his mind racing for a way out.

Maybe if they were fast enough they could reach the next side tunnel. What if that's where the Vix are coming from?

He looked back the way they came. The last tunnel was close, but would they get there before the pursuing Vix caught up?

They were surrounded

"Up," shouted Monkhouse.

Tate looked up. Above them were rows of small pipes that ran the length of the tunnel. There was no time to spare and no other option. If this didn't work, they might just have enough time to suck a bullet before being ripped apart.

"Do it," he snapped.

Everyone jumped up and grabbed onto the pipes. All of them scrambled up except Rosse, who's feet were peddling in the air as he struggled to climb up.

Fulton and Monkhouse grabbed him and pulled his solid frame with everything they had. With a final heave, he clamored up.

Tate looked at the pipe's supports bolted into the ceiling above and prayed the rusted steel would hold their weight.

"Fulton," he hissed. "Douse that light."

Fulton stuck the chem light in his shirt, but it glowed through the fabric. He took it out and shoved it down his pants but was still visible.

"Throw it," hissed Wesson.

Fulton threw the chem light away as if it burned his hand. It landed in the mucky water, casting ripples of muted green light on the tunnel walls.

A second later, the pursuing Vix rushed into view. At the same time, a herd of Vix came boiling down the tunnel from the other direction.

The two mobs blindly smashed into each other. Blind from years in the tunnels, the frenzied mass tore into each other with manic savagery. The tunnel filled with howls and screams as the Vix tore into each other. Teeth shattered and bones snapped in the ghastly green-lit vision from the putrid bowels of Hell itself.

Perched inches above, the team watched, hardly daring to breathe; knowing what would happen if even one of those things saw them.

Bodies and limbs scattered as the slaughter finally burned itself out. As suddenly as it started, it was over. A handful of Vix could still move but were so dismembered that they weren't a threat to anyone.

The team waited, suspended above the wreckage of death, waiting for more Vix to come.

Long minutes passed until, finally satisfied, Tate swung down from the pipes. The rest of the team followed.

Wordlessly, they quickly finished off the remaining Vix and headed out.

Twenty minutes later, they reached the sewer exit. They stood, basking in the pure light of the sun, soaking up the warmth, hoping it would cleanse their spirits.

19

EYES ON MISHA

Misha watched as his men heaved on the chains bolted to the concrete wall. Fractures spiderwebbed across its surface, but it refused to move.

Streaming with sweat, the men grunted and swore, their faces red with effort, their knuckles white as they pulled.

Misha stripped off his shirt and took his place among his men.

"Comrades," he said. "Prison lost its battle of wills against you. How much chance does this mindless slab have?"

The men cheered with angry defiance.

"*Adeen, dva, tree*," counted Misha in Russian. "Pull."

Together, the men hauled. Cement dust puffed around the edges of the great, cracked wall.

"Again," called Misha.

They pulled again and the wall shifted. Once more they strained at the chains. The wall gave with the sound of grinding concrete and a groan of twisted steel.

The men hurried out of the way as the huge block tipped then fell with a fantastic crash, shaking the ground under their feet.

Beyond the steel-reinforced, three-foot-thick chunk of wall gaped a black maw. Cool stale air washed over the men as they took a moment to recover from their efforts.

Misha jumped onto the fallen wall like a victor on a fallen foe.

"Well done," he said. "Rest before you remove the debris. Have a good meal. You've all earned it. Luca."

"I am here," said Luca.

"Bring torches," said Misha. "Let's explore our new find."

"Now we will finally know if we have been on a fool's errand," said Luca.

"Cheer up, Luca," said Misha grimly. "There are many roads to the same destination. We may be delayed, but we will not be denied."

Luca tossed him a flashlight and the two men entered the dark void.

Once inside, the temperature dropped several degrees. The sweat on their skin quickly chilled them.

Their lights shined on a broad concrete floor that stretched out several feet to either side. Solid walls rose up high above them before curving into a ceiling. Industrial lights hung from the ceiling and a network of conduits disappeared into the dark.

The quiet and dark melded together to warp the sense of distance and time. Or would have for the average person, but the training and experience of these two men made them highly adaptable. Subconsciously, they'd been logging their steps and knew exactly how far they had walked.

"Another empty one," said Luca. "Just like the others. We are picking over someone else bones."

"Perhaps you are right," said Misha, "but we only found this one by luck. It may be no one else..."

Both men stopped as their beams of light fell on large, hulking shapes against the distant tunnel walls.

Excitement and expectation filled them as they broke into a jog until they were close enough to touch one of them. Standing before the huge tarp, they swept it with their lights. The fabric was treated with oil to resist the elements and shone with a semi-gloss.

Together, they gripped the thick edge of the tarp and pulled. The tarp resisted for a moment, having become stiff over the decades, but the men broke it free and the big tarp rustled loudly to the ground.

They turned their flashlights onto the thing that had rested, long dormant. Although it hadn't been touched in nearly eighty years, it looked brand new.

Misha patted Luca solidly on the back as they both grinned.

Brooding over them was twenty-seven tons of armored self-propelled artillery. The 152mm howitzer barrel was twenty-five feet long, only half the length of the armored chassis that powered it. The gun could throw ninety pounds of high explosive destruction ten miles away and do it four times in sixty seconds.

There was not a speck of dirt on its treads, or carbon scorching on the muzzle of the barrel. This machine had rolled off the factory floor in Yekaterinburg, Russia, and shipped directly to Cuba in a disguised cargo ship.

Off loaded, the SPG was stowed in one of several secret bunkers hidden under Havana, waiting for the inevitable day American soldiers invaded Cuba's shores. That day never came.

Fidel Castro hadn't come to power in Cuba in 1959. He'd taken it. He ruled with brash passion and protected his power as absolute authority over Cuba with force.

Smaller than the state of Florida, Castro rightly felt he was a target of the United States. Believing it would ensure his safety, he allowed the Soviet Union to install multiple nuclear missile sites in his country. He could not have been more wrong.

The United States had three and a half thousand nuclear warheads, six times more than the Soviet Union. The morning after, an American U-2 spy plane discovered the missiles; Castro woke up dead center in Target Zero.

For the first time in history, the world was looking at the very real possibility of a full-out nuclear war. The incineration of civilization would begin with the obliteration of Cuba.

More concerned with his hold on power than the Cuban people, Castro urged the Soviet Union to threaten the US with a nuclear strike. Instead, sanity prevailed and the Soviet Union withdrew their missiles.

Furious over the betrayal, Castro began a campaign to fortify Cuba and remove its dependence on anyone else for protection. He had hundreds of miles of tunnels dug, deep beneath key areas of the island. Then began the stockpiling; Castro did not hold back. Huge containers, sealed and pressurized, held more than a years' worth of food for his soldiers. Anti-ship mines, artillery, antiaircraft guns, armored personal carriers and main battle tanks were only part of the complex of tunnels. Along with these were support facilities, barracks, hospitals, and mechanic bays for the repair of equipment and more.

Banks of overhead lights snapped on casting the two men in weak, yellow light.

"After all these years, the generator still works," marveled Luca.

"Of course," said Misha. "It's Russian."

Both men laughed. The sound rang down the dark throat of the tunnel. Soon another bank of lights came on, followed by another.

Behind the self-propelled artillery, they'd just uncovered stretched columns of similar covered objects. Behind them were more tarp-covered objects.

They continued for another mile, following the turns and splits of the tunnel.

"These tunnels go forever," said Luca. "It could be weeks before we find what we're after."

"I think we should return and see if anyone has discovered a working cart," said Misha. "These tunnels..." He stopped, recognizing Luca's haunted expression.

It's true, thought Misha. These tunnels reminded him of the Black Rat. The hole he and his men had been thrown into and left to rot for years. Many of his men died there, or worse. The brutality of Kovkiv prison showed no mercy. A life had no value. Luca never spoke about what he endured before Misha had saved him.

The prison was a colony, each building run with its own individual rules and bosses.

Misha's Colony Four almost broke him. Beatings, torture, starvations. But he, even at his lowest moments, scrabbled for the will to resist. As he got stronger, meaner, even cruel, he stopped resisting and began fighting. He did what he needed to survive. In time, he took over Colony Four. He was still under the heel of the guard's boots, but as long as he was able to pay them off in contraband, they were lenient.

Luca was in Colony Two, only a few hundred meters away, but it could have been on another planet for all the difference Misha could make. But he had a plan.

Misha was a man who loved his country and hated the government. He was not unique. Risking immediate execution, Misha began to carefully send out feelers, looking for sympathizers among the prisoners. Some quickly answered his call. Others, less so. They feared Misha's message was another government trap, aimed at weeding out dissidents.

Over time, Misha collected a strong following. His primary goal was achieved when the prison baker joined his ranks.

Timur, the baker, had the personal hygiene of a rotting carcass and his bread was hard enough to beat rats to death, but he was one of the few people who could move freely between the colonies.

After months of separation and endless worry for his friend, Misha could communicate with Luca.

It was not good news. Three days after they'd arrived at the prison, the gang leader running Luca's colony decided to break in the new inmate. He didn't know Luca was Spetsnaz.

By the time the guards broke up the fight, the gang leader was missing an eye and had an arm and five ribs broken. Soon after, the gang had their revenge. Luca spent a month in the infirmary. After the doctor released him back into general population there wasn't a week that didn't go by without the gang ambushing him.

All of that changed when he received the first note from Misha. Luca began spreading Misha's message and soon Luca was second in command of a following of hardened prisoners; men with nothing but resentment and anger at the government, looking for something or someone to vent it on.

Luca knew exactly who to begin with.

The sound of running feet broke both men from the haunts of their past. The echo of footfalls was coming from somewhere deeper inside the tunnel; somewhere untouched by the living for a very long time.

A distant growl prompted Luca to reach for his pistol.

"I do not think this place reacts well to bullets," said Misha, gesturing to the crates of ammunition lining the walls.

Pale faces appeared in the distant light.

"How ironic something as human as laughter should produce the boogeyman," said Misha.

"This is our world now," said Luca.

They could clearly see there were seven Vix as the undead closed the distance.

"Don't make us wait all day," shouted Misha, clapping his hands and throwing the Vix into a renewed frenzy.

With a blur of his hand, Misha's Kukri whipped through the air. The sickle-shaped blade drilled into the head of a Vix. The thing toppled back, tripping another behind it.

The two men readied themselves, unaware of the grim smiles they wore. Like all Spetsnaz, they were trained in Rukopashni boi martial arts. While other arts were considered hand-to-hand, the Rukopashni boi philosophy embraced a purely Russian attitude that the enemy could bring anything they want to the fight and the Spetsnaz would use it to dig their enemy's graves.

It had been too long since they had used their skills to their full extent. They felt the yearning to be tested. The greater the risk, the more they relished the challenge.

And then the Vix were on them.

One leapt, sinking its bony fingers into Misha's shoulder. Ignoring the pain, he grabbed the Vix by the neck and crushed its face with a powerful fist.

No sooner had he let go of the Vix, another grabbed him. Misha wrenched down on its arm, ripping away bone and putrid flesh. Nothing registered in its cloudy eyes. The thing snapped at Misha, who jammed the severed arm into the thing's jaws.

With its remaining arm, the Vix clawed at Misha's face. He ducked low and grabbed its legs and lifted. With a guttural roar, he slammed it into the concrete floor, headfirst.

Luca dodged and slipped the Vix, his slight build giving him agility over brute strength. Two Vix lunged at him, snarling, their decomposed faces twisted and grotesque.

Luca darted behind them and kicked one in the spine. Vertebra cracked and the Vix folded backwards, over itself. The other Vix spun and attacked as Luca kicked low, snapping its leg. As it toppled forward, Luca jumped, bringing down the heel of his boot in a vicious axe kick. Bone and slop scattered across the floor and the Vix lay still.

Misha saw movement behind him and flinched away an instant before a Vix's jagged teeth sheared off the side of his face. Its jaws clashed together on empty air, spraying Misha's cheek with chips of teeth.

The near miss sobered his overconfidence and focused his killer instincts.

He spun around, battering the Vix in the jaw with his elbow. The jaw broke with a terrific snap, not even fazing the Vix.

winced as the putrid corpse tightened its grip with terrible strength. Spots of blood oozed from his shoulders. Misha pulled around his assault rifle from behind his back. Gripping it by both ends, he drove the rifle up, catching the Vix under the arms. It's arms shattered with an awful wet crunch.

The pressure released, Misha yanked himself free of its grip and shoved the Vix back. Its useless arms flopped at its sides as the Vix hunched, ready to spring on the big Russian.

The Vix leapt. Misha grabbed his rifle by the barrel and swung. Steel and bone collided, caving in the Vix's skull, sending it cart-wheeling across the tunnel.

It's body skidded across the floor in a motionless, sticky heap.

Both men crouched, glancing for their next kill. Broken, grotesque Vix lay at their feet, moving no more.

Misha muttered a curse and spat on the carcasses on the floor.

"I think we're a little rusty," he said, examining the cuts in his shoulder.

"You are the one bleeding," smiled Luca. "They never touched me."

Both men chuckled as they straightened themselves out and

checked for wounds. Satisfied neither were seriously hurt, they started back for the tunnel entrance.

Half a mile to the west, Ota shifted to a more comfortable position, keeping an eye glued to his scope. Nestled on the roof of an old factory, he was shaded from the unforgiving heat by generous spread of shrubs and creeping vines that had taken root over the years. Built near the bay, it gave him the added benefit of a constant breeze. In spite of the advantages, the Cuban sun and humidity would not be denied. Beads of sweat trickled down his face, dripping off his squared jaw.

The factory rose eight floors, giving an unobstructed view of the Russian's fishing trawler, the dock it was moored to and most of the dock yard.

As recon went, yesterday had been far from exciting. All he saw was the Russians splitting up in twos and searching the area; for what, he didn't know.

Today was turning out to be interesting. Interesting enough that he called Tate up to the roof to report it.

Tate reached the roof by way of a rickety steel maintenance stairway. Other than the bolts holding it precariously to the inside of the factory wall, the structure had no supports.

Vertigo pulled at Tate every time as walked along the narrow catwalk. Once he'd made the mistake of looking down. He could see the factory floor, seventy feet below, through the open steel mesh decking of the catwalk. It took a while for his stomach to stop twisting.

Reaching the roof, He made his way to Ota, while keeping low, and settled in next to him.

"What's up?" asked Tate.

"I think they found what they were looking for," said Ota. "Yesterday they were all over the place. Today they grouped somewhere behind that warehouse. The one with the red roof."

Tate looked through his binoculars at the distant docks. A group of men appeared from around the corner of the warehouse. Two of them were shirtless and all of them looked tired.

"They're hard at work on something," he said.

"Look at the edge of the dockyard, closest to us," prompted Ota. "Near the wall."

Tate shifted his view. At first there was nothing noteworthy to see. The area running the length of the wall was a clutter of shipping containers, spools of cable, a pile of tires and a mix of bulky junk. Then he saw an orderly row of large freight trucks. One of them had the hood up and a Russian was working on the engine.

"Whatever they found," said Tate, "it must be big if they need a truck to move it." He made a mental note of the area circling back to the fishing trawler. "There's no room for anything large on the trawler's deck. Maybe tow a barge."

"Too unstable in the open sea," said Ota. "They're not planning on moving the mystery object on the water."

Tate glanced at him for comment.

The quiet sniper's deep-blue eyes never left the lens of his scope. The man's shirt was dark with sweat and his hair was matted flat.

"I'm sending Wesson up to take over," said Tate, checking his watch.

"I like it here," said Ota.

"You can stay up here," said Tate, "but she's taking over the scope."

Ota didn't reply or complain and Tate, knowing he wouldn't, headed for the maintenance door and relief from the sun.

The weathered metal door closed with a clunk, but Ota didn't hear it. He was focusing on a group of men wheeling sets of metal cylinders on handcarts. The details were hard to make out through the distortion of heat waves, but he was certain they were oxyacetylene torches.

The thick vault door towered over Misha, who patted his hand on the cold steel in admiration. Metal tanks and tools clattered as his men set up their equipment.

"This is a waste of time," said Luca. "Why don't we blow the hinges off? We have our choice of big guns."

He gestured to the far side of the tunnel wall lined with armored personal carriers.

Misha rapped his knuckles on the thick steel, unsurprised there was no hint of echo or ringing. These doors would still be standing long after the tunnel's reinforced concrete walls were pulverized to dust.

"The tunnel would collapse on us before we made a scratch," said Misha. "It's after that we don't disturb the beast on the other side of the door. How is the other work progressing?"

"Latkav could only get two of the trucks running," said Luca. "But we found another side tunnel with all the armored personel carriers we need to tow what the trucks can't carry. Materials for the platforms are readily available and construction will be finished by tomorrow." Luca's expression flickered as he moved on to the next part of his report. "Our scouts detected an unexpected development. We are not alone."

Misha's good mood became serious. All humor left his eyes. "Do they know we've seen them?" he asked.

"No," said Luca.

Misha clenched his jaw, his expression hardening as the oxy-fuel torch blazed to life behind him.

Luca squinted and turned away as the operator adjusted the torch to a point of blue flame.

"Collect what men you need," frowned Misha. "Kill everyone."

"I anticipated your decision," said Luca. "The kill-team is already on the way."

The welder put the tip of blue flame to the vault's lock. The torch superheated a small diameter of steel to over four thousand degrees. Soon, a rivulet of molten steel trickled down the face of the vault.

Misha's thoughts swirled around the pool of glowing slag as he considered how he was about to shape history.

Tate was readying his next report to the spooks while most of the team occupied themselves between watches on the roof.

He stopped mid-sentence when his earpiece crackled.

"You better get up here," said Fulton.

His voice was laced with worry and Tate headed for the long flight of stairs at a run.

"Everyone make sure you're weapons ready," said Tate, calling over his shoulder.

"Huh? What's going on?" asked Rosse, waking from a nap.

Wesson and Ota grabbing their weapons was answer enough for Rosse, who reached for his medkit.

The sun punched down on Tate as he stepped onto the roof and raced over to the hide concealing Fulton.

"Report," said Tate, bringing up his binoculars and training them on the distant docks.

"A bunch of guys just pulled out in a truck," said Fulton. "They were in a big hurry. All of them had assault rifles, like they were going to a fight."

"Where'd they go?" asked Tate, feeling his gut tighten.

"I lost them behind the warehouses," said Fulton.

Tate took out his data pad and checked the map of their area. Except for a dirt track, there was only one main road that lead to the factory. He scanned the road closest to their location and backtracked towards the docks.

"Got' em," he said. "Two o'clock from our position. Exhaust smoke behind the green building."

Fulton panned his scope and saw it; a smudge of black smoke rising behind the structure.

They watched in silence, holding their breath, waiting to see if the truck was coming for them. The next billow of smoke would tell them.

"There," sighed Fulton. "They're going away from us."

Tate saw it too and felt his grip on the binoculars relax.

"That's weird," said Fulton.

"Not the word I'd use," said Tate, feeling relief settle over him. "What do you mean?"

"I saw another truck go that way a couple of times," said Fulton. "Nobody was armed to the teeth before."

"Hey," said Rosse over the radio. "You wanna share what's happening up there?"

"Stand down," said Tate, smirking at Fulton. "Sergeant Wesson?"

"I'm here, Top," she answered.

"Would you please reacquaint the meaning of radio discipline with our medic?" said Tate.

"That's a clear copy," said Wesson.

They could hear Rosse complaining in the background.

"What are *you* smiling about?" Tate asked Fulton.

The young radio operator's smile faded, his brown eyes a mix between confusion and worry.

"Why didn't you report about the other trucks?" frowned Tate.

"I was..." started Fulton. "I mean, they were... I wrote it down." He held up his notebook, showing he'd logged the time and activity. "I thought it could wait until my watch was over."

"Any movement," sighed Tate. "You need to keep me updated."

"I think I know where they went," offered Fulton, taking Tate's map. "Both of the other trucks headed north to the highway. The road's elevated, so I could see them pretty good, but then they'd get off here and drop down out of sight." He pointed to a set of off-ramps. "The only thing around there is this big stadium."

Tate zoomed the map into the stadium and surrounding area. He nodded in approval at Fulton's conclusion. "Not bad, Private" he said. "From now on, keep me updated."

"You got it, Top," smiled Fulton.

20

ALL BECOMES CLEAR

The once-groomed, lush-green athletic field of the Estadio Panamericano stadium was a patchy stretch of dead grass and bare earth. Built to host the Pan American Games in 1991, it was now home to the few refugees that remained. The people had found the high walls and easily reinforced gates made for a safe zone on an island of prowling horror.

The stadium's fabric dome had been a shady relief from the Cuban sun back then. But years of storms and harsh weather had pulled and torn at the fabric. Each year there was less and less shade.

Tents and shacks of corrugated tin and plywood randomly dotted the field, making the most of the shade that remained.

Alba stepped out of her shack, angrily clutching a handful of toys.

"Javier," she shouted. "You hear me? Come home right now and do your chores."

She tossed the toys, scattering them in the dirt. She scanned the bleachers that ringed the stadium. They were an unhappy reminder of a time when the stadium rang with cheers and applause. A time when there were people. Sometimes she caught herself wishing the sounds would come back. Then she'd snap at herself for being a fool. She knew it would never happen.

Irritation flooded back as she heard squeals of children echoing out of the north tunnel entrance.

She swore to herself as she headed towards the noise, angrier than ever. Javier knew it was against the rules to go near the gates. Noise brought the Vix. The double-door gates were supposed to be strong enough to hold them back, but she never felt completely safe.

Alba had no way of knowing she was about to learn how horribly right she was.

She rounded the corner to the tunnel entrance, instantly jumping back in fright as a knot of children came running out of the shadows, laughing and screaming. Any leniency she might have felt for her son had just been startled out of her.

"Javier," she called, seeing him among the kids. "Go home and do your chores, or I'll have you cleaning fish for a week."

The young boy stopped chasing his friends and stomped his foot in frustration.

"Carlos gets to play," he said, undecided between whining or shouting.

The other children stopped to watch who would win between one of their own and a grown-up.

"I'm not his mother," snapped Alba. "Go home. Rapida."

The battle decided, the other children lost interest in the argument and ran off to play somewhere else.

Alba cursed under her breath. She glanced down the tunnel at the gates. Even on a sunny day the tunnels seemed unnaturally chilled and dark. Light filtered around the cracks of the gates and for an instant she thought she saw a fleeting shadow behind them. She stared as her breath came in shallow gulps, but nothing moved.

"Don't be stupid," she told herself, turning to leave.

She stopped. A low rumble was building behind her. A vibration trembled up through her feet. Earthquakes weren't uncommon, but everything about this was different.

There was shouting somewhere in the stadium; voices filled with surprise and alarm. She took a hesitant step to see where the commotion was coming from and the gates, behind her, blew open.

Something big crashed through, slamming one of the steel doors into the tunnel wall with a clang. The other flew off the hinges and bounced up the tunnel, gouging the concrete in a spray of sparks. The heavy door skidded past a terrified Alba.

Across the field, the air filled with muted pops and people began screaming. She froze, her eyes wide. Her heart hammered in her chest and her mind shrieked at her to run.

Adrenaline slammed through her body. Alba broke into a run, not knowing or caring where. Just away from here.

"Mama," cried Javier. "What's happening?"

His voice cleaved through the fog of panic.

My boy. Shame welled up inside her for forgetting her son.

"Come on," she said, scooping Javier up in her arms.

She could feel her heart pounding against her son's body. Her mind raced with thoughts of escape. *But where?*

She didn't know what she was running from, but her ears were filled with people screaming.

She'd taken two steps when a deafening slap jolted her and the world slowed down. Everything was in fantastic but silent detail.

Swirls of dust created shifting pillars of light through the holes in the dome above. Cracks in the ground were sharply defined. Colors were oversaturated.

She looked into her son's face, contorted in terror, puzzled why she felt nothing.

She turned and saw a stranger behind her, his face partially hidden behind a rifle. Jets of fire gently spread from the barrel. She watched, hypnotized, as brass shells ejected from the side of the gun. It spun, lazily through the air, winking as it caught the sun.

She dropped her son as something powerful pushed against her. The ground floated up to meet her, and Alba's world went dark.

"It just stopped," said Fulton.

"Are you sure it was gunfire?" asked Tate over the radio.

Fulton looked towards the distant stadium with a furrowed brow before deciding on his answer.

"Yeah," he said. "I'm pretty sure."

"Yeah?" asked Tate pointedly.

"Uh, affirmative," said Fulton. "I guess they ran into some Vix."

"Anything else to report?" asked Tate.

"Nop... negative," said Fulton.

"Copy," said Tate. "Out."

Fulton blinked his eyes before going back to the boredom of watching the Russians do nothing interesting.

"The stadium is ours," said Luca. "We can start on the platform as soon as we clear away the bodies."

"Did the men perform their duty well?" asked Misha. He knew more innocent people would die before they were done. A man distracted by his conscious was a weakness he could not afford.

"Da," said Luca without hesitation. "They are committed to the cleansing of Russia. No matter the cost."

"When you chop wood, splinters fly," said Misha.

"I have never heard you quote Stalin before," said Luca.

"Until today I didn't appreciate his irony."

With a pop, the cutting torch turned off, bringing Misha's attention back to the task at hand. After the blazing flame of the torch, the overhead tunnel lights seemed useless.

"All right, comrades," he said, not waiting for his eyes to adjust. "Let's get this open."

The gathered men all grabbed a part of the vault door and pulled.

Nothing happened.

They tried again, grunting with the strain, Misha unconsciously biting his lip. If the vault had a secondary lock, it would take weeks of cutting through the hardened metal to reach it.

His thoughts were interrupted as the tunnel filled with a low grumble. Dust cascaded from the edge of the vault door as it gave way. Relief flooded through Misha and he joined his men.

Chilled air spilled out of the vault like the long-dead breath of a great beast. The men recoiled, expecting undead to spew from its darkness.

They shouted protests of alarm as Misha stepped into the dark vault and disappeared. The men glanced at each other, unsure what to do. Then, in unspoken agreement, all of them headed after their leader and comrade.

Just as they started, the vault lit up. The men stopped short, their eyes wide in shock.

Columns of missiles rose above them, reaching to the vault ceiling, each resting on an inclined support, their conical warheads coming together like an arch of sabers.

As Misha strode under them it was as if the lethal darts were saluting him.

"Comrades," he announced, his voice echoing off the walls. "This is the rewards of your labor. Sixteen, FKR-1 nuclear missiles." He patted the cold skin of a missile with appreciation. "Now you can understand why I kept this secret to myself. With these missiles we will eradicate the rotted soul of the Kremlin. We will return to our motherland and help build a new government. One that loves our country with the same fierceness that beats in our chests."

The men looked at the antiquated missiles dubiously. At only twenty-seven feet long, the weapons looked more like a scaled down MIG-15 fighter jet, complete with wings, rear stabilizers and rudder.

"But they're so old," said one of the men. "How do we know they will fire?"

"Why did we go through all that work for relics?" said another. "We could have easily smuggled enough explosives to kill those Kremlin pigs in their homes."

"And risk even one of those *shlyukha* getting away?" growled Misha, "And what if we're caught. We'd be branded as traitors. Killed, if we're lucky. Worse, banished to a distant prison, never able to return to our motherland again."

Taking a deep breath, he pushed down his anger. "With these we will obliterate all of Moscow's leadership and nobody will know we did it." Misha paused, waiting for his men to settle down. Arguing would not win them over to his plan. He needed them to understand the genius of his master stroke.

"These are short-range missiles," grumbled someone. "How can we possibly smuggle them within striking distance of Moscow?"

"These aren't meant for Moscow," said Misha. "Our target is the American Central Command headquarters."

The men gaped at Misha in stunned silence as they tried to wrap their minds around the magnitude of his words.

"It is located in Tampa Bay, Florida, and well within reach of our missiles. That base is the primary headquarters for operational combat planning and military intelligence. A strike there will be a crippling blow that demands a response."

"We're shooting nuclear missiles at the United States?" said one of the men, his face pale in shock.

"True, but they're Russian missiles," said Misha. "The process of enriching Plutonium leaves a distinct radiation signature. Did you know that? When a nuclear warhead explodes the signature can be detected in the radiation. How do you think the American's will respond to an unprovoked strike on their central command structure... by Russian nukes? They'll believe this is the opening salvo to destroy their military infrastructure. The Americans will immediately launch a retaliatory strike. American nuclear response doctrine states their first and only target will be the head of the snake."

"The Kremlin" said Luca. "The swine that betrayed us, betrayed the Russian people will be wiped off the face of the earth."

Misha saw Luca walk into the vault and admire the missiles.

"Our brothers in Moscow are prepared," said Misha. "They will seize control and wait for our return. When we return, I promise to create a new people's Russia."

"Can it really be done?" asked one of the men.

"We have toppled countries with much less," chuckled Misha. "Now, my brothers, let's get these to the launch site."

Misha and Luca walked away from the men as they organized how to move the missiles.

"Can you get them to work?" asked Misha.

Luca shrugged his shoulders. "They have rubber lines which

might be cracked. If they're brittle they could break during flight. The lubricant around the rudders will have to be replaced. I'll have to test the electronics and see if the batteries still hold a charge. There's..."

"Will they work?" insisted Misha.

Luca glanced around the inside of the vault, shrugging again. "If the vault maintained the seal and the nitrate didn't leak it might have slowed the core of the nuclear warhead from decaying."

Misha crossed his thick arms over his chest, staring at Luca impatiently.

"Da. Da, they'll work," said Luca, feeling pressured. "They might not deliver the full yield, but they'll be enough."

"How much is enough?" asked Misha.

Luca looked up at nothing as he calculated the numbers in his head. "If one of them hit... sixty-four kilometers," he said.

Misha nodded approvingly. The base was only a third of that size, but it was important to ignite the American's rage. These missiles would certainly accomplish the task.

On the factory roof, Rosse swore into the radio. "How should I know what kind of bomb?" He'd been watching the Russians from the factory roof for a couple of hours, cursing the heat the entire time. In spite of the shade, his clothes were soaked in sweat. He was constantly swatting the back of his neck, not knowing if it was trickles of perspiration or another megalithic mosquito.

"I been sweating in places a shower don't reach. I ain't in the mood to play twenty questions."

He glared at his bottle of water. It was nearly as hot as the weather. He knew he had to stay hydrated, but if he had to drink anymore warm water he'd puke.

When he saw the Russians had started doing something interesting, he wanted to run over there and hug each one of them for giving him a distraction from his misery.

He looked though the scope as a forklift appeared with a silver object with what looked like wings or fins on it. The forklift driver lowered the object onto the back of a waiting truck. As it backed away, two men quickly secured it to the truck bed. Belching smoke, the truck drove out of the dock yard.

"Do I look like a bomb expert?" said Rosse. "You want me to go over there and ask 'em?"

Down below, on the factory floor, Tate tried not to chew the side of his mouth into a hamburger as he listened to Rosse complain. It was another thirty minutes before Monkhouse took over on the scope, but Tate was sorely tempted to send him now. Anything just so he didn't have to deal with Rosse.

"Take a picture of the bomb and send it to my data pad," said Tate. "Out."

"Out?" said Rosse. "Maybe I had something else important to say."

He centered the scope on the forklift as it brought out another bomb and took several pictures. "I didn't, but he didn't know that. Out. I'd like to be out. Out of here."

As he checked the images on his data pad, sweat dripped onto the screen. He tried wiping it away with his hand, which was also sweaty. All he did was smear the screen. With a string of curses, he looked for something dry until, giving up, he mashed the *Send* button.

Tate examined the pictures but didn't know what he was looking at. To him they looked like mini jet planes. He considered waiting to ask the spooks when he sent his next report, but something in the back of his mind told him not to wait.

He transmitted the pictures, asking about the missiles, then sat back. It would be a while before they got back to him.

Forty-eight seconds later, the radio buzzed in his ear.

"Grave Diggers actual," said Tate, giving his call sign.

"Good news," said Jones, ignoring radio protocol. "You're done. Your exfiltration point is set up for tonight."

"What about the pictures?" asked Tate, feeling very confused. "What are those?"

"Yeah, I got them," said Jones. "Good work on the Russians. We'll debrief when you get back."

"Hang on," said Tate. "What are those things?"

His answer was the soft crackle of static. Tate waited, not sure if Jones had cut the transmission.

"This operation is over," said Jones. "Understand? It's shut down. Grab your people and head for the extraction point."

"What are you talking about?" said Tate. "The Russians are moving bombs and you want us to leave? We don't know what they're doing..."

"Hey," snapped Jones. "I'm running this op and I'm telling you it's over. Don't try contacting us. This channel is closed."

"Hey," said Tate. "What's going on?"

"For security purposes," said Jones.

The line died. Tate ran his fingers through his short, ash blond hair in frustration. He hated how spooks always kept him in the dark. They always over or under reacted, making it impossible to know what to do next.

Like it or not, the operation had just been shut down. There was nothing Tate could do about it.

He switched his radio over to the team network to announce they were bugging out. *This'll make Rosse happy.*

"Looks like a Salish," said Ota, over Tate's shoulder.

"Crap," barked Tate, startled. "Don't sneak up on people like that."

Ota shrugged an apology while scanning the pictures.

"What did you say?" asked Tate, working on getting his heart rate and annoyance under control.

"A Salish," said Ota, looking at Rosse's picture on Tate's data pad.

Tate looked at Ota, waiting for him to go on, but the sniper was content to leave it at that.

"Ota," Tate said with thinning patience, "What is it?"

"That was the NATO name for it," said Ota absently. "The Russians called it a FKR-I. Huh, never thought I'd see one of those."

"See one of what?" asked Tate. "What am I looking at?"

"The Cuban missile crisis," said Ota.

"I might have heard about it," said Tate sarcastically.

"The Soviets got caught putting their ICBM's in Cuba," said Ota.

"Yes, and Kennedy made Khrushchev take them back."

"He only took the ones we knew about," said Ota. "The Soviets snuck more than a hundred other missiles under the nose of US intelligence."

"Other missiles?" said Tate, beginning to feel a creeping up his spine. "These missiles?"

"Those," said Ota, tapping the image on Tate's screen. "Castro wanted to launch them on the US, you know, show us he was the boss. Naturally, Moscow freaks out. They gave Castro the missiles to shut him up. They didn't expect him to start a war, so they took them back. I guess Castro hid a few from the Soviets. I wonder why he never used them."

"Ota," said Tate, trying to control his patience. "I need you to explain what I'm looking at."

"Sure," smiled Ota. "Those are short-range tactical nukes. They carry a fourteen-kiloton warhead. Maybe thirty-five thousand fatalities, you know, depending on the density of population."

"Rosse," said Tate into the radio. "Did the Russians put any of those bombs on their boat?"

"Nah," said Rosse. "All of them went on trucks somewhere. The last one left a few minutes ago. I was about to tell ya. All the Russians went with 'em."

"Get down here," snapped Tate, feeling his gut tie into a knot. "Do you know the missile's range?"

"Three hundred," said Ota. "Three hundred and fifty miles."

"Fulton," shouted Tate as he opened the map on his data pad.

Fulton jumped, startled from his sleep. He looked around, frightened and confused. He puzzled together Tate had called him and scrambled off the floor and hurried over.

Wesson and Monkhouse looked over, alarmed at the urgency in Tate's voice. They didn't know what, but something was happening. Something bad.

"Is this where you lost sight of the Russian trucks?" asked Tate, meeting him halfway.

Fulton blinked the sleep out of his eyes as he looked at the map. He traced his finger along the route he'd seen the trucks take to where they disappeared.

"Yeah," he said. "I think they were headed to that stadium."

"And that's where you heard the gun fire come from?" said Tate.

"Affirmative," said Fulton, hoping Tate noticed he didn't say, 'yeah'.

"What's going on, top?" asked Wesson, looking worried.

Tate ignored her as he flipped through the mission files he collected.

"We came in though a main sewer," he said to himself. "We passed eighteen side-tunnels. Fourteen run-offs, but only one other main... There."

Pointing to a map of the sewer system they had used to infiltrate, Tate showed them where it intersected with another tunnel that lead to the stadium.

Wesson puzzled at Tate, confused about what was happening.

"Sergeant," he said, "I want everyone combat ready immediately. We're going to be moving fast. I'll brief the team on the way."

"I'm on it," said Wesson.

She turned and started snapping off orders. The team jumped into organized chaos as some put on boots, others grabbed their weapons and ammo.

Slinging his assault rifle over his shoulder, Tate tried to figure out why the Pentagon spooks suddenly shut down the mission. They had to know what those missiles were.

There was nothing in Misha Kilmonikov's profile that suggested a motive for attacking the United States, but that hadn't stopped him from sinking an American war ship.

Now he had short range tactical nukes and the only land mass within range was Florida. Highly-skilled in counter-terrorism, Kilmonikov understood terrorist methodology. Limited to small-scale weapons, terrorists often linked attacks to inflict maximum damage.

The Russian felt betrayed by the Kremlin. That should be his obvious target. *How would nuking the US hurt Moscow?* Tate paused as the pieces fell into place.

He's going to start a nuclear war.

21

SHOCKWAVE

Tate and his team charged past the rusted sewer grate and into the dark with weapons ready. Stealth and caution were sacrificed for speed.

He glanced at the timer on his watch. He had roughed out how long it would take to reach the stadium. If they didn't reach the stadium by the time it went off, it meant they likely turned down the wrong tunnel and were lost.

No one had forgotten the hordes of Vix slaughtering themselves, but Tate was gambling most of them had been wiped out.

As they ran, the beams of their flashlights danced over the rough sewer walls as they desperately tried to see an attacking Vix before it saw them. The wind moaned through the tunnels as their boots echoed back at them. If there was any danger coming for them, they wouldn't hear it.

Globs of foul sludge splattered them from head to foot as they raced for the stadium.

A gunshot slapped Tate's ears as a bullet sizzled past him. Blinded by the flash, he hunkered down, expecting the next second to feel the clutch of a Vix.

"Sorry," yelped Monkhouse. "Sorry. I thought I saw one. It was just trash."

The team's nerves were stretched taunt, ready to pull the trigger without thinking. The combination of darkness, anxiety and automatic weapons was a dead teammate waiting to happen.

"Sling your weapons," said Tate, blinking the spots out of his eyes. "Hand weapons only."

Before they could protest, he disappeared into the sewer. Without a word, they ran in behind him.

Where the tunnel widened, they ran two abreast. Tate felt better as Wesson appeared on his right. If they encountered any Vix, it would be head on, and he had the most confidence in her.

They approached a side tunnel and Wesson shined her light down the passage. Snarling, a Vix rose out of the murky water directly in front of them.

Before Wesson could react, Tate's tomahawk flashed out. The Vix halted as the top of its skull tumbled in the air. It swayed a moment as the team raced by then collapsed, disappearing under the water.

The tramp of their running boots echoed through the tunnels like vibrations of a spider's web. Miles of sewers came alive with Vix.

Their only saving grace was the confusion of the echos. The sound bounced in every direction, making it hard for the Vix to detect the source. Several were too far away, or went the wrong way, but not all.

Something blurred past their lights. A Vix jumped at Rosse.

He swung blindly with all his might. The iron rebar looked like a twig in the beefy medic's hand.

Rosse connected with the Vix in mid-flight. The iron bar crushed in its chest in a spray of splintered bone. Hurled back, the Vix toppled into the water, snagging itself on a pile of junk. It thrashed and snarled but couldn't break free.

The team kept running, hoping the thing wouldn't break free and come up behind them. Tate's heart was thudding in his chest. He was pushing his team to exhaustion. He couldn't keep this pace or there'd be no fight left in them when they reached the stadium.

He lost his sense of time in the dark. He could only guess how long ago they had turned into the tunnel leading to the stadium.

He slowed to a jog, wondering how much further. The pale light of his watch painted his expression of dread as the timer reached zero. They should have reached the stadium exit.

Where was it? Doubts squeezed the breath from his chest. *Did I miss a turn? Was the map wrong? Should we turn around? There's no time. There's no time!*

"There," said Wesson, snapping Tate out of his inner dialogue.

In the distance was a weak shaft of light from a manhole cover.

"Good job," puffed Tate.

He paused at the vertical exit to catch his breath, then grabbed onto the steel ladder and climbed. The top of the tunnel was blocked by the heavy metal cover.

Putting his shoulder against it, he pushed up with his legs.

The iron lid gave with a groan and Tate shoved it out of the way. Bright spots flashed in his eyes until the headrush passed, then he climbed out.

The team filed out of the sewer, next to the stadium. Before they could adjust to the bright sun, Tate was leading them up a ramp and into a concourse.

Their boots echoed dully off the grit-covered floor as they quick-walked along the thoroughfare.

Hollow concession stands sunk into the walls between thick, concrete pillars that reached up to the high ceiling. In a place normally filled with the bustle and clamor of fans, it made the team feel like they were intruding in a forgotten mausoleum.

Mingled with the gritty smell of dust was another scent that caused them to slow with caution. An all too familiar mix of sickly sweet and rot; Vix.

Silent weapons in hand, they approached the next corner, the smell overpowering. They fought against gagging from the stench and rounded the corner, ready to fight. They stopped in their tracks in stunned disbelief.

Piled against the wall was a stack of fresh bodies. Men, women and children were callously heaped in a gruesome mound surrounded by a black pool of blood.

"This is what they were shooting," said Fulton, barely above a whisper. "I... I didn't know."

"Stop," said Tate. "None of us knew. You couldn't have done anything."

"How could they...?" stammered Wesson. "Why?"

She wanted to look away but her eyes were drawn to the corpses. Among the jumble of bodies she saw some of them were small. She involuntarily put her hand to her mouth as she recognized the delicate features of tiny hands. Little bare feet stuck out.

"They slaughtered these people," said Rosse.

"They were children," hissed Wesson.

He felt the dead deserved more reverence than a passing thought, but Tate knew if they didn't move on there'd soon be a thousand times more bodies stacked up.

"We can't help them," he said. "But we can stop this from happening again. Let's go."

Tate took off, trailed by the grim faces of his team. What should have been an easy reconnaissance op had turned into one of the most punishing missions Tate had been on. And it wasn't over. He was about to put his rookie team up against battle hardened soldiers. But they were still mortal. They could bleed and after seeing that stack of bodies, Tate knew his team wanted vengeance.

Around the next corner he turned down a hall leading to the sports field. The entrance to the field was blocked by a makeshift wooden gate. It was sturdy enough to keep out Vix but held closed by a simple latch. Peering through the cracks, Tate saw the Russians hard at work.

Two trucks and an APC were parked on the field, nearest his position. In the center of the field stood a row of six launch platforms, each of them equipped with a nuclear missile.

Several Russians appeared to be checking the platforms, ensuring their stability. Some of them wore pistols, but their rifles were several yards away, propped against a truck.

Thick cables snaked out from a generator, running between the rear of each platform and a bench, littered with electronics. Tate guessed it must be the launch control equipment.

He scanned the faces of the Russians, but curiously, Kilmonikov wasn't there.

The Russians had left the docks twenty minutes ago. More than enough time to get to the stadium. *Where did he go?*

Tate put the question aside and turned back to his team. He instantly had their attention.

"This is it," he said. "I count twelve men. Most are around the missile platforms in the center of the field."

"The nukes are right out there?" asked Fulton. The fear in his voice was evident.

"We're going out this gate, quietly," continued Tate, ignoring Fulton. "Ota, find a high place to shoot from, but get there quick. Fulton and Monkhouse, stick to the stands. Go right about thirty yards. Rosse, hold this position in case we need to get out. Wesson and I will go left."

Tate studied their sweat-streaked faces, each one drawn and tense.

"They won't last long in our crossfire," said Tate. "Everyone check your comms."

They checked their radios were working and nodded.

"I'll give the signal to fire," said Tate. "Stick to the basics. Stay in cover. Controlled shots."

"What if we hit a nuke?" asked Fulton.

"Bullets won't detonate them," said Tate, but inwardly he wasn't sure how Russians engineered their warheads. He tried to find comfort, thinking if a nuke went off he'd be dead in a fraction of a second. It didn't help.

"Let's go," he said.

The Russians turned as a big armored personnel carrier rolled into the stadium. The armored shell of the Soviet-made BRT-40 sat on four beefy all-terrain tires. Even thought it was an antique by contemporary standards, the open-top troop carrier was tough and rugged.

The APC squealed to a stop behind the electronics bench. Tate felt his pulse quicken as he saw Misha and Luca climb out.

They walked over to the bench and Luca picked up a small, rectangular device. "Here," he said, handing it to Misha. "This will allow you to fire the missiles from cover."

Misha looked from the device and peered at Luca questioningly.

"A safety precaution in case one blows up," shrugged Luca. "It is limited to ninety meters, so, let's hope it is a small explosion."

"You do not fill me with confidence," said Misha.

"The missile's solid fuel might be unstable after all these years," said Luca. "Instead of a controlled burn... boom!"

Luca spread his hands apart, mimicking an explosion.

Misha kept his expression free from the unwelcomed catastrophic image playing out in his mind.

"The missiles fire in sequence," explained Luca. "One missile for each press of the trigger."

"How long before they're ready for launch?" asked Misha.

Luca bent over the laptop computer and typed in a command. "Only a few minutes. It's loading the internal guidance systems to the missiles onboard computer."

"We should have launched hours ago," said Misha.

"It's a necessary delay," said Luca. "Without the IGS there's no telling where they'll go. Turn on the remote so I can test the signal strength."

Misha examined the remote control and flipped on the power switch. A green indicator light came to life.

Concealed behind bleachers, Tate had crawled along the third row of seats until he was about a hundred feet from Kilmonikov. The Russian wasn't as tall as he'd expected, but he was thick and powerfully built. His lanky companion picked up something from the bench and gave it to him. Tate was trying to figure what it was until he saw Kilmonikov look from the device to the missiles and back.

It's a remote. Tate could feel himself tensing. *He can't launch with his men next to the platform, would he? Does he care if he kills them?* Tate's

225

mind raced, wondering if Kilmonikov would so easily throw away his men's lives.

He glanced down, checking his weapon as he impatiently waited for Monkhouse to signal they were in position. When he looked back up, he saw Kilmonikov switch on the remote.

Holy crap! He's going to do it.

Tate snatched his radio. "Open fire. Now, now!"

As he shouldered his assault rifle, the stadium exploded with gun fire.

Three Russians fell to the ground, dead. The others didn't hesitate, instantly moving. Some risked crossing into the open and ran for their weapons.

The men fell with each sharp crack from Ota's rifle.

Kilmonikov was already in motion when Tate opened fire on him. Bullets chased him, kicking up the dirt at his feet. Kilmonikov dove for cover behind the bench with Luca scrunched up next to him.

Other Spetsnaz pulled their rifles from the nearby truck and the chop of gunfire doubled as they returned fire.

Concrete chips flew as Tate and his team ducked into cover.

"We have to launch now," shouted Misha.

"No," yelled Luca, his face going pale. "The guidance hasn't finished. You could bring a missile down on us."

Misha didn't know who was attacking and didn't care. After years of careful planning, he was seconds away from exacting justice on the cowards that had betrayed him and killed his men. For years, when all other hope had abandoned him, the one dim light that fueled his resolve in the fetid bowels of the penal colony was knowing this day would come. The day he would deliver the blow that would crush the Kremlin.

No. He demanded justice and would not let these intruders steal it from him.

Misha mashed the trigger.

"Have you lost your mind?" screamed Luca. Horrified, he swatted the remote out of Misha's hand. It bounced into the open, eight feet away.

The stadium shook with a tremendous roar as the rocket booster shot out a pillar of flame. Screams of agony were cut short as the men near the rocket were instantly killed.

The launch platform was consumed in a cloud of smoke and fire. The gunfight halted as the living stared in awe as a streak of silver shot through the fabric dome and into the sky.

The missile traced a line of smoke as it continued straight up.

"If it doesn't turn soon," screamed Luca, "it'll fall on top of us."

The missile was lost from sight; all eyes followed the finger of smoke as it climbed higher and higher, unbending.

The missile's onboard altimeter tested the atmospheric pressure hundreds of times a second. At two hundred feet the missile had met its preset pressure value and armed the warhead.

The activation sequence successfully completed and powered up a new set of circuits. The processor took over the missile's system, feeding the altimeter with a new preset and command instruction.

Re-programmed with a new value, the altimeter began to monitor for a drop in atmospheric pressure.

Another set of circuits sent test voltage to the eight detonators surrounding the plutonium core. The detonators all responded as active and primed. All systems were working and waiting.

At exactly fifty feet above sea level, the altimeter would detonate the warhead.

Inside the booster, the solid fuel lined the interior combustion chamber like a sleeve. Exacting measurements were used to ensure the hole running through the length of the solid fuel was uniformly smooth. Any deformity could create uneven thrust, pushing the missile off course. The exacting engineering did not account for the effects of age.

Over the long decades, the fuel had developed dangerous micro fractures, invisible to the naked eye.

Incredible g-forces and friction pummeled the missile's frame and it sliced upwards into the sky. The intense vibrations tore at the fractures, creating hairline fissures. Heat and fire burned into the fissures to the wall of the combustion chamber, sheering off a chunk of fuel. The jet of escaping gas rammed the loose piece against the nozzle with tremendous force.

The fuel inside the chamber glowed white hot at over two thousand degrees, but with the nozzle blocked there wasn't oxygen to burn.

Inertia carried the missile for only a couple hundred feet more. It slowed then stopped, hanging in the air, just for a moment, then toppled over and began its return to earth.

Ice water shot through Tate as the smoke trail abruptly stopped. Something high above winked in the light.

"We are dead men," said Luca, eyes fixed on the sky.

As the missile picked up speed, the air flow over its wings and tail-fin stabilized its fall, keeping it nearly perfectly on course to the stadium.

Although the engine of the missile had failed, the altimeter continued to work perfectly and it registered the accelerating decent; *180 feet, 160 feet, 120, 98...*

To the souls in the stadium, the missile appeared as a tiny dot in the sky. In a moment that dot would blaze with the light of a thousand suns. Everyone beneath it would be instantly erased from the earth. All they were and hoped to become, gone.

83...

"It's been a damn pleasure," said Tate over the radio.

71...

The heat shield inside the missile's combustion chamber was engineered to withstand fifteen hundred degrees kelvin. With the nozzle blocked, the intense heat of the solid fuel was turned back on itself, effectively turning the combustion chamber into a forge.

67...

White-hot fuel burned through the chamber wall, flooding it with oxygen. The solid fuel blazed to life. With the nozzle blocked, the burning exhaust shot out the chamber wall. The missile's shell channeled the exhaust back and out the rear.

The accelerometer registered the missile had achieved enough thrust to fly and handed flight control to the internal gyroscope in an attempt to resume its previous course.

Everyone watched in disbelief as the missile roared to life. Turning sharply, it leveled out and streaked away, a jet of fire crackling behind it.

"What now?" asked Rosse after a moment's silence.

Tate shrugged, not conscious that Rosse couldn't see him. Nobody knew what to do. Fight, run, wait for the inevitable explosion?

Racing at over a thousand feet per second, the missile needed to fly another fifty-eight seconds before the stadium was outside the blast radius of the shockwave.

At twenty-seven seconds the missile's skin melted from the immense heat. One thousandth of a second later, the gyroscope failed and the missile toppled out of the sky.

Two Russians tentatively moved towards their weapons leaning against a truck.

"Do we shoot?" asked Wesson, startling Tate out of his trance.

He looked at her as if she'd just appeared.

"It's not over," he whispered.

22

AT ALL COSTS

"Cover your eyes," said Luca with a trembling voice. "And hope the sound of the explosion is not the last thing you hear."

Misha buried his face in his hands, trying to control his quaking body.

Wesson's pale-green eyes searched Tate's for some kind of guidance. He was suddenly struck by her eyes as something nagged at the back of his mind. *Her eyes.*

"Cover your eyes," he yelled, shoving his fists against his eyes. "Everyone cover your eyes."

Everything disappeared in a wave of brilliant light. Screams of pain wailed off the stadium walls as Tate counted the seconds. The light winked out and he opened his eyes. In the sports field, the two Russians writhed in pain from the flash-blindness.

"Hang..." began Tate, just as the shockwave hit with an impossible roar.

Eighteen thousand tons of steel and concrete jumped as the shockwave slammed into the stadium. The ground punched up sharply, knocking the wind out of everyone.

The stadium walls buckled as blocks of concrete were hurled across the field. Dust boiled down, only to be sucked away by the tremendous winds. The world cracked and groaned around them in a maelstrom of chaos.

Wesson dug her fingers into Tate, begging for it to stop and suddenly it was over. A sigh of wind brushed through the stadium as people lay dazed, groping for their senses. The only sound was the occasional clatter of loose rubble. The ground was motionless.

By the fallen bench, Misha groaned as he struggled to sit up. Wheezing, he dug the grit from his eyes and got his bearings. Seeing the scattered launch controls, he quickly looked for his missiles.

He found them in a jumbled heap and his face fell in ruin. He hardly dared to look around to see what else he'd lost.

Close by he found Luca. Misha scrabbled over to him, checking for blood but found no wounds. Coughing, he unscrewed his canteen and washed Luca's face.

"Can you hear me?" asked Misha. "Luca? Wake up."

With a panicked gasp, Luca's eyes flew open. He looked, uncomprehending, at Misha's dirt-streaked face. Then his eyes became clear.

"If you are the first thing I see," groaned Luca, rubbing the knot on the back of his head, "then I must be in Hell."

"As if Hell would take you," grinned Misha, relief washing over him.

Luca saw the toppled platforms and chuckled. "Misha Kilmonikov, you are a mad man."

Misha remembered they had been attacked and ducked behind the bench. Risking a shot, he glanced over the bench before grabbing Luca and pulling him to cover.

"Come, my friend," said Misha, getting into a crouch. "This mad man is not finished yet."

Tate reached to help up Wesson when he saw Kilmonikov's head pop up from behind the bench. He fumbled for his gun, but the Russian disappeared.

Tate fired off a quick shot, missing, as a lanky man broke cover and dashed behind the APC. He knew, any second, Kilmonikov was going to follow.

Tate pre-aimed, his finger on the trigger.

To his surprise, Kilmonikov appeared, going the other way. Tate instantly shifted his aim and fired. Just as his sights were on Kilmonikov, he scooped up the remote and reversed, scrambled back into cover, disappearing behind the APC.

Tate swore, knowing he had missed. His frustration turned to confusion as he looked at the wrecked missiles.

Why'd he risk getting shot for the remote?

They were useless. Kilmonikov had to know that.

Tate snapped his eye behind the gunsight as APC growled to life. The tires dug into the dirt, kicking up a spray of dust as the armored vehicle spun around.

The remote's useless, thought Tate. Suddenly a cold knot sank into the pit of his stomach.

"Oh no," he said. "He's got more."

"What?" asked Wesson, confused.

"Come on," barked Tate, yanking her to her feet.

The remaining Russians saw them break cover and took hurried shots. Bullets cracked the air around Tate and Wesson as they ran for the remaining APC.

"Give 'em cover," yelled Rosse over the radio.

Bullets rained down on the Russians, sending them ducking for cover.

Tate jumped into the driver's seat and hit the ignition button. The big machine lurched forward. The heavy armored door slammed closed with a thud, narrowly missing Wesson's foot as she dived in.

Tate rammed the gearshift and stomped the accelerator. The APC slewed sideways and he spun the wheels and shot after Kilmonikov.

Wesson braced herself as the APC flew off the curb onto the street.

Tate saw the distant APC race up the freeway onramp and steered after it.

"What's going on?" asked Wesson, her knuckles white as she held on for dear life.

"He took the remote," said Tate. "It means he's got more missiles."

Wesson's jaw almost fell open as the gravity of his words hit home. How could anyone live though the hell they'd just experienced and want to unleash that destruction again?

Tate needed more speed and downshifted. The gears clashed together as the engine howled in protest. The tachometer shot into the red as the big machine cut the distance.

The wind roared in their ears, whipping through the open-top vehicle. Wesson could hear the whoosh as they tore past abandoned cars.

Ahead, Kilmonikov's APC swung wildly as it dodged the derelict cars that littered the freeway.

White smoke billowed from the tires as Tate skidded around the same car. Losing control, they smacked into the guardrail in a spray of sparks. Wesson turned white as the APC threatened to veer off the forty-foot drop from the elevated freeway.

The APC righted as Tate pulled them back from the edge.

Misha saw the other APC growing larger in his sideview mirror, cursing the fates for this useless machine.

"The gun," he snapped.

Luca nodded and grabbed the overhead bar. Wind whipped around him as he pulled himself up behind the 7.62 machine gun. The heavy gun sat on a swivel mount, giving it the ability to shoot over the armored sides of the APC.

Luca braced his back against the metal frame of the windscreen and gripped the machine gun's handles.

"Crap," said Tate, as he saw a figure appear behind the gun.

He yanked the steering wheel as the machine gun spat fire. Bullets gouged the hood of this APC as Wesson ducked.

They could hear the chop of the machine gun as Tate fought to get closer.

Bullets ripped the air over their heads, slamming into the inside of the rear hatch.

"What are you doing?" yelled Wesson. "Any closer and he can shoot down on us."

Tate glanced up then back at their own mounted machine gun.

"Get behind that gun," he said.

"Are you insane?" she snapped.

No. If anything, Tate was more clear-headed than any other time. It was like an embrace from an old friend; the more dangerous and chaotic things got, the more centered and focused he became. Wesson was brave, but she hadn't experienced the acid bath of repeated, prolonged combat. She didn't understand, but there was no time to explain. He knew what he was asking of her.

There was nothing gradual about being shot at. He was throwing her in the deep end and hoping she wouldn't freeze.

"Stay low," said Tate. "The second he starts reloading, start shooting."

Bullets slapped into the ballistic windshield, spider-webbing cracks across it.

Tate swore, yanking the wheel and throwing Wesson into the hard frame of the back seat.

Metal screamed as he careened into another car, peeling off its skin. Sparks and flecks of metal few though the open shutters in the driver's door.

Misha crushed the accelerator pedal into the floor. His leg threatened to cramp as he willed the APC to go faster.

Above him, Luca's machine gun hammered the air, spewing hot casings all over the metal floor.

234

Glancing at his sideview mirror, Misha saw it filled with the big steel grill of the other APC. It was almost on top of him and he was running out of time.

He leaned forward, trying to peer though the dull, bullet-proof glass. In the distance he saw it. A lone lighthouse.

Misha grinned, knowing at its feet slumbered six more nuclear missiles, prepped and ready to go.

He looked down, making sure the remote was still in reach. All he needed was ninety meters.

Closer, swore Tate.

They were inches from the rear of the APC and the lanky Russian was chewing them up.

"Get ready," yelled Tate, and downshifted. The gauges were buried in the red as the engine screamed. The APC jumped forward, slamming into the back of Kilmonikov with a crunch. The lanky Russian folded over the machine gun and fell.

"Now," yelled Tate.

Wesson jumped to her machine gun, racked the slide and fired. Wind snapped her hair, lashing her face as flame and smoke pulsed from the barrel.

She was practically shooting down on them as bullets chewed into the Russian's cab.

Kilmonikov swerved wildly side to side. Wesson shot wide, blasting out chunks of asphalt.

She swung the heavy gun back, her thumb pressing on the trigger. Impossibly, the big Russian turned in his seat, his pistol aimed directly at her head.

Wesson dropped as his gun popped. Bullets shattered off the machine gun as hot fragments bit into her skin.

Steam began shooting out from under the hood. The temperature gauge was in the red. The engine was on the verge of blowing.

Tate had to stop Kilmonikov now. The Russian's APC was slowing too, breaking down under the strain of the chase.

Tate steered around and along the side of Kilmonikov. Suddenly the passenger door opened and the lanky Russian appeared, nearly sticking his pistol through the shutters of Tate's door.

Tate flinched as gunpowder scorched his cheek, the pistol's bullets seared by his face.

Tate torqued the wheel, slamming into the side of the Russian's APC. Metal screeched as Tate ripped Luca's door away.

Luca flailed to save himself as he fell out of the open APC. Misha's hand shot out and grabbed the back of his shirt, pulling him back in.

"We're almost there," said Misha.

His chest heaving in panic, Luca's mind could hardly comprehend he was still alive.

Misha had to get off the freeway, but Tate was blocking him.

"Hang on," growled Misha, and twisted the wheel, crashing into the other APC.

The wheel twisted out of Tate's hands as Kilmonikov slammed into him. Rubber burned and smoke billowed as his front tire was shredded. He wrestled for control as he saw the Russian was driving them off the edge of the freeway, but it was too late.

The APCs burst through the guardrail. Tate and Wesson held on, bracing for the long fall.

To their surprise, the front of the APC bounced as it landed on a dirt berm that sloped down to the street below.

Across the street was a steel and concrete wall that surrounded a parking lot. Further on was a brightly-painted lighthouse.

The APC rattled violently as the mangled tire dug into the soft dirt. They bottomed out on the street below, gouging chunks of asphalt.

Metal snapped as Tate mashed the gears, trying to stop as they raced at the wall.

Misha kept his foot anchored to the accelerator, throwing plumes of dirt as he flew down the slope.

Desperate to reach the missiles, he decided to ram through the wall. They hit the street in a jarring shower of sparks and crushed metal. The axel snapped, folding a tire under the APC as they hurtled forward.

With all his strength, Misha fought the wheel as the APC violently shook and then they hit. The APC had no more to give as it plowed into the wall. The combination of concrete and steel crushed the front of the armored car like a tin can. The back end flew up and over, flipping it into the air.

Misha saw Luca thrown out of the open door but could do nothing to save him. He squeezed his eyes closed, bracing for impact.

With a gut-wrenching crash, the APC hit the ground. Twisted metal and debris flew as it rolled, two, three, four times. The battered machine came to rest on its side.

Smoke curled above the wrenched carcass as a broken tire wobbled away. Nothing else moved.

Wesson blinked the stars out of her eyes, trying to make sense of where she was. Her ears were ringing and her head thudded painfully. Chunks of concrete were scattered across the mangled hood. She coughed in the swirling dust.

She heard a groan and saw Tate next to her. He clutched his leg, pain carving lines in his face.

"Tate," she muttered, still groggy. "What's wrong?"

"Check the Russian," he gasped through short breaths. "Destroy the remote."

She looked at the distant, smoldering wreck of the other APC and shook her head.

"Nobody's walking away from that," she said.

"You gonna bet a nuclear war on that?" he grimaced hotly.

The warped door fought Wesson as she forced it open wide enough to get out.

"Wait," said Tate. He held out his Colt 1911 pistol.

Wesson took it, too dazed to check if she still had her own gun.

Climbing over the remains of the wall, she could feel her head clearing. But the bright sun hurt her eyes. Far to the right she saw Luca, his crumpled body laying in distorted angles. He wasn't getting up again.

She could hear the hiss and tick of the wrecked APC as she got closer. Its open top was turned towards her and she could see it was empty.

Where's Kilmonikov?

She'd seen the Russian stare down the barrel of her machine gun without flinching. He was fearless and dangerous. Was he dead, too, or waiting to ambush her?

Wesson cursed herself for not checking her gun before now. She quietly switched off the safety and pushed the slide back. A quick glance told her there was a round in the chamber. Cocking the hammer, the big .45 was ready.

Shielded behind the wreckage, she inched out, careful not to expose herself as she looked around the corner, a sliver at a time.

No bullet sizzled past her. Expecting Kilmonikov, she saw a trail of smeared blood.

Broadening her search, she saw him crawling across the parking lot towards the lighthouse.

She knew he could hear her footsteps as she approached, but he ignored her.

His eyes were fixed on a row of glinting darts, shimmering near the base of the lighthouse.

He held the remote in his stretched-out hand, pressing the trigger over and over.

Even in the baking sun, Wesson felt a chill clutch her as she realized what he was doing.

"Stop," she ordered, pointing the gun at him.

With a grunt, he pulled himself closer to the row of missiles. Stretching out the remote, Misha jabbed the trigger again and again.

"I said stop," yelled Wesson, glancing at the missiles, terrified to see if one of them was launching. But they continued to lay dormant.

"Or what?" chuckled Misha. "You will kill me? Do you know how many times I have died? My country has killed me a hundred times over." He dragged himself again. "Today they will know a better death than they ever gave me."

The Colt trembled in Wesson's hand, her fingers white, squeezing the gun as if it might escape. She had killed countless Vix without a second thought. It wasn't long ago that she'd killed a living human being, but she was defending her life and the lives of her teammates. The man at her feet was defenseless. Pulling the trigger felt like murder.

He reached out the remote again. Her mind screamed *shoot...SHOOT*.

His finger closed on the trigger.

With a scream, Wesson fired. The gun bucked in her hand with a deafening boom.

Misha screamed as the remote exploded in his hand. Plastic and electronics scattered over the pavement.

Wesson tucked the Colt in her waistband. "You're done."

If she expected the big Spetsnaz to give up, she was wrong. Misha raised his head and winked at her, then began crawling... towards the missiles.

"Your Thomas Jefferson, I think, said, 'The tree of liberty must be refreshed with the blood of tyrants'."

Wesson wasn't listening. She was looking at the smear of blood, turning black in the heat. Black blood, like the sticky pool around the bodies in the stadium. Blood that speckled the child's tiny hand, frozen in death.

A single image, she'd fought to bury in the dark of her mind, slowly pushed out of the gloom; forcing her to remember.

The angry buzz of flies. The air thick with stench. Too horrible to look at, but she did. Her eyes stopped roving, beckoned by something silently calling. She wanted to look away, but she couldn't. The tangle of limbs blurred, losing their meaning as her focus was pulled to a shape almost hidden in shadow.

Like a fog lifting, clarity and grief gripped her as she saw the small, perfect face of a child, its one milky eye staring back at her.

She recoiled from the memory with a gasp, instantly transported to the present.

Wesson looked down on Kilmonikov. His only goal to manually launch those missiles. No matter the cost.

"Tyrants?" said Wesson. "What about the blood of innocent children?"

"Don't be so naive," snapped Misha, his face twisted by anger. "There is no innocence."

His surprise never registered on his face when Wesson shot him. The gunshot echoed flatly across the parking lot. Wesson absently heard the clink of the spent case bounce off the pavement. She stood over the dead body, prepared for the twist of guilt or rush of triumph.

Nothing came. There was only the hot wind ruffling her hair.

She lost track of time, standing over the body, alone in her thoughts.

"Hey," called someone.

Wesson blinked, breaking out of her trance and saw Tate steadying himself against the Russian's APC. She felt his eyes looking at the body by her feet and the gun in her hand.

A sad smile crossed his face as he limped over to her. "I think we've spent enough time on this rock," he said. "Don't you?"

"I've never so far away from home," she said.

"It takes time," said Tate with a weary sigh. "But, you'll get there."

THE END

YOUR REVIEW HELPS

Reviews are a huge support for a self published author, like yours truly. If you enjoyed this book, please leave a review and tell your friends about my books.

Thank you.

You can leave your review here

ENJOY THIS FREE BOOK

Add this free prequel to your library!

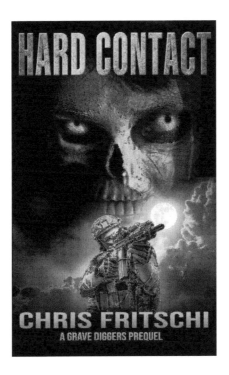

A simple mission turns into terrifying fight for survival.

This special forces team is about to walk into something more horrifying and relentless than they could ever imagine.

BOOKS IN THE SERIES

Is your Grave Diggers library complete?

———

The Grave Diggers

The Suicide King

Grave Mistakes

Deadly Relics

AUTHORS NOTE

Digging Into The Story

While reading this book you may have asked yourself, 'When did this happen? In the future, or is this a parallel world, or what?' You might (even) have gone back and reread some of it, thinking you missed the key sentence that explains it. To answer your (assumed) second question, no, this isn't a parallel world. In answer to your (equally assumed) first question the answer is *the near future*. I know. That doesn't exactly put a pin on a year, but if it's any help in narrowing down a date, you probably have enough time to work out your evacuation plan and stock up on MRE's before society is cannibalized by the undead.

I kept to current military gear because most equipment has a long service life before something new comes along. Look at the M14 rifle, for example. It first saw action in 1961 and is still in service 55 years later. I did cave to the temptation to come up with a fictitious weapon because, come on, it's cool.

One Last Thing

If you think you've seen all there is to the Vix in this book you'd be very mistaken. I've grown up on zombie lore and, like you, feel that once the monster has stepped out from behind the curtain you've seen it all. What kind of storyteller would I be if I did that to you? There's more to the Vix you haven't seen yet, and judging by how creeped out people got from reading the early copy of my next book, I think you'll enjoy it.

ABOUT THE AUTHOR

Chris grew up on George Romero, Rambo, Star Wars and Tom Clancy, a formula for a creating a seriously good range of science fiction, action, paranormal, and adventure novels.

Chris is currently working on The Grave Digger series, an action packed thrill ride that will have you hooked right up to the last page. It's Tom Clancy meets Dawn of the Dead and X-Files, and it's guaranteed to keep you on the edge of your seat. Jack Tate, ex-Delta operator, has assembled a rag-tag team of rookies and motley group of wannabes is all he has to go up against a secret cabal who are plotting a takeover of the United States. Can they do it before time runs out?

---

website: chrisfritschi.com

Printed in Poland
by Amazon Fulfillment
Poland Sp. z o.o., Wrocław

65012341R00153